The Judge and the Barfly

Mary McCarte Johnson

To Sadie
Another Irish Scot —
Cheers! Mary McCarte Johnson

PublishAmerica

Baltimore

First printing

ISBN: 1-59286-479-1
PUBLISHED BY PUBLISHAMERICA BOOK PUBLISHERS
www.publishamerica.com
Baltimore

Printed in the United States of America

For the love of my life, Charlie.

ACKNOWLEDGMENTS

I am grateful for the help of many people during the writing of this book, particularly Jan Tew, whose love and help and encouragement spurred me on. Without her, this book might never have been launched.

I am also thankful for the assistance of Melanie Paas, Lynn McKay, Ann Tamboline, and Ken Babcock—the first person to put my hand on a computer mouse and tell me it didn't bite! David and Donna, my grandnephew and his wife, provided me with my first computer, for which I will be forever grateful. Thanks to Norman David, my nephew, for his sharp wit and encouraging words. Lloy Falconer encouraged me from the first with my short story writing, and my grandnephew Richard Joss provided me with a listening ear as I read to him from the first draft of the novel during our tour of France.

In addition to these, I appreciate the invaluable support and encouragement from my many friends and family members, including my nephew Douglas and Claire Boyack, Felix Teh, Paul and Simone Ledet, Ken Sherwood and Dr. Peter Yam. I am grateful for the legal support of Phil Williams and Jim Drake and the incredible tech assistance from Ziggy Haque. Thanks to Terence Teh, who had the faith that I would write this book someday! As well, I appreciate the "ear" of Mary Dolan who listened to my many excerpts.

CHAPTER ONE
The Parting

The dawn slowly unfolding across the fields cast a hazy glow over the two women as they embraced in a tearful farewell. Anne Jordan couldn't believe that her beautiful and talented daughter was being banished under a cloak of darkness and shame. She hoped and prayed that Elizabeth's father would eventually yield and forgive his daughter. But his unyielding way of thinking would be difficult to change.

Many minutes passed as Elizabeth and her mother held each other's gaze as though they were trying to imprint a lasting image.

Sadly Elizabeth turned around and approached her father with outstretched arms but he refused to acknowledge the gesture. For a second she looked imploringly into his granite countenance and heart brokenly whispered, "Oh Father, I loved you so…"

As she walked down the steps to her father's car a feeling of irrevocable finality passed through every fibre of her being…and she knew she might never see her parents again.

Elizabeth entered the car and tried to avoid looking back at the pathetic figure of her mother standing on the threshold. Torrey the chauffeur glanced at Elizabeth's face as he tucked the car blanket on her lap and was appalled at the sadness he beheld. His thoughts took him back to the time when she was a little girl and the day she had brought a tiny bird wrapped in a white handkerchief and tearfully explained that the little sparrow couldn't fly and begged Torrey to fix it. He had his doubts about that because the broken wing hanging from the poor little creature's body…didn't bode good news. Nevertheless, he assured her that he would make it fly again. On hearing this she skipped off happy as a lark.

That evening Torrey buried the little bird in his garden. Sure enough Torrey barely had time for the night's sleep to leave his eyes the following morning when Elizabeth knocked on the door to inquire about the sparrow.

"Lord in heaven, that little bird flew away this morning singing a song that was music to the ears. Aye, it was a sight to see, do you know that he flew around my head a few times, that was his birdlike way of saying thanks!"

'Twas a worthwhile fib! The little girl eyes filled with admiration cried, "Oh Torrey I just knew that you'd make the little bird well again."

Now sad to say here was that lovely little girl facing more serious tragedy, but this time he had no way of helping her. He didn't know all the details of this banishment...but the little he did know cast a despairing shadow across his spirit.

When the car pulled up in front of the forbidding doors of the convent... neither Torrey nor his passenger made a move to get out of the car... Elizabeth sat ramrod straight as though she was frozen in time.

Then with a sigh ending in a sob, she said, "Torrey I shall miss you," and choked with emotion, added, "Please, keep me in your prayers."

That did it! Torrey was so overcome he couldn't utter a word. He unrolled the car blanket from her lap and handed over the small valise. Only then did he look into her beautiful eyes, "Miss Elizabeth, all these years I've loved you like one of my own and this tragedy is tearing me apart. May God bless you and keep you. Aye, and I'll be praying for you until there's not a breath left *in* me."

Having said that he got into the car and drove off as though the devil himself was chasing him! Elizabeth looked up at the fortress like walls of the convent and *wished she could turn around and run away!* But there *was no escape route*, where could she go?

Hesitatingly she pulled the iron knocker and heard it resonating like a cannon shot. At eye level a slot in the door was opened and she found herself being stared at...then the massive tall door opened and a voice from within told her to step inside. She obeyed and came face to face with a nun who introduced herself as the Mother Superior and without further ado... this formidable person's only greeting was an icy… 'Follow me.'

Elizabeth, valise in hand, followed behind the nun's measured steps until they reached a door with an enamel nameplate bearing the title, 'Mother Superior.' Pulling a long chain from around her waist, Mother Superior selected a key dangling at the end of the chain and silently motioned Elizabeth to enter.

The sparsely furnished office contained a wooden desk and the customary statues and holy images hanging on the walls. There was a stillness in the room that gave Elizabeth a feeling of complete separation from the outside world and without warning her knees began to buckle! She looked for a chair and finding none she remained standing in the center of the room. Only sheer willpower kept her from toppling over.

Mother Superior shuffled the papers on her desk for what seemed like an eternity then straightening her glasses on her beak-like nose…she contemplatively scrutinised Elizabeth. Under this frosty gaze, Elizabeth's body settled into a cold uneasiness and the next words spoken did not relieve the anxiety that was tearing the last remnants of Elizabeth's composure into shreds.

In a cold and deliberate manner Mother Superior stated the rules under which Elizabeth would have to abide by during her stay in the convent. First of all she must remain in her room and have no contact or conversation with anyone other than the priest. Required religious reading would be at her disposal, however, she would not be allowed to attend daily mass. A priest would visit her on a daily basis. Rising from her chair, Mother Superior thrust the door open and once again said, 'Follow me'.

Elizabeth was taken to a cell-like room containing a narrow bed, a crucifix and a picture of the Sacred Heart. Beneath a statue of the Virgin Mary there was a votive lamp and by the bedside there was a small wooden chair. As she surveyed this cell like room… sharp slivers of fear slithered down her spine!

The Mother Superior left and Elizabeth was jolted back to reality when she heard the door being locked on the outside. Alone in this chilling cell like room… apprehension spread its wings around the vulnerability that had taken hold of her. An insane desire made its way through her befuddled thoughts... should she laugh or should she weep? She was sure that she would never last in such an environment as this.

Sitting stiffly upright on the wooden chair by the bed, she pondered the predicament that she found herself in. Total isolation such as this... she had never experienced before. Alienated from the love and comfort of family, the atmosphere was so oppressively stultifying that she wished for death!

The months following the birth of her baby had a dire effect on Elizabeth's health. Mentally and physically it had taken its toll. The time spent in the convent hospital was a blurred version of what had actually occurred. The fever that almost consumed her after the birth was fogged over with vague memories of asking to see her baby and the request being denied.

However, she remembered a young nurse whispering that her child would have *his* needs met and that he had been taken away. Upon hearing this Elizabeth turned her face to the wall and wept bitter tears. And again she reverted into that remote corner of her mind where life was no longer a reality.

The doctor who had delivered her child was a close friend of Elizabeth's mother. His name was Dr. Pearce and he had given his word to her parents that he would keep the birthing of Elizabeth's child absolutely confidential. This promise was just one more addition to the patchwork of broken dreams and heartbreak that he had already acquired throughout his years of practicing medicine.

Attending to this young woman whose beauty reminded him of her mother made his heart ache. Alas, there wasn't much he could do because her father had made him promise that regardless of what happened he must not contact them with information about their daughter. As far as he was concerned she no longer belonged to the family.

However, when Elizabeth's condition worsened, the doctor decided to inform her father hoping that he would soften his stand. Dr. Pearce was shocked at the cold indifference shown by her father, he sternly said that Elizabeth's illness was of no interest to him. The kindly doctor was made aware that Elizabeth would have no source of comfort from family or friends! God help her, she would pay dearly for flaunting Ireland's strict code of premarital behaviour!

CHAPTER TWO
The Orphanage

The classroom door opened and a small boy stepped out into the hallway. He scanned the hallway and finding it empty he cautiously walked towards the short dark tunnel that connected the school to the orphanage. The swish of his ill-fitting shoes was the only sound to be heard … as his little feet uncomfortably slid in and out. He curled his toes desperately trying to keep the shoes on his feet.

His spirits spiraled downwards as he drew closer to the kitchen and the noxious odours of boiled cabbage assailed his nostrils. Doing kitchen chores for Sister Fatima wasn't something he anticipated with joy. Whenever he arrived in the kitchen she microscopically inspected him from head to toe and during this inspection he felt as hopeless as a lobster marking time alongside a pot of boiling water.

Sister Fatima was an embittered, miserable hunk of humanity, with a razor edged tongue. Young Patrick was sure that she was one of God's *good* intentions gone awry. She seldom spoke to him; all conversations were limited to his duties.

Before he commenced his duties she motioned him to the table with a sweep of her fat pudgy hand…then a bowl of steaming watery soup and a hunk of dry bread was placed before him. Although his belly was always empty… the soup did nothing to appease his appetite. He blew on each spoonful trying to cool the scalding soup as it made its way over his gullet. Sister Fatima barely gave him time to finish the scalding soup. Halfway through she would poke him sharply in the back and bellow, 'are you going to sit there all day?'

Fatima took full advantage of being in charge of the kitchen and enjoyed showing her authority. She bullied the young novice nuns who were sent there to help prepare the meals and scowled ferociously at the tradesmen who crossed her path. However, there was *one* person whose appearance in the kitchen filled Fatima with terror: and that personage was Mother Superior!

Sad to say, young Patrick was terrified of *both* Sister Fatima and Mother Superior and in turn they detested him. He had no idea what he had ever done to arouse their wrath, but it seemed their greatest pleasure was batting the hell out of him at the least provocation. And for such a young lad this was a lot to handle, mentally and physically. Patrick learned to control his emotions until he reached the drab dormitory. And there beneath the old grey blanket he would empty the contents of his sad little heart allowing his tears to flow in privacy until sleep gently closed the sordid happenings of his day. And well he knew that all the other narrow beds in this miserable Dorm held lonely little orphans …all unwanted and unloved!

One afternoon when he entered the kitchen he was surprised to see Fatima feverishly sweeping the floor. This took Patrick by surprise because the sweeping of floors was one of his chores.

With her fat face flushed red with the exertion of sweeping, she cried, "Aye, 'tis high time you showed up. Get on your knees and search for my gold wedding ring."

"Wedding ring? I didn't know you were married."

With a pride filled voice she replied, "I am a Bride of Christ."

He hadn't the slightest idea what she meant, after all; he had never heard that Christ was a married man. So Patrick shrugged it off… believing that at last… old fat Fatima had gone off the rails. Bride indeed! What a bloody bride she would be. Sure even the Devil himself would make a fast exit from Hell if she arrived on the scene intent on marrying him.

That night as he did most nights he prayed beneath his old grey blanket that God would send Fatima and Mother Superior straight to Hell as soon as possible.

Patrick knew that the sounds of the gloomy cavernous kitchen would be imbedded in his memory forever! The loud ticking of the clock on the wall dolefully chiming each quarter hour… methodically erasing each fifteen minutes from life's allotment! The sound of the soup simmering in the tall stockpot and Fat Fatima puffing her way across the cold stone floor…grunting and burping unabashedly. Patrick was always fascinated by the satisfaction on her round fat face as each burp... grunt or *whatever*...escaped from her ever-burgeoning girth.

Sometimes for his own enjoyment he would take the chance of addressing her as Sister Fat-Am-I. Immediately she would scream and make him repeat her name properly. Enjoying her wrath to the hilt Patrick would obey her command with false *solemnity* and pronounce her name properly.

One incident he would never forget was the time she had left him alone in the kitchen. As she waddled out... she called over her shoulder, "I'll be back in ten minutes and I'll check what you've done in my absence, so don't think you can slack off."

As soon as he heard her shuffling steps retreating down the hallway, he had the daft notion to find out what was in the stockpot. All sorts of scraps of leftovers found their way into that big pot and yet he had never seen it being emptied or cleaned out. To satisfy his curiosity he stood on a chair and stared down into the tall stockpot. He was amazed at what met his eyes... colourful vegetables were bubbling and bobbing in the soup...and then it dawned on him; no vegetables ever adorned his soup bowl. Evidently that old bitch skimmed off the thin watery stuff just for him. No wonder his ribs stuck out like the teeth on an old comb and his backside was so small it looked like two eggs wrapped in a hankie.

As he was about to jump down from the chair... he caught sight of a big stone jar on the shelf marked 'pickling salt'. Before his courage had time to evaporate, he grabbed the salt jar and emptied the contents into the soup pot. He just had time to stuff the empty jar into the bottom of the garbage, when Fatima shuffled back into the kitchen.

Patrick's heart was pounding a mile to the minute! Why was she staring at him? And as she stood with her eyes glued to his... guilt played havoc with his stomach! Should she ever find the empty salt jar... *he* would never live to tell the tale!

But all she said was, "Get a move on, take the garbage out and start finishing up in here."

Did she say garbage? The outside garbage was cleared every morning and that was his only chance to bury the jar at the bottom of the heap where no one would find it!

For sure someone up there must be listening to his prayers because when she returned to the kitchen all she said was "What kept you so long with the garbage? At the rate you're going we'll be here 'til midnight."

She clouted him hard in the ribs with the soup ladle and losing her grip on the ladle it clattered to the floor. He watched as she bent down to retrieve it wheezing and grunting like an old sow. The broad expanse of her bottom instantaneously filled his horizon and the temptation to kick her fat arse was difficult to resist! Just the thought of doing so alleviated the tension from the salt escapade.

Slowly she unfurled her massive hulk to its' five foot stature and waddled over to the pantry and emerged rubbing a ripe pear on her big blue and white striped apron. A look of glutinous anticipation spread over her full moon face as she shuffled towards the wide wooden chair at the end of the kitchen. The voluminous black habit puffed out as she descended like a deflating balloon into the chair. Upon receiving the full impact of her burgeoning girth the chair creaked like an antiquated wooden fishing vessel.

Safely ensconced in the chair, she sucked the juicy pear until the denuded stump held between her fingers was the only witness of her fruity feast. With the back of her dimpled fat hand, she wiped a few remnants that had *miraculously* escaped the cavernous mouth. However, the pleasurable satisfaction vanished when her gimlet eyes caught Patrick staring at her and he speedily focused on a safer target.

Whenever Mother Superior came to inspect the kitchen, spasms of terror passed over Fatima's face. Mother Superior strutted around…tight-lipped…stiff arsed… nose tilted upwards as though she was inspecting an odorous abattoir. Her inspection time was usually in late afternoon when the dinner preparation was in full progress. The untidiness and mayhem in the kitchen was just too much for Mother Superior. She strode from one cupboard to the next nursing her wrath to keep it warm… as she observed the feckless efforts of Fatima's household skills. A terror stricken Sister Fatima followed in her wake, oblivious to the fact that Patrick was savagely enjoying her discomfort. He gloated in the fact that for once she was getting the dirty end of the stick. And as she waddled behind the tall austere figure of Mother Superior... Fatima had the appearance of a bedraggled old hen fished out of a well.

CHAPTER THREE
Sister Rose

The day after the salty soup had made its way into the Nuns' dining room, Patrick entered the kitchen to be greeted by a smiling young nun. Wearing a big white apron draped over her habit.

"Hello. Are you Patrick?"

"Yes Sister, I work in the kitchen every day after school."

"I'm Sister Rose. Mother Superior said you would be around after class to lend a hand. I need to know where everything is around this kitchen. How about giving me a guided tour? From now on you and I will be working partners here, so we'll have to rely on each other."

Never before had an adult asked him for advice. And his thin chest expanded beyond its usual bony boundary. Young as he was, he cautioned himself to take it all with a grain of salt, at least until he knew which way the wind was blowing. Salt …why had that word popped into his head again? Where *was* Sister Fat-Am-I, what the hell had happened to her? Why this sudden change? He decided to bide his time and wait for things to happen. Alas, curiosity got the better of him and he heard himself asking rather timidly…

"Sister Rose, where *is* Sister Fatima, is she ill?"

"No she is not ill. Patrick from now on I'm going to be head cook and bottle washer in this kitchen. And come to think of it you and I may have to discuss a thing or two that's for our ears only. Do you understand?"

"Yes, Sister Rose, whatever happens I'll never tell a soul. Anyway, I have only one person to talk to and that is Sister Elizabeth."

"Yes, Sister Elizabeth said you were a sensible young fellow and she warned me that if I didn't treat you right she would stop praying for my redemption. Quite frankly, I think I'm *past* redemption." Having said that, she laughed heartily!

'Twas like a summer breeze for Patrick being greeted everyday by Sister Rose instead of the old harridan Fatima. At last God was answering his prayers. He wondered if God ever got fed up listening to his tale of woe. Aye, maybe he should give God a rest for a while now that Fatima had been removed.

He had prayed for the burden of Sister Fatima to be lifted from his shoulders for such a long time. He had even gone as far as ask God to remove her from the face of the earth. Ah, well, his prayer had been only half answered; she hadn't been removed as far as he had hoped, but at least she was to hell out of the kitchen. Silently he thanked God for granting this big favour.

"When you stop daydreaming Patrick, I'll tell you about the commotion in the nuns' dining room last night. We were served soup that was so salty; the nuns had to leave the table in a panic. Their faces were as white as the driven snow and Mother Superior departed in such haste she didn't take time to excuse herself. I'll bet the well is running dry this morning because the nuns drank water all night long trying to quench their thirst. Thank goodness I never take the soup, so I'm well and hearty today. Anyway to make a short story longer, I was called to the Superior's office and appointed to kitchen duties. I love to cook, so from now on Patrick you and I will be eating decent meals. Sister Fatima has been transferred to the laundry room where she will be less of a menace to the digestive health of the community."

"You mean she will never be in charge of the kitchen again?"

"That's right, Patrick, and you can wipe the 'cat that ate the canary' look off your Irish mug and start working."

Tut-tutting in disgust, Sister Rose viewed the clutter in every nook and cranny of the pantry. Before long she had the trash can bulging with preserves that she declared had been there since 'The Last Supper'. Two novice nuns scrubbed and cleaned until their hands were the colour of a lobster. When everything was in tip-top condition, Rose rolled up her sleeves and started cooking.

Later she called Patrick to the table and placed before him a plate with roast lamb, potato and vegetables. Never in all his born days had a feast like that been set before him. He ate with gusto and when his belly was stretched to the limit… a blissful look of satisfaction declared to the world that he had never tasted such delicious food. "Well now, if you're not bursting at the seams, have you space for a piece of hot apple pie? And before you leave, take this orange with you to the dorm, it will wet your whistle when you wake up in the morning."

An orange! God almighty, he couldn't believe his ears. The only time he had been given an orange was on Christmas day. But then wasn't that the *one* day of the year when everyone's heart should be filled with unstinting charity? After all, it *was* Christ's birthday! But some folks celebrated *His* birthday in queer ways. Maybe Christ had forgotten to stop at the orphanage and inform everyone what *His birthday* was all about.

Sister Elizabeth the music teacher was the only person Patrick adored. She taught music to the wealthy students who came from posh private schools. Patrick enviously observed these students, wearing their dark green school blazers with a gold crest on the breast pocket and a skip cap to match. Their shoes so well polished one would think they must walk on their hands to keep their shoes so clean! Patrick wondered what their lives were like…he tried to imagine what it was like to have a mother and father, plenty to eat and a good clean bed.

The gift of the orange from Sister Rose reminded Patrick of the time he had stolen an orange from the storeroom. He had just started peeling it when Sister Fatima rounded the corner and grabbing him by the ear she pulled him all the way to Mother Superior's office. By the time he reached the office he was sure his ear was hanging at half-mast. Sister Fatima's dramatic rendition of his thieving ways was enough to bring Mother Superior to her full height and with the poise of an executioner she reached for the cane. With savage pleasure she pelted his skinny bottom until the throbbing pain seared through him like a fire out of control. Patrick left her office barely able to put one foot in front of the other, but somehow that severe caning was a turning point for him. It strengthened his resolve: never ever again would he allow his tormentor the satisfaction of seeing him cry! 'Twas a small victory…but an important one! He crawled into his cot and the only way he could ease the pain was by lying face downwards. Black despair sucked its way through every nook and cranny of his being…and he prayed that he could go to sleep and never awaken!

The following morning, Mother Superior, with her hands stuffed up the wide sleeves of her habit was waiting outside of the classroom. He tried not to look at her, but she blocked his passage and in her usual grim tone said, "Come with me to my office."

What in the hell have I done now? Patrick wondered.

He didn't have long to wait for answer. Opening the door to her office she unceremoniously pushed him inside. The prodding stopped only when she had him placed in the centre of the office. Standing ramrod straight she appeared to be deciding which part of him she should dissect. Her thin lips were like the slits on a child's penny bank.

"O' Grady; I'll not mince words, so listen carefully. You are what we call a destitute orphan; you have no relatives to contribute to your upkeep. The daily chores you perform in the kitchen are a small repayment for the care we give you and stealing will not be tolerated."

"Mother Superior, that orange was the first thing I've ever stolen."

"Perhaps it was the first time you were ever caught. You may return to your classroom and keep in mind that we have harsher forms of punishment to administer should you continue misbehaving."

He left swearing under his breath…'May you die groaning you old bitch.'

Now that Fatima was no longer in charge of the kitchen, Sister Elizabeth visited more often. She and Rose were great friends. Their personalities were as different as night and day, Sister Rose bubbled over with endless energy and laughter and Sister Elizabeth was of a quieter nature. Elizabeth walked with a dignified aura of tranquillity and Rose on the other hand was always going at a fast pace. Rose seemed to enjoy every minute of the day and cracked jokes with the men who delivered the groceries. The deliverymen never left her kitchen without a cup of tea and a scone or two. Sometimes when the day was cold and wet she would hand them a couple of big hot spuds right out of the pot. As they held the hot spuds in their cold hands she would smother the spuds with thick yellow butter. Their weather beaten faces would glow with pleasure with this bit of human kindness!

One time when Mother Superior caught Sister Rose giving spuds to the two deliverymen, she asked for an explanation. Sister Rose solemnly explained that she was following in the footsteps of Jesus. Hadn't He left the message to feed the poor and the hungry?' With that Mother Superior flounced out of the kitchen as though her knickers were on fire. After this hasty departure Rose burst into laughter!

A few days after the meeting and chastisement at the hands of Mother Superior, his teacher told him to report to Sister Elizabeth in the music room. He had no idea why, and he didn't care because he loved being alone with her. She was the only nun who had ever smiled or spoke to him. Patrick thought she was beautiful, tall and graceful and she walked so softly it seemed her feet barely touched the floor.

He remembered the day a sheaf of papers slipped from her hands as they were passing in the hallway. Simultaneously they stooped to pick up the papers and their heads bumped, she laughed and whispered, 'Patrick if your head is as hard as mine there will be no damage done.' As she spoke Patrick looked into her smiling eyes and thought they were the most beautiful eyes he had ever seen. And Elizabeth had the greatest desire to caress his little face.

From that day forward Patrick had a fanciful dream to light up his dark moments. He imagined Sister Elizabeth taking him by the hand and running away from the orphanage and living happily ever after.

'Twas a fleeting dream, but momentarily the bleakness of his existence faded into oblivion.

So now, on his way to the music room along the gloomy hallway he stared at all the life-size statues lining the walls. He thought they were the dourest group he had ever clapped an eye on. Were these the Martyrs who were fed to the lions? If so, their sour expression was enough to ruin the lion's digestive system... or a notion to change their diet.

When he came to a huge brown door marked 'Music Room' he opened it noiselessly and heard Sister Elizabeth playing the piano. She was not aware of his presence and appeared to be in a world of dreams. A golden shaft of afternoon sunlight slanted across the room and rested on her beautiful face. Young Patrick imagined she looked like an angel and his heart filled with happiness as he stood in silence admiring her.

Suddenly she stopped playing, and putting her face in her hands, she bowed her head so low it almost touched the keys. Patrick was quite sure she was weeping, and a strange emotion took hold of him. How good it would be, if only he could snuggle into her arms and weep with her... allowing their tears to wash away their combined sadness. 'Twas pure fantasy on his part, after all he had never snuggled in anyone's arms or known what it was like to be hugged.

He cleared his throat and she swung around at the sound.

"Ah Patrick, there you are standing as quiet as a mouse and scaring the daylights out of me."

"I didn't want to startle you Sister Elizabeth, but the music was so beautiful, I had to stand still and listen. I've never heard music like that before."

"I'm always happy when someone tells me they love music. Have you ever thought of learning to play an instrument?"

"I've always wanted to play the flute."

"The flute? Well now, I have a flute that belonged to my dear brother. He was a grand Flutist. Would you like to learn to read music and play the flute?"

"Sister Elizabeth that would be grand. But it will never happen."

"Yes Patrick it will happen. I shall arrange to give you lessons every Monday after class and you may use my brother's flute."

"I don't think Mother Superior will give me permission to take lessons."

"Patrick, I requested that you come here to help sort out the music for a forthcoming concert. And now that I know you are interested in music I will make sure you have lessons. I will make arrangements with Mother Superior as soon as possible."

"Mother Superior hates me and wallops me every chance she gets! I know that she will not allow me to study music. Every time she canes me I go to the dormitory and weep. Then I pray that my own mother or father will come and take me away from here forever."

"I'm quite sure she doesn't hate you. And why on earth does she beat you? Patrick an orphans life can be terribly lonely, but keep in mind that when you reach the age of fourteen you will leave here forever."

"I can't imagine staying here until I am fourteen years old. That's such a long time from now."

"When the boys leave this orphanage they receive a small amount of money and a letter. I believe those letters might provide information about their parentage."

"Sister Elizabeth, I like talking to you. There is no one else as kind as you are."

"Patrick, you haven't had the opportunity to meet many people, but I can assure you there are plenty of kind people in this world of ours. Unfortunately, you have stumbled across a few who aren't quite up to scratch, probably because they never knew kindness in their own lives. I'm not offering that as an excuse for their behaviour...perhaps they have forgotten that regardless of our station in life we are all equal in the eyes of God."

Seeing how hopelessly unhappy he looked, she put her arms around his thin shoulders and wished she could do something to assuage his misery. Then she asked him where he went on Sundays after Mass, "You should go for walks through the woods, and get some good, fresh air in your lungs."

She was thoroughly shocked when he told her he had never been outside the main gates, because he had to work in the kitchen every day of the week including Sunday.

"I'll have a word with Mother Superior right away and you can be sure that from now on you will be free of all chores on Sundays. Then you can spend a few healthy hours strolling through the countryside."

"Sister Elizabeth, aren't you afraid of Mother Superior? I'm filled with fear from my head to my toes every time I see her coming towards me."

"No, I can't say I'm afraid of anyone. Why do you fear her?"

"Because she beats me every chance she gets."

"Patrick, I do hope you're not exaggerating. Meanwhile, I'll make sure you have Sunday's free in the future."

"Did you say I should go for a walk in the woods? I can't, I'd get lost. I don't know how to get there. I've never been outside the gates in my life."

"I'll draw a map for you and explain it to you before you leave."

That night as he lay in bed, his mind was full of dreams about passing through those big, formidable iron gates for the first time and heading out to the unknown world. Perhaps he should just keep walking and never return to this miserable hellhole?

CHAPTER FOUR
Patrick's First Outing

Saturday afternoon Sister Elizabeth arrived in the kitchen with a hand drawn map. She and Sister Rose guided Patrick through the winding, little roads on the map. As they spoke, they recalled the games played there when they were children.

Sister Rose said that he must go as far as the Babblin' Bridge. "When I was a child I used to pitch stones down into the gurgling waters, it was great fun until my little brother almost fell over into the water below. I was frightened to death that day until I managed to pull him back over the stone wall. Then my fright turned to rage and I smacked him one on the backside. So for goodness sake be careful, we don't want to lose you."

"Rose, don't frighten the lad on his first outing."

"Sure Patrick is made of stronger stuff than that. Don't coddle the lad or you'll make a real 'Tea Jessie' out of him."

The morning of his keenly anticipated adventure into the outside world, he combed his hair at least three times. He washed his face until it glistened and by the time he had finished, the skin on his face felt as thin as a cobweb. Meticulously lining the soles of his well-worn shoes with new cardboard, he knotted his laces so tightly that he was sure he would never be able to undo the laces again. He glanced at his image in the old cracked mirror and what he saw was not reassuring. Even after all the combing, his thick wavy hair seemed to be standing at attention.

Gingerly making his way to the main entrance hall he was greatly relieved when he saw Sister Elizabeth waiting at the desk for him. He always felt safe and comfortable in her presence and his love for her was immense.

She waited patiently as he laboriously finished the task of applying his name to this his first sign-out document. Sensing his anxiety she wanted to give him a reassuring hug, but this wasn't the time or place…so patting him on the shoulder she reminded him to return before curfew.

"Sister Rose has made a lunch for you," and she handed him a brown paper bag.

They walked together down the tree-lined path to the main gate. Bidding him goodbye, she pressed a shilling into his hand.

He stared at the round silver coin nestled in the centre of his small palm and anxiously asked, "What will I do with it? I've never had money before."

"I thought you would treat yourself to a bar of toffee or anything else your little heart desires. There used to be a little shop selling all sorts of Sweeties at the end of the first road, I'm sure it is still there. Don't be shy, just walk in and buy what you like. Patrick, don't worry about all the newness of this little outing, observe, absorb and enjoy all that comes your way. If perchance you lose your way, which I don't think is going to happen, just go into any farm…tell them you're from the orphanage and they will have you back here safe and sound. Off you go now and I'll be waiting for you when you return. And may God go with you."

Once out on the road by himself for the first time in his life, he squared off his shoulders and planted each step down on the unfamiliar road as though he *actually* knew where he was going. Nevertheless without moving his lips he asked God for guidance. He couldn't talk out loud to God, in case someone passed by and thought he was daft. So he tried to spiel off a holy conversation with closed lips–the words hitting the back of his teeth–ending with "Heavenly Father, you're the only father I have… so please don't let me get lost". Patrick continued on his way quite confident that *someone* up above would take care of this… his first big adventure.

The road veered off just like the drawing on the map and to his great delight the trees and shrubs thickened and he knew he was entering the woods. When he reached the winding path with all the green foliage and an umbrella of green branches above, there was a hushed silence…just like the lull in church before communion.

Through the narrow path he went, looking up through the tall trees at the blue glimpses of the sky. 'Twas a feat he could accomplish in spurts, because he found that when he brought his head down again he was a bit dizzy. But oh, what a beautiful sight it was! A flood of happiness surged through every nook and cranny of his being. He breathed deeply and slowly exhaled. The teacher instructed them to do the breathing exercises in the classroom every morning before they planted their backsides on the narrow seat at their desks. She opened the windows wide as soon as she entered the classroom in the morning and told them to face the open windows and fill their lungs with the good morning air. She told them that the brain required oxygen to function properly and this was attained through filling their lungs with fresh air. None of the children knew what the hell she was talking about; however, they obeyed to avoid a clout on the ear-hole.

Finally he came to a shady knoll, and throwing himself down on the lush green grass, he lay there looking up through the sun-dappled trees with glimpses of the blue sky adding to the beauty. The birds filled the air with songs as they flew in complete abandon from tree to tree.

Closing his eyes he imagined himself flying over the treetops. Jaysus…if he had wings he would fly away from that orphanage and never go back. Right then and there the notion of escape began to form. Aye, why not just keep on walking this fine day in the opposite direction from the orphanage? He wondered how far a shilling would take him? Since he had never used money, he had no idea of its value.

But deep down he knew he had to go back. He imagined the state Sister Elizabeth would be in if he pulled a stunt like that on his first day out. He knew the pleasure it would be for Mother Superior to heap the blame on Sister Elizabeth if he ran way. But then again, why not just keep on walking? Supposing he never got another chance to leave the orphanage? The thought of never having to return to that dismal place almost blotted out the consequences.

With the notion of escape temporarily abandoned, he opened the lunch bag. What a treat! Two sandwiches with sliced white chicken, a tiny jar of chutney, an orange and a piece of iced fruitcake. The fresh country air had whetted his appetite and Patrick devoured every morsel with gusto!

Smacking his lips he lay down on the green grass, enjoying the tasty aftermath of his little feast. After a most enjoyable 'think' he decided to leave his bed of lush sweet smelling grass and search for the 'Babbling Bridge'.

As he rounded the path he heard the sound of water and there it was! 'Twas built with huge rough-hewn rocks of all shapes and sizes and the centre was rounded almost like a beehive. Walking to the middle of the bridge he braced his feet on the rocks, and climbed until he was at the right height to look over and down at the gurgling waters below. He could feel the rough-hewn rocks boring into his belly as he curved the top half of his body down towards the water.

He went to the outer edge of the bridge to find stones to pitch into the waters below. Rolling the front of his jersey up he made a sort of hollowed out apron and filled it with stones of various sizes. He pitched the stones one by one into the water below. Taking careful aim, he tried to hit the crests of the little foaming waves as they frolicked and frothed above the water.

Were there other boys somewhere along the way pitching stones into these same waters? Did they have shoes with sturdy soles that never allowed their feet to get wet? A nice cosy home with a clean bed covered with a creamy coloured wool blanket? Had their mother made hand-hooked rugs to put on the floor by their bed, so their feet wouldn't freeze when they stepped out of bed in the morning? Did their mother hug them every day? Jaysus, if he had a mother he would hug her every time he saw her.

Having no idea of the time, Patrick decided to start walking back to the orphanage. As he reached the winding road, a farmer came along in a horse drawn cart and asked him if he would like a lift.

"I'm just roaming the countryside on this fine day, Sir."

"Well," said the farmer, "you will see more of it from this cart than you will on foot, so hop aboard lad before Old Champion gets restless."

Patrick jumped up and the farmer gently flicked the reins and Old Champion took off in a trot. Patrick had never been on a horse drawn cart before. He sat in silent happiness enjoying this new sensation…and sure wasn't this the grandest day in his life?

"Why would a young lad like you be out walking alone? Don't you have any friends your own age?"

"No Sir, I don't have any friends, but I don't mind being alone. This is the first time I've ever been allowed to leave the orphanage."

"Now, is that a fact? Well it wouldn't be a bad idea if we knew each other's names. I'm Sean Murphy and I'm pleased to make your acquaintance."

"I'm Patrick O' Grady. Could I call you Sean, or Mr. Murphy?"

"Maybe you'd better put the mister to my moniker until you meet my wife, she appreciates youngsters being respectful to their elders. Now let's head over to my farm, I have some fine animals I'd like you to see. Maybe my wife will have a cup of tea ready and some of her good scones. Are you due back at a certain time?"

"I don't know what time it is now, but I must be back at the Orphanage before curfew at five o'clock."

"Well my lad, we'll make sure we have you back on time. Now, here's the road to my little farm; we'll be there in a jiffy."

"I've never been to a farm before."

"Tis a little bit of a farm, but it keeps us well supplied with fresh eggs, meat and vegetables. We have cows to give us good milk and plenty left over to make butter. Aye, we have all of God's blessings on our wee bit of earth."

Sean led him through the barn, and every animal received a pat on the rump as he passed.

Patrick thought it was funny listening to Sean calling the animals by name and chatting with each one as he patted their rumps. And strange to say… each of the animals turned their heads towards Sean as though they understood everything he said. . After the barn chores were done Sean doused his hands and face beneath a spigot of water and dried them with a big red and white hankie.

Mrs. Murphy was standing at the door of the little white washed cottage and she called out.

"Aye, you two stragglers timed it right, the scones are hot off the griddle and the tea is infused. Who is this young lad you have in tow?"

"Shivaun, this is young Patrick, he's from the orphanage. I came upon him roaming the countryside on his own and thought the two of us could do with a bit of company. He tells me this is the first time he has been allowed away from that dismal hellhole."

"Well now, I'm pleased to meet you. Come on in and share a meal with us. As Sean just stated, it's grand indeed to have a bit of company."

"Shivaun, that's a mouth-watering aroma coming from the kitchen. Lord bless us, it's tantalizing enough to resurrect the appetite of a corpse. What are you cooking?"

"I have a roast of lamb and all the good things that go with it. Aye, but just wait until you see what I have for Sweets afterwards."

'Twas a fine supper indeed. There was fresh strawberry pie with big red strawberries resting their fat bottoms on top of the thick cream. Patrick scraped every last bit from his plate and heaved a sigh of contentment. Mrs. Murphy watched with satisfaction and asked if he had space for another helping.

Not waiting for a reply she filled his plate with a generous portion.

When it was time to leave, Mr. Murphy hitched old Champion up to the little cart as Patrick bid a sad farewell to Mrs. Murphy. She made him promise he would return the following Sunday for dinner. Mrs. Murphy kept on waving until they were out of sight.

As they neared the orphanage Patrick could feel the warmth of the past few hours evaporating. Leaving Murphy's cosy home to go back to the orphanage was as piercing as a cold blade of steel. It was the first time he had ever been inside a home and he wished he could have stayed in that cheery kitchen forever!

This was a roller coaster of a day with the happy and sad moments vying for attention. These fast changes tripped him up when he least expected it. Was that what life was all about? Today he had tasted both happiness and sadness, whereas inside the grey walls of the orphanage there was only undiluted misery.

Remembering that next Sunday he would be visiting the Murphys was something to look forward to. Heavenly Father, he prayed, I just don't want Mother Superior to forbid me to leave next Sunday.

Sister Elizabeth was waiting at the gates when he arrived back at the orphanage. Taking him by the hand she said, "I'm so glad to see you back safe and sound. Sign in and then we'll go to the music room, I'm anxious to hear all about your first day in the outside world."

The warm welcome from Sister Elizabeth was all he needed to begin relating the events of the day. Relating how much fun it was when he came across the Babblin' Bridge and pitched stones into the water. How he enjoyed listening to the birds sing as they flew from tree to tree in complete freedom. He told of how he lay on his back on the lush grass and made skyscapes out of the white curling clouds in the sky.

He told her how he had fallen asleep on the grassy slope, after eating the delicious lunch that Sister Rose had made for him. His eyes lit up when he told her about Mr. Murphy giving him a ride in his cart and that the seats were all sideways, making it easy to see the countryside as they passed along.

"Those carts are called 'jaunting carts,' Patrick. Where did you go in his cart?"

"Oh, he took me to his farm and I visited all the animals in the barn. Then he took me over to his home. Mrs. Murphy sat me down to a fine supper of roast lamb and afterwards she brought out a strawberry cake lathered in cream with big fat bottomed strawberries sitting on top of the thick cream in rich red juicy glory. And do you know what? I had two helpings! I'd like to be a glutton for the rest of my life, except that Sister Fatima told me that gluttons go to hell. Is that true?"

"By the look of Sister Fatima she's had more experience with gluttony than most people and may God forgive me for that remark. However, I don't think your little feast today will be recorded by Saint Peter."

29

When he finished relating all that had happened, he tried in vain to stifle a yawn. The yawn was so enjoyable; he didn't want it to end. Sister Elizabeth laughed heartily and said it was his bedtime.

Again yawning with abandon he mumbled, "I'm so sleepy. I've never felt as sleepy as this in my life."

"That's the good fresh country air, now off you go my lad, and have a good sound sleep and sweet dreams. God Bless you."

Elizabeth sat in deep thought after his departure with her mind tossing a slew of ideas back and forth. First of all she feared that she was becoming too attached to Patrick and she was amazed at his resemblance to her brother. After all these years of erasing the memories, now Patrick was reopening the pages of time.

She began to question her decision to become a nun. Now it was apparent that she had taken the vows to avoid the disgrace, there was no place in Ireland where she would have been accepted as an unwed mother with a child. Now this sort of raking through the past was ravaging her peace of mind. All the reasons that had prevailed at that time still rankled her.

The Murphys taught Patrick how to milk cows, churn butter and do a host of other farm chores. He was scared to death the first time he fumbled beneath a hen to retrieve the eggs and the fluttering hens sent him reeling backwards into a pile of hay. Mrs. Murphy laughed at his timidity and taught him how to gather the eggs fearlessly, saying, "Patrick you mustn't ruffle their feathers too much, but at the same time you have to let the hens know you mean business."

As time went by Patrick learned how to cut turf for the fires, paint the barns, whitewash the cottage and dig up the potatoes. Sean showed him how to plough the fields, walking behind old Windy the plough horse. But it didn't take long before Patrick understood that Windy knew more about ploughing than he did.

As time went on Sean and his wife grew very fond of Patrick and each Sunday when it was time for him to leave their farewells were tinged with sadness.

Mrs. Murphy offered to pay Patrick for the work he was doing, but he refused, saying, "I have never been so happy in my life. Shure and I couldn't be taking money for happiness, wouldn't that spoil it all?"

"Child I don't understand it, but sometimes you say things that are far beyond your age. God bless you, and may you bask in the warmth of His great love all the days of your life."

"Thank you Mrs. Murphy, I wish all the nuns at the convent were like you."

"Well Patrick, shure and I wouldn't want to change places with any of those nuns. Bundled up in black robes from head to toe, wearing blinkers on the side of their eyes like horses, aye, that's not for me. I can't imagine cutting myself off from the rest of the world and walking around all day as though I had a dozen funerals to attend. It's been said that they spend all their spare time praying for the sinners of the world. I think the sinners should take time out from *enjoying* their sins and pray for their *own* redemption. Come to think of it I've often wondered why *some* sins are so enjoyable."

The following Sunday they told Patrick they had opened an account in the Post office for him and that once in awhile a few shillings would be added to his account. They showed him a small wooden cupboard in the kitchen where he could keep his savings book and personal items. The Murphy's weren't wealthy but they were rich in the warmth of love and kindness and their little farmhouse was an embodiment of love.

Sister Elizabeth arranged his music lessons for every Monday and Patrick headed to the music room as fast as his legs would take him. Passing the statues of the dour looking saints in the gloomy hallway no longer bothered him. His anticipation of the music lesson filled him with such joy it lifted him into a world he had never known.

Sister Elizabeth was happy when the two of them were alone in the music room and she began to feel a protective love for Patrick. For the first time she allowed herself to dream of leaving the convent and taking him with her...but where would they go? Quickly she would sweep these fantasies away. However, they began to flit back and forth in her mind more frequently to the point that her sleep pattern was badly disturbed.

Patrick had no trouble at all learning to read music and was thrilled to the tips of his toes when Sister Elizabeth told him that he was a born musician. This was one compliment he *did* believe, because when he played the flute he felt that he was floating on air. The music lifted him to heights far and beyond his immediate surroundings. Sometimes when the last note was played, he and Sister Elizabeth sat quietly...wrapped in a magic silence.

The months passed swiftly for Patrick now that he was taking music lessons twice a week. He also spent many hours in the music room practicing. The long practice sessions were necessary because Sister Elizabeth had secretly arranged for him to play solo in the upcoming concert.

One afternoon when he was practicing in the music room, Mother Superior walked in and demanded Patrick return to the kitchen for the rest of the day. Sister Elizabeth, in a very determined manner, told Mother Superior that would not be possible. In addition, he had to be excused from kitchen chores due to the fact he had two lessons each week and required time to practice.

With lips tightly compressed, Mother Superior strode to the door. She aimed a look of venom in Elizabeth's direction.

It always surprised Patrick when he heard Sister Elizabeth going against Mother Superior's commands. Elizabeth never kow-towed to her in the way Sister Fatima did. She simply stated her requests in such a way that she expected no opposition from Mother Superior. But he sensed that Sister Elizabeth didn't really care how much Mother Superior's feathers were ruffled. Needless to say Patrick enjoyed these encounters.

On the Sunday before the concert Patrick was walking towards the Murphy's farm, when he heard the clip clop trotting of Champion. He couldn't explain the happy feeling he had inside, whenever Sean and Champion came to meet him. Patrick had grown so fond of the Murphys he couldn't imagine a Sunday without them.

Having Sister Elizabeth, Sister Rose and the Murphys in his

world was wonderful, and Patrick was sure his Heavenly Father had arranged the whole thing. He remembered telling Sister Elizabeth that his heart smiled every time he thought of playing his flute. This reverie came to an abrupt end when he heard Sean calling out. "There you are me lad, for a minute you looked as though you were in another world listening to the Wee Folk spinning yarns."

Patrick laughed and told him that he had good news and that he could barely wait to tell. Sean, I've been taking music lessons and I am learning to play the flute.

"Where did you get the flute?"

"Sister Elizabeth has one belonging to her brother and she allows me to use it."

"Hmm, is that a fact? Mrs. Murphy will be a happy woman to hear that bit of news. I used to play the violin and my wife sings like a nightingale."

"Do you still play?"

"Well, we had a tragedy in our lives and the music stopped."

Instinctively Patrick sensed that he shouldn't ask any more questions. For the rest of the way home they remained silent, the peaceful clip clop of the horse's hoofs being the predominant sound. The boy stole an occasional glance at Sean's face and found it deadly serious. A shadow of fear passed over him, had he said something wrong? He appealed to his Heavenly Father to change things back to where they had been...before he had started talking about music.

Mrs. Murphy was at the door to greet him. As she held him close to her well-cushioned body, she said, "I declare you've grown taller since last Sunday."

"Shivaun, let's go in and have a cup of tea and listen to the good news Patrick has for us."

Patrick related all that had happened and why he had refrained from telling them about his music lessons. He didn't want to tell them until he was sure that he could play. His face lit up as he said it was the happiest thing that had ever happened to him!

Ruefully he added, "I wish I could practice and play the flute every day of my life. Someday I will buy a flute and I'll leave it here.

Then I will play for you on Sundays."

Sean glanced over to Shivaun; "Don't you think the time has come for us to start a new chapter in our lives?"

"Aye, Sean, it's time to turn the tide and God only knows why this lad was sent into our lives. I suppose there's a reason for everything. Go ahead and fetch the instruments."

Sean went over to the big wooden chiffonier and brought forth a violin, and then he pulled out a box filled with sheets of music. Some of which were yellowed with age. Then he placed a green and gold case on the table and asked Patrick to open it.

Patrick felt an inexplicable current in the atmosphere and was surprised when he saw tears coursing down Sean's cheeks and Shivaun also on the verge of tears. He carefully opened the green and gold case and therein laid the most beautiful flute he had ever seen.

The silence in the room was shattered when Sean removed a big white linen hankie from his pocket and thunderously blew his nose. It's a known fact that the Irish have the ability to slide from tragedy to humour with the greatest of ease. So the emotionally charged moment was cleared…when Shivaun said, "Sean, it's a wonder you didn't blow a hole right through that hankie…shure it sounded like a clap of thunder."

That brought a smile back to Sean's face and he reached over and started spreading the sheets of music on the table. He told the boy to look through the pile of music and find something that hit his fancy. Then Sean started tuning the instruments.

Typical Irish music filled the room. Some tunes lively enough to make your toes tap with joy and some so poignant they could tear your heart in two.

Sean beamed when he heard Shivaun singing in her sweet Irish voice and silently thanked God for the wonder of it all.

Patrick's happiness spilled over when the Murphys congratulated him on how well he played.

"We are lucky indeed to have you with us, Patrick. Every Sunday when you visit us we will share this beautiful gift of music. God in His heaven is happy that three little bits o' driftwood like us have found each other."

The time flew past and reluctantly the instruments had to be put away. What a wonderful day it had been. Sean put the instruments into the cupboard in the big Chiffonier. "There they are, Patrick, and there they will stay until you and I play again next Sunday. Would you look at the time now? God almighty, if 'Old Champion' could run as fast as this day has gone, sure and we'd enter her in the next Derby. Let's get her tacked up. I'll take you as far as the crossroads. We don't want you to get into any trouble by being late."

CHAPTER FIVE
Returning to the Orphanage after Meeting Sean

Patrick said goodbye to Sean, and without a backward glance passed through the orphanage gate. The joy of the day evaporated as the bleak stone building came into view. He hoped Sister Elizabeth would be there to meet him. Sure enough, she was waiting outside the tall wooden door. He was so happy to see her that he ran the rest of the way to where she was standing. Patrick wanted so much to race into her arms and hug her. Instead, he just stood looking up at her, the story of his heart in his eyes. Elizabeth understood that it would be a terrible letdown if he went straight to the dormitory without the 'telling'. So, off they went to the music room where they could talk in private.

Closing the door she walked over to the piano bench and motioned Patrick to join her. "Now, let's hear all about your day. I also have news for you, too, but that can wait. I'm anxious to hear all about your day."

"Well I was so happy when Sean came half way to meet me and do you know I think old Champion was glad to see me too. When I patted him he talked back to me with a ho-ho deep in his throat. Mrs. Murphy had a fine dinner ready; I could smell the goodness of it the minute she opened the door. Sister Elizabeth, their only son was a musician and he died a long time ago. Mrs. Murphy wept when Sean spoke about their son, and he had to go over and comfort her to make her stop crying."

"Yes, now that you mention their son, I know which Murphys you are referring to. Their son Seamus and his chum were drowned when their boat capsized. Their bodies were never found and that fact added more sorrow to the tragedy. Seamus won a scholarship for music; he was an accomplished flutist. All Murphys in this village are talented musicians. As a matter of fact Sean was a fine violinist and Shivaun his wife sang like a nightingale. Before the accident occurred they played and sang at all the gatherings in the village, but after their sons' death they never played again. It's wonderful that they have opened up their hearts to you. God works in mysterious ways."

"Well now, here is the good news I have for you. I want you to play a solo in the concert and I will accompany you on the piano. Patrick, don't look so frightened, you'll have plenty of time to prepare and practice. I've arranged for your kitchen duties to cease from this day forward. You have a gift and I intend to nurture that gift to its full potential. I want you to keep reminding yourself that it is a gift from above."

Timidly he told her that he would study hard but he would be too nervous to play in public. Then he stammered, "Sister Elizabeth, please don't be angry, but I just know that I could never go out on stage all by myself."

"Patrick, you've just started playing and already you have surpassed students who have taken lessons for years. Some students of mine play without the emotional power to raise their music to its magical glory and this type of student continues to take lessons because their parents insist on it. You have a God given gift. Off to bed now, you've had quite a day. Tomorrow when you come for your next music lesson, we shall discuss this further."

Even though he was dog-tired, he couldn't fall asleep. Eyes wide open he lay in the dark, trying to digest all the changes that were flowing into his life. Finally and almost against his will he drifted into the arms of Morpheus. He dreamed that he had found his mother and she was young and beautiful and had held him in her arms. The dream had been so real...that even after he was awake... he felt warm and cosy. That warmth evaporated when his eyes swept across the long row of beds in the Dorm...each bed with the little mounds of unwanted humanity huddled beneath the threadbare grey blankets.

Sister Elizabeth tried to instill in Patrick the need to cultivate happy thoughts; she told him that good healthy thinking acted as a buffer when the going got rough.

In his wildest dreams he had never imagined he would have the chance to study music and every lesson was a joy to look forward to. With all this change in his life even his schoolwork improved. For the first time he had top marks in his class. Now with coaching from Elizabeth he walked with shoulders straight and his chin a little higher.

When the teacher read the monthly report to the class, she called out his name and asked him to come to her desk. With a smile she handed him a piece of notepaper and when he read it he could feel his face and ears burning. He had come first in the class and he was absolutely speechless! Then she gave him a small slim parcel wrapped in stiff brown paper.

"Patrick this book is my gift to you for your outstanding improvement. I want you to finish reading it before the end of the month. Then I want you to write an essay on what you have read. I congratulate you on your good marks this month and remember if you can do it once–you can do it again."

He returned to his seat in a daze with the book clutched tightly in his thin chest. Holy Jaysus, that was the first gift he had ever received. How many prayers had he sent to the Holy Mother asking her to help him to come first in the class? He had prayed such a long time for this favour; he figured she must have gone abroad on a long holiday. One time in confession he had told old Father Devlin that the Holy Mother never answered his prayers and the old priest had bellowed, "Ah, yea of little faith."

Suddenly the excitement of coming first and the gift got the better of him and he, holding his belly, raced out of the classroom without asking permission. Once outside the classroom he stood leaning against the wall still clutching the book against his belly and not knowing what to do. His breathing seemed to be exploding in little short heaves and his heart was hammering hard enough to break loose from its moorings.

That is where his teacher found him standing with his back to the wall as though he was glued to it. Sensing that the lad was in a highly emotional state she told him to take the rest of the day off. She suggested that he should go to the music room and tell Sister Elizabeth about his scholastic achievement. Giving him one of her rare smiles she returned to the classroom.

Ah, but his dream world crashed in a helluva hurry when Mother Superior cast her dark shadow across his path, barring his way she asked, "Where do you think you are going before class is over?"

"I am on my way to the music room, I have permission to start my music lesson earlier today."

"Who gave you permission?" and before waiting for an answer, bellowed, "Follow me, I'm going to find out why you have these special privileges."

So he walked in the wake of that rustling black bundle of hatefulness and thought how wonderful it would be... never to set eyes on her again. Maybe, just maybe, if he started sending a few extra prayers to the Holy Mother she'd get Mother Superior transferred to another convent.

She barged into the music room and in a voice dripping with loathing...demanded to know why he was being excused from class. Sister Elizabeth sent Patrick an inquiring look and seemed to understand that something unusual was happening. She studied the little watch pinned on the front of her habit and said in an off hand tone, "Ah yes, I've been waiting for Patrick to arrive, we have a special piece of music to go through today."

With the wind knocked out of her sails... Mother Superior stalked out.

"Well Patrick, now that I've blackened my soul with a white lie on your account, will you please explain what this is all about?"

Words tumbled rapidly as he told her that the teacher had given him a gift for being first in the class. This had made him so nervous that he ran out of the classroom. Then the teacher came out and told me to come here and tell you the good news. Mother Superior saw me in the hallway and asked me where I was off to before class closing. I told her I had an early music lesson so she brought me here to find out if I was telling the truth.

"I'm glad you are here early, I have a new piece for you to

practice. I'm so glad that your lessons have improved and I'm sure that you will keep up the good work. Now before we commence, have you anything further to add to your story?"

"Well Sister Elizabeth, I just want to tell you how it happened that I came first in class. You see I prayed for a long time to the Virgin Mary but she took so long to answer that I gave up. But sure enough as soon as she returned from her holiday abroad, she got busy on my petitions and answered my prayers."

"The Holy Mother was on holiday? How did you find out that she took holidays?"

"Do you remember when the old priest was in hospital and they sent a young priest to take over? Well, I went to confession and this is what happened."

"Bless me Father, for I have sinned," says Patrick.

"Have you now?" said the young priest. "In that case we'd better get started on your particular list of sins. How old are you?"

"Father, I'm almost eight and three quarters."

"Well now, isn't that a ripe old age. When will you make up the other quarter?"

"Oh, a long time from now."

"Hmm, is that a fact? In that case I'd better start hearing all the sins that you've committed in your long past."

"Well Father my sins are usually just make belief sins, you see, I've no way of making them happen. I always need the help of the holy Mother, but lately she hasn't worked on my problems."

The young priest was thoroughly enjoying this encounter and marvelled at the sheer innocence of the boy's faith. And not wanting to put an end to the dialogue, he said, "Perhaps when the Virgin Mother becomes wearied listening to all the whining requests we send to her, she just takes off for a wee bit of a holiday."

This amazed young Patrick; he believed that once you were inside the pearly gates you were there forever. "Father, I didn't know that once we got into heaven we could leave on a holiday."

"Frankly, I didn't know about it either until a very short time ago.

These vacations are given as rewards to the saints who spend their heavenly days listening to our pleading requests. Faith can work wonders... so be sure that the Good Lady will take care of you in her own good time."

The confessional was silent for a moment and then in a whisper filled with wonderment, he inquired, "Father, how does The Virgin Mary travel on her holiday, do they have trains up there?"

He waited anxiously for a reply, but it seemed the young priest was having bit of trouble with his throat, finally Patrick inquired, "Father is it a bit of a cold you have?"

"No I've been in here so long I need something to quench my thirst. Now to get back to your question about heavenly transport...it's been said that the angels spread their lovely silvery wings in a circle and the Blessed Virgin is transported to whatever destination her heart desires. So you see, there's no need for noisy old trains puffing around up there and leaving smoky stains on the lovely white clouds."

"I've never been on a train, but I'd pass that up, if I could float around in a nice soft cloud away up in the sky. Anyway, I think the Virgin Mary is lucky indeed to be able to travel by floating on a powdery soft cloud."

"Well child, if the Holy Mother of God doesn't deserve a bit of luck, who does? Now how about revealing some of those 'thinking' sins that are playing such havoc with you."

"Father, it's like this, I don't like Mother Superior or Sister Fatima, and as a matter of fact I hate the very sight of them. Putting up with those two is a lot worse than walking with a stone in my shoe, and that happens often when the cardboard inside my shoes wears out. I pray every night for the holy Mother to get rid of those two nuns, but so far she hasn't seen fit to shift them elsewhere. It looks as though they are here to stay and their life's enjoyment is cuffing my ears or paddling my backside."

"What in the name of God do you do to warrant such punishment?"

"I don't know Father...and that's the truth. Shure the two of them wish I'd never been born…and sometimes in bed at night I wish the same for myself. Father, have you ever felt so sad that you wished you had never been born?"

"Well now that you ask, I've had moments when I felt like a rudderless ship. Nevertheless, I believe life is a great gift and now I welcome every day that comes my way. I know that your life in the orphanage doesn't provide many happy moments, but you must have faith. Just think when you leave the orphanage you will have a blank canvas to fill with life's comings and going's… and it will be up to you what you fill it with."

Patrick turned to Sister Elizabeth and continued, "Having said that, he gave me absolution."

"When I left the confessional the young priest came out of the narrow middle door and winked at me and said, "Shure and it was a pleasure making your acquaintance. And Sister Elizabeth, no one had ever said that they were glad to know me and I was happy as a lark for the rest of the day. But that wasn't all; he ruffled through the pocket in his long black robe and gave me a half bar of treacle toffee. He said he knew I'd like the toffee, because the first half had tasted pretty good to him. Then he said now that we are out of the confessional, will you tell me how you want the Virgin Mother to dispose of these two nuns?"

"I told him, I don't care how she gets rid of them as long as they are miles away from me. Truly I wish they were out of this world forever."

He said to me, "Son, I think it would be a sensible idea if we kept this conversation just between the two of us."

I told him not to worry because I only had you and Sister Rose to talk to. Then he said that you and Sister Rose would be so upset to hear that I was trying to make an executioner out of the blessed Virgin.

With great effort Elizabeth managed to control her mirth and said, 'let's get on with our music now.'

They practiced every day for the concert and as time passed,

Patrick's nervousness loosened its hold …that is…as long as he didn't think ahead to the concert. When he disclosed his feelings to Sister Elizabeth, she said it was natural to have stage fright and that the most seasoned actors often suffer the pangs of stage fright. That didn't comfort him too much; he told himself that if he had to suffer like this just thinking about it…how could he summon up the courage to walk on stage?

As the concert date drew near his nervousness became acute and many times he sought reassurance from Sister Elizabeth. And again and again she assured him that he would be a success and that she wanted him to make a mental picture of himself—playing with complete abandon. "Every time you feel your courage deserting you, close your eyes and imagine you can hear the applause from the audience ringing in your ears. It is going to happen that way and you *must* start believing it."

So the nun and the small boy spent many hours practicing. When they played together he was transported to another world and it always came as a surprise when he had to return to the drab reality of orphanage life.

He was concerned about appearing on stage with his threadbare clothes. His jersey draped over his thin frame as though it had landed there by mistake. Whenever he passed a glass door, he made sure he looked the other way, because what looked back at him was no Prince Charming. He promised himself he would never wear gunmetal grey clothes after he escaped from the orphanage. His hand-me-down boots were too large and too wide for his feet. Well he thought there is nothing I can do with my clothes, except make sure everything is clean.

One afternoon when he arrived in the music room, Sister Elizabeth told him that the following day they were going into town to buy new clothes for his concert. She had arranged for him to be absent from class and told him to meet her in the front hall at nine o'clock.

The following morning he and Sister Elizabeth walked towards a big black square cab at the front entrance. The chauffeur tipped his cap and held the door open and Sister Elizabeth swept into the back seat with one graceful motion and beckoned Patrick to follow suit.

What a surprise! He had never been inside a cab in his life and his eyes were swivelling from side to side trying to see everything at once as they drove through the small town.

The cab pulled up to a shop with a sign above the door marked 'O' Byrne's Haberdashery.' Three women standing in a clump with their dark wool shawls wrapped tightly around their bodies were furtively eyeing the tall nun and the small boy as they passed by. Their gossip was momentarily silenced…but not for long.

"In the Name of God," said one woman in a hushed tone, "Do you know who that was?"

"Indeed we don't, so for God's sake tell us and don't take all day," and their eyes lit up anticipating another morsel of juicy gossip.

Annie enjoying her moment of importance pulled her shawl across her ample bosom and stretched the story of the tall nun as far as it would go. When they could no longer bear the snail pace of the story, they cried, "Christ, you're not on the pulpit at Sunday mass with a bloody hour to bore the arse off the congregation. Get on with it!"

"Whisht, will you hold your tongue and I'll get to the point…and if the length of the story has stuck in your craw, I can put an end to it right now."

Annie got the reaction she wanted, the other woman told the complainer to keep her tongue behind her teeth and her mouth shut.

The upshot of the gossip was that Sister Elizabeth was one of the Jordan's from the *big house* on the banks of the river. No one understood why she had turned her back on all the privileges her parent's wealth provided and not only that she was the most beautiful girl in the whole county. Annie's cousin had been a servant at the big house and had heard all the gossip, which was running rampant in the servants' quarters at the time of Elizabeth's departure. Annie the servant girl said that Miss Elizabeth had bid farewell to her family one morning and had been driven away to the convent. The mistress was in tears as her daughter walked down the steps to the family car.

Elizabeth, looking forlorn, stepped into the car without a backward glance towards her heartbroken mother.

It was said that the mistress went up to her room and never came downstairs again until the day they carried her coffin to the church for the mass of the dead. And from then on it was a terrible house to work in. The master barked out orders to the servants as though his words were hot coals. The servants bandied gossip around and the tales expanded with each telling. There was talk that her father had caught Elizabeth and the handsome groom holding hands in the stable.

"Och sure," said Annie. "Where there's smoke there's fire. I heard some of that story a long time ago. It was said that the young groom was sacked a few days before she left the big house. Her father had caught the two kissing in the stables. I'd bet any money there was more to it than an innocent kiss. But would you just look at her this morning walking like a proud peacock as though she had never stained her soul with a sin of any size. Aye, there's more to it…but I'm saying no more!"

That did it—the others protested vehemently, "Annie, in the name of God tell us the rest of the story or we'll kick your arse from here to hell and back."

At that moment the Angelus bells tolled and the three women solemnly made the sign of the cross. Maureen, one of the three…lowered her head in mock piety and said aloud. "Dear Jesus, keep us free of sinning by *word* or deed." With the emphasis on 'word' Maureen enjoyed the look of anguish on Annie's face.

At that moment Annie felt like disregarding the Ten Commandments and belting Maureen a right hook to the chin, which was an easy target because it jutted out like the handle on a jug.

Furiously pulling her well-worn shawl around her shoulders, Annie walked off in a huff, and over her shoulder she called out, "and that's all you're ever going to hear from me."

The other two followed and tried to smooth Annie's feathers by reminding her about their longstanding friendship and sure it wasn't worth a farthing if they fell out now.

Annie, knowing that the feverish pitch of curiosity would not abate until the rest of the story unfolded walked homeward bound with the two women scurrying behind her like baby ducklings. Finally they caught up with her and pulling her by the arm, said… 'Come on into the Snug for a pint of stout and the treat's on us today.'

"Sure and I'd rather drink with the Devil himself than drink with you two. I'd die of thirst before drinking to your health again, off with you now and leave me in peace"

"Och, sure and you don't mean that at all at all." Having said this they took her by the arm and headed for the Pub. Inwardly Annie was delighted, the reason being…that at the moment she didn't have a penny to her name, having just paid her overdue rent that very morning. To tell the truth a pint of stout would go down nice and easy.

At this time in the day the pub was empty so Paddy the Publican welcomed them with a little more enthusiasm than was called for. But inwardly he hoped they had money to pay and not be asking him to put it on the cuff until their man came home with his pay docket. Raising their glasses to the good health of themselves and to Paddy the Publican they took a hearty slurp of the stout. As the stout trickled down their gullet it cleared away the bit of animosity that had sprung up between them. Although they never brought up the topic of Sister Elizabeth—it was still as fresh as a newly laid egg in their thoughts.

Annie was biding her time…well aware that having to wait for the rest of the story was almost killing her two friends. And if buying her a pint of Stout was going to loosen up her tongue they had better think again! She'd be damned if she'd disclose anymore this day.

Deirdre tried to keep the flow of conversation on an even keel. No doubt hoping that since a nun was involved in the half- told tale that it would be a good idea to steer the talk back to religion; so she asked the other two what was their opinion of the new young priest.

"Och, it's a bit too soon to know what he's all about, sure he's only been here two weeks. I missed Mass the first Sunday–may God forgive me for that! You see 'Himself' was going through the pangs of hell after a binge in the pub the night before. He had dried out for the previous two weeks to get in shape for the football game. Aye, it was a hard fought game and by God they only won by the skin of their teeth. So wouldn't you know…with a win like that the team headed for Clancy's Pub and drank until their kidneys were floating in Guiness's Stout! My man came down the road singing at the top of his lungs. Shure, 'twas loud enough to bring all the corpses to their feet in the graveyard! Every house on the street was in darkness as he passed by. His drunken rendition of 'Danny Boy' disturbed old Peggy O'Hara's sleep… she opened her window and threw a bucket of water down upon him. Aye, he cursed her for five minutes steady until I went out and dragged him home by the muffler that was drifting in the wind halfway around his neck. I felt like kicking his arse from here to Tipperary.

The following morning being Sunday I shook him until his teeth rattled and ordered him to get up and go to Mass. He glowered as though I was the Devil's second cousin and took such a swipe at me that if I hadn't ducked…I wouldn't be here to tell this tale today. Since I hadn't slept all night meself–I left him in bed and had a good sleep on the old squeaky couch in front of the fire. It was so peaceful lying there looking at the dying embers except for his snorts and snores and sometimes it sounded like he had swallowed his tongue…so I tiptoed over and hit him a clout with a wet towel. Jaysus, he yelled so loud it was enough to make the poor souls in the graveyard turned over back to front. I hid behind the curtain—until his snoring was in full swing again. And to this day he never knew who clouted him!

Aye, and he didn't come to…until one o'clock that day. Jaysus he looked so bad I thought I'd have to call the priest in to give him the Last Rights of the Church. To tell the truth he looked like a corpse someone had forgotten to bury. I told him right to his face that I was so bloody fed up with him and his boozing that I wouldn't do any cooking for the rest of the day."

"That's the best news I've heard all day," sez he, "now will you shut your gub and leave me in peace."

"Aye, It's terrible indeed the things we women have to put up with after those bloody football games," said Maureen. "Our men stumbling home three sheets to the wind...walking as though they had two left feet. And not giving a damn whether we like it or not. Aye, I'd like to see the reception we'd get if we staggered home drunk to the eyeballs. Shure 'himself' would be ashamed to show his mug to any of his cronies. And when he did they'd probably tell him to put an end to it by giving me a damn good leathering with his belt. But I'll tell you something by, if he ever lay a hand on me, he'd never live to do tell the tale!"

"Aye, it's true, women spend their young years yearning to catch a man. Then when the chase is over and we've worked them loose from their mother's fireside...we wonder why the hell we bothered. By the way is it true the new priest is Polish?" Annie asks.

"He is indeed."

"Mother of God, what's Ireland coming to? Half the lads in our country can't find work and they haven't enough sense to go and study for the priesthood. At least it's a chance to get an education and three square meals a day. Imagine having to bring a priest all the way from Poland. Shure at one time... didn't Ireland provide priests and nuns for every corner of the world?"

"Aye, but they had no choice in those days...sure the poor lads had to either become a priest or fight for the freedom of our country. And to think that after all the years of oppression, killings and starvation...the conqueror's heel is still in our necks! Why in the name of God in a small country such as ours, would the English still want to hold onto six counties? I pray every night that Ireland will be united and free before I'm on the other side of the sod."

"Here we are bemoaning the fact that we have to send to Poland for a priest, do you think it's possible they are also God's chosen people? The Jews are supposed to be the chosen race. Even Saint Peter was Jewish and he was the first Pope we ever had."

"In the name of God, where did you hear such a thing? Saint Peter wasn't Jewish, he was a Catholic."

"Aye, well I have me' doubts about that. I've heard that Saint Peter was circumcised a few days after he was born... so you can be sure he was Jewish!" said Deirdre.

Annie, with superiority dripping from her every word replied, "Don't let anyone hear you spouting such rubbish, my brother was circumcised and he's Irish to the back bone."

"In the name of God and him a Catholic... why was he circumcised?" cried Maureen.

"How the hell would I know what for? I just know the deed was done before he was ten days old. Maybe they thought he had too much of a good thing and decided to lop a wee bit off. Anyway my brother is not Jewish and that's that!"

"Ah well, when all is said and done, what's the difference, aren't we all created by the same God? That should make us all kin? So tell me, why do we all have a *go* at each other? Fighting and warring and the calling of names! I often wonder why God made us all different in colour, language and religion...'shure it's the cause of all the wars. Aye, we're different all right, but we just don't bother to understand each other's differences. I think the maybe God got fed up creating white people and started dabbling in black, yellow and bronze colours just for a bit of fun."

"Aye," said Maureen, "I can't say I blame God for changing things around a bit just for the hell of it... I often get fed up doing the same things day in and day out. Even making the same scones every day gives me a pain in the arse. And so I start tossing all sorts of currents and stuff into the mixture just for fun. And when his 'Nibs' sees... what he calls *foreign* objects peeping up at him from the insides of the scones it drives him daft. Aye, he tells me if I used my head for more than a hat rack, I'd make sensible scones just like the scones his dear old mother's used to make. Anyway throwing currents and raisins into recipes that never ask for them is my way of having a bit of a change. Jaysus, imagine what my life has become ... when the highlight of my day is tossing currants and stuff into scones where they have no right to be. And do you know that when I left school I had ideas that I might become an actress?"

"An actress? Jaysus hadn't you a high opinion of yourself."

"Well let me tell you something, I wasn't hard to look at in those days! But now when I look in the mirror shure I scare the living daylights out of 'meself. I'll tell you something if I had the money I'd be away from here like a shot out of hell. Off to Paris I'd go and anywhere else that caught my fancy."

"Mother of God, surely you wouldn't leave 'Himself,' all alone here?"

"You're bloody right I would. Think of all the nights that I spend alone waiting for him to come home soused to the gills. I'll bet you a shilling if I left him–he would be in the confessional the next day moaning to the priest that he was hard done by. Of course the priest would console him by saying him that I would roast in hell forever and a day for not performing my marital duties. Aye, I may roast in hell, but I'll make damn sure I've had a helluva good time before my hide starts singeing."

As soon as the first Stout was down the Hatch, Maureen suggested one for the road and the treat would be hers. Of course she was hoping the second one would loosen Annie's tongue on the unfinished story of the nun. She didn't have long to wait. Annie took a long slurp of stout and noisily cleared her throat, *as was her way* when she had something important to say.

"H'm, as I was saying earlier, there's more to that story about that nun than meets the eye. It was said that after she'd been in the convent a few months that she had a nervous breakdown. Aye, being wrapped in those black clothes with women all dressed the same would be enough to break down anyone's nervous system." And with a look of secrets still to be told, Annie arose and said it was time they all went home.

With that they made their way out of the Snug Pub, two of the women veered off in a different direction, Maureen whispered, "Aye, I'm damned sure Annie knows more about that nun's story than she's telling us. I've got a feeling that it will take a few more treats of Stout to make her unwind more of the story. Isn't she the proper bitch dragging it out…like a clock that needs rewinding?"

CHAPTER SIX
Kevin O'Byrne's Haberdashery

Sister Elizabeth told Patrick the history of the O'Byrne Haberdashery, which had been in the O'Byrne family for a couple of generations. "So with all that experience in men's clothing he should be able to make you the best dressed Flutist an audience ever clapped an eye on."

A young salesman walked towards them, and couldn't hide the curiosity on his face as he saw the nun with a young boy in tow. And was further taken aback when Mr. O'Byrne rushed forward and gave the nun a big bear hug.

"My God, will wonders never cease? Only yesterday you were sifting through my mind like sand in an hourglass and here you are today! Elizabeth, it's a treat for tired eyes seeing you again."

"Kevin O'Byrne you've kissed the Blarney Stone once too often. Anyway I'm glad you are here because I need your advice. I was hoping that you'd be here instead of gambling your money at the racetrack. If my memory serves me well, your pockets never held money too long during the horseracing season."

"Ah yes, but life has straightened out some of the knots in my brain since last we met, so don't be too hard on me."

"Well then; let's get down to business. I'd like you to meet Patrick, a young protégé of mine. He will be playing in the concert this month. Now, Kevin O'Byrne, lets see how much you have learned about men's clothing since taking over your father's business. I want this young fellow clad from head to foot in the best outfit you can lay your hands on for his first public appearance."

"Elizabeth, your wish is my command. Come on Patrick my boy...follow me."

Patrick was whisked into the fitting room and when he emerged sometime later, he looked like a different person altogether. A robin's egg blue shirt and a softly coloured tie complemented his dark blue suit. He was shod with the nicest black leather shoes he had ever worn. These new shoes would never require cardboard stuffed in the heels to keep them on his feet. The tie was a different kettle of fish, having never worn one before; he began to feel a slight strangulation creeping around his neck.

With self-assurance he didn't actually feel... he walked towards Sister Elizabeth. He knew by the expression on her face that the transformation in his appearance had surprised and pleased her. Indeed he had surprised himself when he caught sight of his image in the mirror. Somehow the excitement of the moment took hold of Patrick... he smilingly bowed to the three of them as though they were his audience.

Sister Elizabeth and Mr. O'Byrne laughed heartily.

"Elizabeth, I think you have found a born actor. Would you look at him now, strutting around like a rooster in a hen run."

"Well, that's a step in the right direction. Lately he has been scaring the living daylights out of me, worrying about whether he would have the nerve to go out on stage. Kevin, I commend you on the clothes you have chosen for him, he looks like a miniature Lord Fauntleroy. Thank you, I'm sure the angels away up there are dusting off a little white cloud in readiness for your heavenly arrival."

"Your industrious angels would be better off dusting clouds for someone else, because I've no intention of departing this world for a long time yet. And by the way, while we have this young lad here, I have a few outfits that I've had in stock for God knows how long and if the size is right they are his for the asking." And once more Patrick went into the fitting room.

The salesman flitted back and forth to the fitting room with garments draped over his arm. When Patrick emerged wearing a lovely Irish wool sweater, corded trousers and a handsome tweed jacket and his feet were shod in sturdy leather tan brogues Kevin guided him towards the Cheval mirror and Patrick shyly gazed at his own image...he couldn't believe that was himself.

When he saw the other three in the mirror behind him with such happiness on their faces, he wanted to run and hug them. Alas he had never known the freedom of displaying his affections, or for that matter receiving affection…so there he stood rooted to the spot not knowing how to handle the tumultuous storm pounding inside his chest.

Sister Elizabeth, sensing that he felt out of his depth, walked over and drew his small thin frame towards her and exclaimed, "Patrick you are the handsomest young man in all of Ireland."

"In that case we can't keep this young lad all to ourselves, let's go to the hotel for lunch and show him off to the rest of the world."

Sister Elizabeth was about to refuse knowing it would be frowned upon by Mother Superior. Yet she knew it would be such a treat for young Patrick… throwing caution to the wind…she accepted.

Kevin drove to the hotel…and as they walked through the lobby… all heads turned when they entered the dining room. The appearance of Kevin, the boy and the tall attractive nun, lulled the buzz of conversation into a *curious* unfamiliar silence. Kevin was well known in the town and he was considered a good catch. Not only was he a handsome man he was also one of the wealthiest…so this scenario of Kevin with a nun and a boy on tow was perplexing to say the least.

The young waitress greeted them warmly and winking at Kevin she asked in a *stage* whisper,

"Shure, and I've never seen you in such '*holy company*' before. In honour of your present company …shall I tone down your usual belt of Irish whiskey today?"

"It's a bit of respect you should be showing for your customers Maureen O'Hara. You're an impudent young scamp. Off with you now and I'll have my usual belt of whiskey. All I can say is that you're damned lucky your father owns the hotel or you'd be out of a job. In regards to the holy company I bet you didn't know that our heavenly Father has no objection to his flock having the odd drink or two. Sure didn't his son tell the apostles he would not partake of wine on this earth again—until he reached his Fathers vineyard? Until I read that in the scriptures, I had no idea that there was a Bar in Heaven. I don't suppose Irish whiskey will be served, but I'm sure their wine will be palatable."

Tossing her tawny head of hair, Maureen laughingly said, "Kevin O'Byrne trust me—you'll never get the chance to suffer a heavenly hangover from indulging *up there*—because you'll be down below with the rest of the sinners—thirsty as hell while you stoke the roaring furnace."

Sister Elizabeth was enjoying the repartee; it seemed such a long time since she had participated in a bit of bantering gab. How strange to think that she had once belonged to this kind of carefree life laughing and talking with a group of friends around a table. Nevertheless she wondered if she had been wise embarking on this shopping spree, but when she looked across the table at young Patrick in his brand new outfit and the wondrous happiness in his eyes, her doubts vanished.

The lunch was marvelous, starting with a creamy potato and leek soup, roast lamb done to perfection, surrounded with golden roast potatoes and vegetables. Kevin derived the greatest pleasure as he watched his two guests eating everything in sight with such gusto. When the dessert tray arrived...Patrick was speechless. Never in all his born days had he seen a plate loaded with such a variety of cakes and tarts. Kevin smiled as he noticed the delight in the young lad's eyes as he viewed the tarts and cakes on his plate. Patrick was solely preoccupied with the joyous consumption of these delights. And was unaware of the amused glance passing between Kevin and Elizabeth as they watched him chase the last crumb around the plate with a teaspoon!

Sister Elizabeth and Kevin talked about bygone days and since this conversation was of little interest to Patrick; he spent the time surveying the lovely dining room. His eyes roamed over the pastoral landscape paintings, the huge chandeliers and the beautiful glass vases filled with colourful flowers. Then his eyes rested on the flickering flames chasing each other in the huge fireplace and he thought how wonderful it would be to stay in this lovely room forever.

When Maureen came over to present the bill, Kevin asked her to put the rest of the cakes in a package for young Patrick to take back with him.

Maureen, having overheard a bit of gossip from the barman...that the nun was from the orphanage therefore, regardless of the lad's nice outfit, he must be an orphan.

With that in mind she said to Kevin, "Sure and I'll do better than that; I'll put a nice bit of sliced lamb between layers of our good home- made bread. God bless him, he has a few nooks and crannies that need a bit of filling out. He's going to be a handsome young man in a few short years and the village girls will be tripping over themselves trying to catch his eye.

"Maureen, you have the gift o' the gab, one of these days it will get you into trouble. Next time I set eyes on your Father, I'll tell him about some of your shenanigans."

"Lord almighty, shure, I'd be trembling all over in fear if I didn't know that you're bark is worse than your bite."

"Maureen when some poor unsuspecting soul asks for your hand in marriage, your father will think he has died and gone to heaven. That will be the happiest day of his life when he finally hands you over for another man to take care of."

As Kevin passed her in the lobby he gave Maureen a light smack on her backside...and not to be outdone she walloped him right back.

"Maureen, what did you hit me with ...a brick?"

"I keep myself in fine fettle in case I have to wallop a young man for trying to do what he shouldn't be doing... he'll know I mean business."

Walking back to the car, Patrick felt he was walking on stilts; the reason being that the soles of his new brogues were the thickest he had ever walked on. He stole a downward glance at his new shoes every chance he got. He wondered where he could store the box of brushes and polish that Mr. O'Byrne had given him, if only he had a drawer of his own to put things into. This was a new kind of worry... before today... the only belongings he owned were the ones on his back. He thought it would be awful to own a lot of things...then he would really have something to worry about. Patrick was so filled with all the different happenings of his day that he felt he had entered into a new world. And the interaction between people was amazing to see!

Kevin suggested driving them back to the convent; Elizabeth was a little apprehensive about accepting. She told him that should Mother Superior find out, it would mean another verbal confrontation.

"Is that old Harridan still in charge there? A couple of years ago I donated clothing to the orphanage. I was taken to her office; she sat behind her desk and looked me over from head to foot as though I was the Devil himself minus the horns. She has a look about her that says she doesn't like herself or anyone else in the world."

"Kevin, surely you feel a lot better getting all of that out of your system. Keep in mind the family she came from, most of the time she and her eight brothers and sisters hadn't a bite to eat. They came to school barefooted with tattered clothing covering their undernourished bodies. Their mother died at a very young age, worn out from a hopeless marriage and too many births. After her death the father was never sober. Whenever he got a few days work, his pitiful wages were spent in Murphy's Pub. Most of the time he was maudlin drunk and bemoaning the fact that he was alone in the world with a brood of children to look after. Frequently beating them was his way of discipline. Is it any wonder that they grew up with warped personalities? My cousin was head master of the school at that time and he reported the children's plight to the parish priest...alas, nothing ever changed. Mother Superior escaped from that dreadful life of deprivation by entering the convent. No doubt she hoped that her life would change and a measure of happiness would come her way. Alas, she never discarded the baggage of Dross held over from her miserable childhood. Lashing is the only type of discipline she knows. Now Kevin, to finish this sad story, I believe the only happiness she has in life is her title of Mother Superior.

"I have pleaded in vain with her to stop caning the children for small misdemeanours. I've tried to explain that these children are bereft of parental love and that was punishment enough. The fury in her eyes was enough to make my blood turn cold. She believes that severe punishment will improve and strengthen their character.

"My family has donated a large amount of money annually to the orphanage for the past decade. I must confess I blatantly use that wedge when it is necessary to get my own way in *some* matters. For instance, it was a battle royal when I told her that Patrick had to be excused from his kitchen chores on the days he had music lessons. When I told her that he was gifted, she snorted and threw her account book on the desk with such fury, that it sounded like a gunshot. I walked out of her office and left her standing there."

"How did she ever become Mother Superior?"

"Because she knows how to cut corners and saves a lot of money for the institution. She runs it in a tight fisted manner; quite frankly the food that is served to the orphans is dreadful. I know you will not discuss this further with anyone and somehow it has lightened my burden just having someone on the outside to talk to."

"How long has she been Mother Superior at the orphanage?"

"She arrived a few years after I took my vows."

"Why didn't they offer you that post?"

With lowered eyes, she answered, "I was not considered for the post and I am thankful for that."

So they drove on in silence, each with their own thoughts bobbing around like churning butter

Patrick's whole attention was focused on everything as they drove past the white washed cottages with their thatched roofs and the cattle grazing in the fields. He was happier than he had ever been in his life. The only dark cloud was the fact that now he was returning to the orphanage. Thinking about it made him cringe inside–why was everything outside of those walls such a happy place? Even the people seemed different; they laughed easily and loved to talk. Why then was everything so dull and lacking in joy within the walls of the orphanage? The only colour within those walls was the Fern plants at each end of the long dismal hallways.

Before going to sleep Patrick's mind began to wander, going over all the new experiences of his day. The love from Sister Elizabeth was the only love he had ever known and if she ever stopped loving him, he knew he would want to die. Dying? What did dying mean, he didn't know–he only knew that when a person died they never came back to visit. The old nun who had worked in the laundry all her life had dropped dead amidst a huge pile of soiled laundry. Patrick thought about that old nun, who had passed him on his way to the kitchen every day. Her face was like parchment paper and riddled with wrinkles…yet he had loved to watch her eyes crinkle when he smiled as he passed her by. She responded with a smile, which was a feeble attempt of an ageing face that had almost forgotten how to smile through lack of use. No one ever paid any attention to her until the morning she was found dead on the cold stone laundry floor. Perhaps she was glad to die, to get away from that steamy hot laundry where she worked six days a week. She walked around the laundry bent over like a half-shut knife; therefore her horizon was limited to a few paces ahead of each step she took. Patrick wondered if she had ever seen the sky. Young Patrick wondered why a person like the laundry nun who always walked at a snail pace, had to leave this life in such a helluva hurry.

Patrick's daydreaming was cut short when the car suddenly stopped at the gates of the orphanage. Within seconds he felt his entire body shrinking within its shell and his belly doing somersaults. His first impulse was to open the door and run back along the road.

Sister Elizabeth turned towards Patrick; instinctively she was aware he dreaded going back into the orphanage. Had she done wrong? Opening a window to the outside world for him…a world he wouldn't be free to explore for a few more years.

Turning to Kevin she was surprised to see that he too was sad. Her thoughts went back to their young years together, how they had cheered each other in moments of sadness and laughed like young fools in moments of lightness. She had always gone to him when she needed advice–except that one time…when her life had fallen apart. Once more her thoughts rummaged back and sifted through those happenings of long ago.

She remembered their last walk along the seashore, when he told her that he was going to Europe for a year. 'I wish you were going with me he had said; alas Ireland being Ireland, we could never get away with it. You would be a marked woman traveling with a man with no marriage label to put the licit sanction on the relationship.' Little did he know the terrible secret that was darkening her world and with his departure there would be no chance to solicit his advice.

During the first dreadful months in the convent she had wanted to write to him and unload her anguished heart. But she had no idea where he was. She was sure he had written to her, no doubt her father would destroy any letters. When Elizabeth had taken her final vows, she tried to banish all memories of the outside world and the friends she had known…including Kevin.

Behind the convent walls she had prayed with all the other nuns as they offered their daily prayers for the sinners of the world. Loss of chastity in dear Old Mother Ireland was the most unforgivable of sins! Particularly the sins of *unchaste females!* Once a woman crossed the line and allowed a man to have *his way* with her as the saying goes… she was beyond the Pale. No other man would ever ask her hand in marriage because he knew that he'd be the laughing stock of the whole county. In other words he would be marrying another man's leavings. But men were forgiven, it was all right for a man to get *his way*, it was up to the woman to be the strong one and withhold.

Turning to Kevin she said, "I thank you for all your kindness today. Those 'so called samples' were a big plus. I may have trouble explaining Patrick's new clothes to Mother Superior. Kevin I do hope you attend the concert."

"I wouldn't miss it for the world. Elizabeth today was the most enjoyable day I've had in years. It was marvelous seeing you again…yet I feel we've left so many things unsaid. I wanted to find out so much about you and that *big why* –is still suspended in mid air. When I returned from Europe and learned that you had entered the convent, I wondered what might have happened if we had been together to discuss the situation. Elizabeth why did your life spin off in this way? There wasn't a better-looking woman in the county and the fellows at the university were all vying for your attention. I remember a law student from Dublin who monopolized your time at the dances, I was jealous as hell."

"There you go exaggerating again."

"I mean every word! Damn it we were such close friends and a big part of my life revolved around our friendship. Remember those early morning rides…racing across the fields before breakfast? Old Paddy the groom wouldn't allow us to go for breakfast until we walked the horses to cool them down."

"Please Kevin, it's too late to rehash what might have been, what good will it do?"

"It appears that I had to lose you to find you—then and only then—did I realise how much you really meant to me. I love you and I suppose I'll carry that torch until I die."

"Kevin, I know you didn't carry the torch too long. You were married a couple of years after you returned from abroad. The parish priest asked me to play the organ at your wedding mass and I refused."

"I was never cut out for celibacy and yes I did marry Mary Eileen Brogan. She was a kind-hearted woman and loved me and I loved her. We had a good marriage and I missed her when she died. I've been alone ever since and it is a lonely road to travel. Throughout the years I wished that you and I had taken the journey through life together."

She studied his face, remembering how well he had handled problems when they were young. But his daredevil attitude was no longer apparent…what had happened in his life to extinguish the spark? She dare not ask…his answer might be one she wouldn't want to hear. She fussed around with the parcel of clothing to bring the curtain down on further conversation. Deep down in her heart she knew that for old time's sake she wanted to take him in her arms and comfort him.

As their eyes met a surge of emotion that he hadn't felt in a long time pulsed through him, 'twas a feeling too deep for words. Elizabeth's expression was strange to say the least and he wondered if she might be experiencing the same emotional turmoil. They clasped hands for a moment and then stood further apart as though to avoid further contact.

To get on safer ground he inquired what time he should pick them up for the concert.

"Kevin, perhaps it would be better if I order a cab. Mother Superior might have something to say about it if she noticed you appearing here too often."

"Really? In that case I will visit Mother Superior in a couple of days with a parcel of children's clothes. During the course of our meeting I will inform her that to save the expense of a cab I will drive you and Patrick to the hall the night of the concert."

"Have it your way, it *would* be easier to go with you. Once again thank you for all you've done for us today. I'll be looking forward to seeing you on Saturday evening."

Taking Patrick by the hand she said, "Come along Patrick, we have to find a spare cupboard in the music room to store your new outfit."

Kevin watched the two of them walking hand in hand, and wondered about this close attachment between Elizabeth and the boy.

Sister Elizabeth folded his new clothes and placed them in a big deep drawer in the music room. She paused as she unpacked the everyday outfit, turning to Patrick she said, "I don't think it would be wise to wear these in the classroom Patrick. Perhaps you should keep this outfit for your Sunday outings. However, you may take the brogues, socks and underwear to your dormitory. Those shoes that you have are past retirement age. Should Mother Superior inquire about your new wardrobe I will explain that they were a gift from Mr. O'Byrne."

"I hope the other boys in the dorm are not upset about my new shoes. Many nights I lie awake and hear some of the other boys crying and it makes me feel sad and sick inside. Y'know I've never once heard anyone laugh in that dorm. I suppose there's nothing to laugh about."

"Patrick, do you always feel lonely and sad before you go to sleep?"

"I often cry but no one hears me because I pull the blanket over my face. I pretend all the time that underneath the blanket is my little home. I won't be sad tonight because I've had such a grand day and when I say my prayers I'll tell God how happy I am. Maybe I'll ask Him to find shoes with no holes...for all the other boys."

Just then Sister Rose entered the music room; "Hello Patrick I bet you're hungry, I made a ham sandwich for you. Did you have a nice day?"

"Shure, it was grand day. I was inside a shop for the first time and then I went to an hotel and had dinner and ate a whole plate of tarts and cakes."

"Holy Mother of God. Sure and you will be bursting at the seams if you eat any more today. I suppose you'll lie on that featherbed of yours tonight and ruminate about the 'birds eye' glimpse of the world you've seen today."

"I don't have a featherbed."

"Sister Rose is just teasing you Patrick, she has a torrent of words that pour forth like a river overflowing its banks. Now Patrick, give me those worn out shoes of yours and we'll toss them out. Remember Mr. O'Byrne in your prayers tonight. Off you go now and have a good sleep."

CHAPTER SEVEN
Patrick's First Concert

Many nights before the concert Patrick lay on his narrow cot praying for sleep to wipe away his fears. But depressing thoughts deluged his young mind and a sense of hopelessness was sustained by the gloom of the dormitory. Whenever he was overcome by helplessness he always turned to his only source of comfort...God! At this moment in time his biggest concern was the upcoming concert!

"Heavenly Father, I need your help to get through this concert. Sister Elizabeth believes you gave me the gift of music and if that is true...then I guess you'll have to wind me up with courage. God, if I was sure that you'd be with me on the stage, I wouldn't have my worries swinging back and forth like the pendulum on a clock."

Soon after that plea for help...a comforting sleep closed the curtains on young Patrick's day.

Patrick was wide-awake at the crack of dawn and his fear-driven thoughts drifted back and forth like a fog spreading over the fields. It was beyond his scope of imagination to envision playing before an audience and now he realized that he was too nervous to go on with it. Then he remembered that Sister Elizabeth would be in the music room early today so he decided to go and tell her how he felt.

With his mind so full of what he had to say, he almost died of fright when his knock was answered by the rasping voice of Mother Superior.

He timidly opened the door and silently she glared at him. Satisfied that she had him squirming, she barked. "What do you think you're doing in the music room at this time in the morning?"

"I have to talk to Sister Elizabeth about the concert."

"She has not arrived yet. Go outside and sit on the bench and you will be called when I'm through with her."

Through clenched teeth he whispered, 'You old bitch'.

Thumping his skinny bottom on to the dark wooden bench in the hallway…his thoughts dragged him into places where he didn't want to go. The rustling of robes brought his eyes from the floor and he was relieved to see Sister Elizabeth coming towards him with her long graceful stride. The boy looked up at her smiling face and thought she had the most beautiful smile in the world.

"Good morning Patrick, it is a pleasure indeed seeing you at such an early hour in the morning. Why didn't you go inside and look over your music, instead of sitting here?"

He whispered, "Mother Superior is waiting for you in there. She told me to wait here and she looked angry when she saw me."

"Really, she may be a great deal angrier when she hears my plans for today. You and I are going to practice for a couple of hours and sort out a few things for the concert. Should she have kitchen chores for you today she will have to find another willing worker. By the way Patrick, why are you here so early?"

"I have something very important to tell you about the concert."

"Oh really? Perhaps you should tell me now."

With great difficulty he started to splutter, "Well… because… well… you see… I don't think I will be able to play onstage."

"Are you ill?"

"No I'm not really sick–at least if I am, it's not the kind that shows, its not like a banged up knee or a big black bruise. Everything inside of me is hammering like blazes and I don't know how to make it stop. I just know that I can't play before a whole slew of strangers and I'm frightened to death."

"Patrick, sit here until I'm through with Mother Superior. Calm your mind by thinking of pleasant things–such as the day we went shopping and dining with Mr.O'Byrne. Happy thoughts will lighten that load of fear that's piling up inside of you. Do you know that even seasoned actors feel the pangs of 'first night jitters' and that is what you are experiencing right now? On the night of the concert we will need each other for courage…so please don't desert me now."

On hearing that his eyes lit up, his thin shoulders straightened and for the first time Patrick reached out and took her hand. With his heart in his eyes he proudly told her he would never desert her.

As she searched his young earnest face she knew that his masculine chivalry was taking its fledging flight. She patted the top of his head and entered the music room.

Upon opening the door she was surprised to see Mother Superior shuffling through papers on her desk. Sister Elizabeth, in a 'no nonsense' tone, asked Mother Superior if she needed help to find what she was looking for.

Without eye contact, and looking thoroughly nonplussed, Mother Superior replied, "No, I was just idly thumbing through some papers."

Taking a hankie from the voluminous folds of her habit Mother Superior blew her nose… as though it was the most important action she had to perform! She had been caught snooping and the disconcerting twinge was unbearable. Her low self-esteem always hit rock bottom when she was in the presence of Sister Elizabeth. At the moment her title of Mother Superior was of no consequence or comfort. There was nothing holy about her feelings towards this snooty nun and she disliked her intensely!

"Patrick is here this morning to run through a few last minute details for the concert. Is there something you want to discuss with me?"

"Patrick's music lessons are playing havoc with his educational routine. What this boy needs is strict discipline to keep him in line. The orphans here do not require mollycoddling. The harsh realities of life should be drilled into them at an early age, hopefully to prevent them from following in the sinful ways of their parents. His music lessons should stop after this concert!"

"In all due respect to you Mother Superior, a child should not be punished for what you term as 'the sins of his parents.' Patrick's schoolwork has improved since he started music lessons; he came first in his class last month. Stop his music lessons? That would be tragic! This young lad is gifted and we should humbly thank God for that. It strengthens ones faith knowing that there is a God bestowing gifts on His chosen few…as in this case… *even* the most humble."

"I am the Mother Superior here… and I say that he should be kept in his place. A good caning once in a while is required to remind him that he is nothing more than a destitute orphan."

"Mother Superior, that form of punishment is now considered detrimental to the development of character. Love can perform miracles and that is precisely what these motherless children are lacking. Unfortunately in the past many caretakers did not believe in that philosophy… and such ignorance spewed a dank suffocation over the spirit and soul of *both* the victim and perpetrator."

"I have no time to listen to such bilge. He came from nowhere and is going nowhere."

"Regardless of one's humble beginnings—no one has to stay at the bottom of the heap. When one allows past injustices to get an everlasting hold on them—it becomes a *self-imposed* burden… forming a putrid bulk that leaves no space within one's spirit for fresh winds to blow freely. I'm determined to develop Patrick's musical talent to the best of my ability. He should be allowed to climb to any height he chooses."

Without further ado Mother Superior stormed out of the room and her face looked like a barrow load of mortal sins. She nursed her raging fury as she walked along the hallway and her warped mind began a plan of revenge. Sister Elizabeth's disobedience would be reported to the Mother General. Then Mother Superior decided to go one step further and request Sister Elizabeth's removal to another convent. That would settle everything! With her out of the way she'd make Patrick toe the line!

Patrick entered the music room and Elizabeth smiled grimly, "I think we won that round, now let's get down to clearing up the last details for the concert."

Little did she know the *plans* Mother Superior was concocting at this very moment!

Mother Superior went straight to her office and sent a request to the Mother General to have a meeting with her as soon as possible. She needed advice regarding a problem with Sister Elizabeth who had broken her vow of obedience. The letter hinted about the coddling of a certain orphan who was now receiving lessons from Sister Elizabeth. She ended the letter apologising for the expense of the train trip and ensuring Mother General that the severity of the problem had to be dealt with immediately.

The reply wasn't long in coming…it was short but *not* sweet.

"I am shocked to learn that you deem it necessary to make a trip to the Mother House over this matter. Your training to become Mother Superior should have endowed you with enough common sense to handle all but the most serious offences. Hence, for your sake I do hope your problem merits my attention. Should you find yourself unable to handle this matter, by all means make your way here as soon as possible."

Waves of terror flooded through as she read this curt response to her letter. Recalling some previous meetings with the austere Mother General she quaked inwardly. However, she was so intent on the removal of Sister Elizabeth that she pushed all fears aside and left by train the following morning.

The train ride should have been a pleasant change away from the convent, but Mother Superior was oblivious to the green fields and the cattle grazing beyond the stone fences. She sat like a mummy staring blindly into space as despair shredded her last bit of self-confidence. Apprehension went out of bounds as she realized what she was getting into. Her only source was God; surely He would help her find a way to have Sister Elizabeth ousted to another convent. Alas, her mind was so clouded with hate for Sister Elizabeth there was no space for God's love to enter.

On arrival at the Mother House she was directed towards Mother General's office. Glancing at the tiny watch pinned to her scrawny bosom, she wondered why she hadn't been offered lunch. It didn't bode well for the meeting with Mother General. Timidly knocking on the door she was told to enter. Sitting at the huge mahogany desk the Mother General neither looked up nor acknowledged her presence… and so she was left standing like a lump on a log. Several minutes elapsed before she gathered enough courage to cough politely…hoping the sound would bring some response. It did… but not what she had hoped for.

Without raising her eyes, Mother General brusquely said, "I am aware of your presence. Please be seated and don't stand there as though you were anticipating a trip to the guillotine."

With such a frosty reception… Mother Superior's hopes slithered down into her stub nosed black shoes.

"Oh Merciful God," she prayed silently. "Please help me handle this ordeal in a sensible manner. Surely you know Heavenly Father, that Sister Elizabeth has been a thorn in my side for a long time."

Then the dreaded moment arrived, the dark blue piercing eyes of the Mother General looked straight into hers and in a frosty voice she inquired, "Now then, is this problem of such magnitude that you deem yourself incapable of resolving it? I have a meeting with the Bishop in half an hour. So please, give me the details exactly and precisely in the shortest time possible."

"Reverend Mother, I apologize for interrupting your very busy schedule, but this is important. Recently I've had trouble with Sister Elizabeth disobeying my orders. An orphan by the name of Patrick O'Grady has taken her fancy and she has beguiled herself into believing he has the gift of music. She gives him music lessons free; therefore these lessons don't enhance the convent coffers. Prior to her discovery of this so-called gift Patrick worked daily after school in the kitchen. But now against my wishes she no longer allows him to work there, she believes it will ruin the dexterity of his fingers. Frankly I've never heard of such nonsense. She has gone as far as having him perform in the upcoming concert. I was under the impression that the convent should be run on my terms; it appears Sister Elizabeth thinks otherwise. I should like you to reprimand her severely. My other request is to have her removed to another convent as soon as possible."

This diatribe was interlaced with dollops of venom and self-pity.

Feeling as vulnerable as a newborn child she searched for some approval from Mother General and she saw anger flash across that usually calm countenance.

Believing that the significance of her complaints had hit the right target, Mother Superior heaved a sigh of relief. Her gratification was short-lived when The Reverend Mother responded with the following...

"It's a pity you hadn't the foresight to put these facts in a letter, it would have saved the expense of your trip. I'm a musician therefore I greatly appreciate Sister Elizabeth discovering this young protégé. The Bishop and I have had the pleasure of hearing Patrick play and we are of the opinion he is a talented Flutist. The Bishop and I are looking forward to the concert with keen anticipation. Now to return to your problem, it appears that your mind and soul are in dire need of restoration, therefore I order you to seek peace on a retreat here at the Mother House. You may leave now, go to the kitchen and your dinner will be served. Enjoy your meal, because for the next seven days you will be on a restricted diet... except for prayers you will observe the code of silence and fasting. Report to me before you return to your convent at the end of the retreat."

Feeling unjustly reprimanded and with tears blurring her vision, she asked, "Reverend Mother may I ask who will replace me?"

"Hopefully Sister Elizabeth will find time in her busy schedule to take charge in your absence."

That was the last straw. With buckling knees she made her way out of the office and lowered herself on to the first bench in the hallway. Holy Mother of God, what had she done to deserve this humiliation? Choosing Elizabeth of all people... whilst she was stuck here cooling her heels. Well that was it! She was quite sure that after having a taste of being in charge that Sister Elizabeth wouldn't want to relinquish the post.

Little did she know it was the *least* of Elizabeth's ambitions.

Head bowed in abject misery she slowly made her way to the kitchen. A rosy faced novice nun with due deference for Mother Superior's title waited on her hand and foot. At some other time this attention would have restored some of Mother Superior's *limited* supply of self-esteem, but today that was impossible. Her esteem had hit rock bottom! Even her appetite had deserted her and after a few feeble stabs at the food on her plate she thanked the young nun and left for the cell like chamber.

A huge crucifix above the narrow bed and the heavy wooden framed picture of the Sacred Heart of Jesus were the only adornments in this dismal cell. The ambience, or rather the *lack* of it, presumably restored one's spiritual health. Alas Mother Superior harboured no spiritual contrition for denouncing Sister Elizabeth… her only regret was this deplorable outcome. The thought of Elizabeth sitting in her office mulling through her papers was sheer agony. Easing her sparse frame onto the narrow bed… all the misery of the day flowed over her like a dark cloud before a storm.

Her bitterness increased the following morning, when the Mother General greeted her with the following; "A retreat can be a wondrous healer if taken with the right spirit. With God's help you will leave with a greater understanding of the frailties of mankind. I will pray that your mind and soul will cease being a wasteland of despair. When you return from your retreat you have my permission to attend the concert. The Bishop and I will have seats right on the same row."

Bowing humbly to receive the Reverend Mother's blessing the latter left without further conversation. The curt dismissal resurrected a memory of the rejection and lack of kindness that Mother Superior had experienced earlier in her life and she was filled with a pungent bitterness! She turned her face towards the wall and wept.

Patrick had no more time to worry about courage or lack of it because Sister Elizabeth kept him busy going through the stage routine. At last all was in order and she handed him his new outfit. She told him to wash and dress in the washroom adjacent to the music room…explaining that she didn't want to lose him until they reached the concert hall. Handing a towel and soap to him… she laughingly told him to make sure he washed behind his ears.

Having completed his ablutions he came over to her and asked, "Am I clean enough?"

Looking him over from head to toe she said, "My dear boy, you look good enough to eat."

"Well, if you make a meal out of me now, who will play the flute tonight?"

This bit of riposte pleased her to no end. Thank God, she thought; at last he is losing the stiffness imposed on him by these harsh surroundings.

"You're becoming a cheeky young scamp Patrick O'Grady. Now let's get you all poshed up for your debut."

Looking him over from head to foot she took a pair of scissors and trimmed his unruly, wavy hair. When he noticed a toothbrush and a nailbrush placed near his clothes, evidently new additions to his worldly goods, he lifted the nailbrush up and inquired what it was used for.

"It's a nailbrush to scrub your nails, when you play in public you must have your hands in fine condition. That is why I asked Mother Superior to release you from your kitchen chores."

"I miss not seeing Sister Rose every day after school and I also miss the good dinners."

"Don't worry she will visit us here periodically and I'm sure she will *always* have a little treat for you. You must know by now that her main goal in life is to fatten you up."

He donned his new outfit with determined concentration…that is…until he came to the tie. How would that ever fit under the stiff collar of his shirt? After studying it carefully for a few moments, he rolled it up very carefully and put it in the breast pocket of his jacket. Then he felt a hand on his shoulder and Sister Elizabeth retrieved the tie from his pocket and deftly knotted it. This action brought back memories of her dear brother rushing into her bedroom in evening clothes and begging her to knot his tie. Looking down into Patrick's dear little face, she kissed him on the forehead and hand in hand they wended their way towards the front entrance. Deep indefinable emotions were streaming through her ... and had her life depended on it she couldn't have spoken a word.

Kevin was waiting for them and as he came forward to take the parcels from Elizabeth, their eyes met and a current of wild excitement flowed from one to the other. Yet the drive to the concert hall was a silent trip and the futile attempts at light conversation died for lack of energy.

Kevin understood that Patrick was nervous and that trying to divert his thoughts with small talk would be of no avail. Arriving at the Hall, Kevin, with feigned seriousness asked Sister Elizabeth if she would like a shot of whiskey sent to her dressing room.

Rolling her eyes to the heavens, she replied, "Kevin, what a grand idea, I never thought you would ask."

Needless to say she was joking. But Kevin saw a flash of the young girl he had known years ago, whose sharp wit and quick repartee had been one of her main attractions.

And thus he made his way to his seat with conflicting emotions. He thought that the world and its inhabitants were a bloody mess of twisted contradictions. With a belly-bottomed sigh he lowered his body into the forest green velvet seat.

Memories came flooding back of long ago when he and Elizabeth had enjoyed performances together in this hall. Never in his wildest dreams could he have imagined the situation that he found himself in tonight. That beautiful lithe body of hers, hidden from the world swathed in that cumbersome cloak of black. Christ almighty, he thought...'I don't believe it's natural to hide one of God's really good creations from the eyes of the world in such a manner.'

Waiting in the darkened theatre for the performance to begin, Kevin wondered what had happened in Elizabeth's life to make her enter a convent. He remembered with sadness the letters that he had sent her and all had been returned unopened. Kevin squirmed deeper into the velvet seat as though the physical comfort would somehow alleviate the weight of his thoughts.

Back in the dressing room Patrick's nerves were jangling like church bells in the hands of a mad carillonneur. He wished he had never started playing the flute. How could he walk on stage in this present state of fright? Everything inside of him was as tight as a drum! He was afraid that this tightness wouldn't allow a free flow of air into his lungs. Worse still his guts felt as though they were going through a mangle and there was Sister Elizabeth walking around like the calm before the storm. He figured she had no idea that he was ripping apart inside and at that moment her voice broke through his panic ridden thoughts.

"Patrick my dear boy, it's time to go on stage. By the time we are through the first piece of music you will have the audience in the palm of your hand. Now let's ask our heavenly Father to calm your spirit."

Without further ado, she took him by the hand and led him from the wings to the center of the stage. She proudly introduced her protégé to the audience. He stood alone…and as she walked towards the piano she silently prayed, 'heavenly father he is in your hands – give him the strength he needs.'

As the hall lights dimmed a soft blue spotlight zeroed in on that tiny bit of humanity standing alone on centre stage. Abruptly the coughs and shuffling rippling through the audience was silenced…and that sudden hush was deafening to his ears.

In a stage whisper a woman murmured, "Mother of God, would you look at the size of that wee lad, sure a good wind could blow him over. Lord bless us, my heart weeps for that poor child standing there alone and knowing all of us gobs are staring up at him."

As soon as he started playing, Patrick's spirit soared. All nervousness dissipated into thin air and a grand feeling of exhilaration sprang through his whole being.

Patrick's rendition of 'Danny Boy' was wrapped in such purity that each note poured forth like crystal clear waters. When the music stopped and as he clasped the flute to his chest an emotion lifted him to a place where he had never been before. Exhilaration coursed through his entire body and he wanted to go on playing forever.

There was a moment of silence after the last lingering note and he stood rooted to the spot… steeped in the *embrace* of the music he had just played.

Like a huge tidal wave the audience rose to their feet and gave him a standing ovation.

Sister Elizabeth, with tear-filled eyes sat very still at the piano leaving Patrick alone to savour his well-earned applause. He took his bows and then he looked anxiously towards her. Only then did she join him at center stage…and hand in hand they took one last bow and stepped out of the footlights.

Even though she believed he was a gifted child, she was surprised by the reverberating applause and the resounding 'Bravo' throughout the hall.

"Why are they still clapping?" He asked.

"Because they want more of your beautiful music. Go back on stage, take another bow and play your heart out. You've got them in the palm of your hand and I'm proud of you my dear boy."

The emotion was so strong that it filled the young boy with a happiness he had never experienced before.

Taking a damp towel Elizabeth wiped his hands and face. Her eyes never left that small figure as he walked towards center stage… to share that magical pivot of power, which emanates between an audience and actors.

The energizing flow from the audience was so potent he could have played forever without tiring. At the end of each piece the applause was deafening. At the finale although he felt drained, he was totally aware of the impassioned strength still coursing through him. It was such a warm emotion he wished he could wrap it around him and keep it forever.

After the concert, tea and savouries were served in the reception room. Patrick was not prepared for this and he shyly whispered to Sister Elizabeth that he didn't want to go in there.

"Patrick just let others do the talking and you will be all right. Do you remember all those lovely cakes at the hotel where we had lunch? Well you'll find plates overflowing with delicious titbits in there, too. A lot of people are waiting to meet you, let's go."

As they entered, Kevin came forward to offer his congratulations. The happiness on his face told her all she wanted to know regarding the performance.

Kevin gave Patrick a bear hug, "From now on my boy you'll be the talk of the town."

Upon entering the reception room they didn't have long to wait for their arrival to register with the crowd. Immediately, congratulatory well wishers surrounded them. Questions shot back and forth like confetti in a wind. Where had the young musician come from? How old was he? Where had he played before?

The Bishop and Mother General made their way through the maze of people surrounding Patrick and Elizabeth. From the sidelines Mother Superior watched in dismay as the Bishop enfolded Patrick in a warm embrace. The Mother General held his face between her hands and with a warm smile told him how proud she was to meet such a talented young musician.

Elizabeth heard a voice from behind her, saying, "When you have a moment, may I have a word with you?"

Turning, she saw a handsome man with a smile that could melt a candle.

"Hello, I believe you are Sister Elizabeth."

"Yes, what can I do for you?"

"I'm Terrence O'Dea, a concert promoter from Dublin and a friend of Kevin O' Byrne's. He promised to introduce us, since he is nowhere in sight I'm taking the liberty to do so. I won't keep you more than a few minutes, because I'm sure a lot of people here tonight are waiting to meet you and your protégé."

"A concert promoter? That's interesting, did you enjoy the concert?"

"I did indeed, and I'd like to know more about Patrick. I found his playing remarkably poignant for one so young. I observed that after his first taste of applause he opened up and played with complete abandon. I should like to meet his parents, are they here tonight? Kevin was quite mysterious about the boy. All he told me was that you were his music teacher and that the lad was gifted."

"Yes, the first time I gave him a lesson I knew he was special. From the beginning he was so wrapped up in his music that it saddened him when the session was over. Patrick started playing a few months ago. But I can assure you that the hours he spends playing are the happiest times of his life. He has no family, he is an orphan and lives in the convent orphanage."

"I would like to have the two of you come up to Dublin and put on a performance there."

"Mr. O'Dea, that would be impossible. I, for one, cannot travel wherever I choose, and I'm afraid Patrick is in the same boat…so to speak."

"Well, whom should I approach to remedy this situation? He could earn good money for a few performances a year. A few pounds in the bank would be a good start in life for him later on when he leaves the orphanage."

"Mr. O'Dea, I appreciate what you are saying, however, I'm sure Mother Superior would not allow him to travel to Dublin. And as far as I'm concerned it is out of the question, I must adhere to the rules. Mother Superior has a jaundiced view about Patrick's lessons. I hope you understand my position, it wouldn't do for my words to be bandied about."

"Perhaps if I approached Mother Superior with an offer to donate so many pounds to the convent's coffers for each concert he plays? Would that ease the way? Or better still, I happen to know the Bishop quite well–perhaps I should have a few words with him."

"Well, that might be the correct route to take. The fact that extra cash would be available for the convent would be welcome news for Mother Superior. Convent Orphanages are always short of cash. As the first step I'd advise you to speak to the Bishop before you approach Mother Superior."

With a mischievous grin he replied, "I had the doubtful pleasure of being introduced to Mother Superior earlier, she looked me over as though I had just been fished out of a stagnant pond. I must say she has a face that could stop even a well wound clock."

"Mr. O'Dea, passing judgement on someone you barely know is not a desirable trait." Then she mischievously added, "On second thought perhaps that's the reason so many clocks in the convent no longer tick."

"I should hate to wake up in the morning and find her sharing my pillow."

Elizabeth laughed, "I can't imagine that happening in the near future. Mr. O'Dea, I find your dry wit just as impossible as our mutual friend Kevin O'Byrne. His brand of humour is sharp and he revels in jabbing the odd person where it rankles most. Thank goodness he is sensitive enough to know when he has jabbed too deep. I hope you have the same knack of knowing."

"Sister Elizabeth, I have two wishes going through my mind at the moment. One, I wish you weren't a nun. Secondly, I hope we meet again. And I also wish that you'd call me Terrence?"

"Mr. O'Dea, I am no longer accustomed to conversations like this so let's put an end to it before it gallops out of bounds."

"My lack of sensitivity to your position is appalling; nevertheless, I meant every word I said."

"Said like a true Irishman …they always enjoy the thrust and parrying of words."

"I will give you my card, please get in touch with me if you can arrange some way for Patrick to perform in Dublin. Now I must not take up any more of your time, it was *truly* a pleasure meeting you."

When he walked away, Elizabeth had a whimsical look in her eyes. It seemed her femininity had not died from suffocation beneath the voluminous folds of her black Habit. And she thought he was the handsomest man she had ever seen! His deep-set eyes conveyed a depth of meaning that one could drown in. Elizabeth felt a sensual stimulation that had been stifled for a long time!

Patrick was sitting on the edge of a big armchair against the wall; he was more or less using the long velvet drapes to shield him from the others in the reception room. His eyes had an inquiring look as Elizabeth came and sat beside him. She knew he was terrified to go into the reception room. However, since he was turning a new corner in his life, he had to learn to be at ease with people. Here I am she thought, dreaming about his future and this is his first public appearance. Well, she believed that dreams could come true if one worked hard enough to bring them to fruition. She was aware that Patrick was tugging at her heartstrings and when the time came for him to leave the orphanage that it would break her heart.

"All right Patrick, you've had time to cool down. Surely you know that you played like an angel tonight. I'm so proud of you. Now let's go in and taste those delicious savouries. By the way, did you notice that gentleman I was talking to? He arranges concerts in Dublin and he was quite impressed by your playing. I have a feeling that we will be seeing more of him."

Kevin joined them at their table. "Well, Elizabeth, what did you think of my friend Terrence?"

"An interesting man indeed! I believe you were responsible for his presence here tonight? Why didn't you tell me about Mr. O'Dea before the concert?"

"Because I thought it might make you nervous knowing that he was in the audience. Patrick's playing deserved to be heard by a professional and that is why I invited him to the concert. Terrence believes that the boy has potential and with a little more polish he could go a long way. You appeared to be enjoying your conversation with Terrence?"

"Yes, what he had to say was a little premature; nevertheless it was most encouraging. Your friend Terrence has an engaging personality."

"I knew that it would be a most inopportune time for me to interrupt your 'tête-á-tête'. A green-eyed devil of jealousy took hold of me and I regretted having invited him."

"Kevin, don't be ridiculous, are you forgetting where I return to tonight after this short foray into the outside world?"

"Elizabeth, I wish to God that you didn't have to go back to that horrible place. I'd love to swoop you and Patrick up and away and leave this county forever."

"There you go again saying the most outlandish things. Kevin, you haven't changed a bit since we used to ride together as youngsters. You always had to jump every fence in sight regardless of the danger involved. It never occurred to you that your horse might not be capable of the challenge. Please don't allow your imagination to run amok as far as our relationship is concerned. Realize that my fate is a done deal, sealed and delivered."

They drove back to the convent in a subdued mood. Tiredness and that peculiar calm that follows an emotional high had seduced them to silence.

After helping to carry the parcels to the door of the convent, Kevin took her hand, "Elizabeth, meeting you again has given me a happiness that is tinged with gut deep sadness." And without a backward glance he walked back to the car.

Elizabeth made her way to the small austere room where she had slept every night for the past decade. The recent 'happenings' were chasing her thoughts into territory where she didn't want to enter. As she lay on the narrow bed ruminating over the evening's events her thoughts were interlaced with Terrence O'Dea's strong handsome face. So delightful were the thoughts she forgot to rein them in!

For years she had struggled to wipe out the worldly life she had once enjoyed. But tonight without guilt she wallowed in the pleasure of picturing her own lovely bedroom in the home she had shared with her parents. Those happy memories had diminished by the rigidity of convent rules. Why in the name of God had they returned to twist a knife in her heart after all these years? Why…Why…Why? She had been so sure that she had conquered those natural longings. But tonight the seeds of forbidden fruit were once again struggling to sprout on hitherto fallow ground.

Lying on her narrow bed she told herself that meeting Terrence O'Dea tonight had stirred up feelings that she had no right to embrace. To say she was alarmed was to put it mildly so she prayed for deliverance from such thoughts. Alas, Terrence's deep-set eyes with their knowing look seemed to mock her feeble efforts for deliverance. She felt the blood rushing through her as she remembered the touch of his hand and how she wanted to hold it just a little longer. Strange that being in his presence for such a short time could disintegrate years of convent discipline. It was absurd to allow Terrence's handsome face to dominate her thoughts...but the feeling was wonderful.

CHAPTER EIGHT
The Concert Aftermath

The morning after the concert Elizabeth was surprised at the wondrous joy hurtling through her like an express train. Once again, as the events of the previous night unfolded, small flames of desire flicked back and forth and in vain she tried to sweep it all aside. Stepping out of bed onto the cold floor she knelt and again prayed that she would recover her usual self-discipline. A melancholy and all-consuming loneliness spread its dark wings around her.

The deep depression she had suffered during the first year in the convent had almost destroyed her to the point where death seemed the ultimate solution. The will to live came to the fore and she slowly expunged all remnants of her previous life from her thoughts. The biggest hurdle occurred when she took her final vows… first and foremost was the question…had she made the right decision?

Glancing at her tiny watch she was surprised to see she had overslept and wondered why no one had come to awaken her. Elizabeth made her way to the kitchen.

When Sister Rose saw her standing in the doorway, she cried, "Well now, so there you are all in one piece. I was beginning to think that you'd never wake up. I looked in on you twice and there you lay as though your dreams were the sweetest in the world. So I left you to dream because I had orders not to disturb you at the request of the Mother General. Mother Superior looked as though she had swallowed a bottle of Castor Oil when she heard that you were not to be disturbed."

"Hush Rose, do be careful what you say. If this ever got back to Mother Superior you'll be wearing a hair shirt for the rest of your life in some backwater convent in the west of Ireland."

"I won't be sent away from here, because I'm the best cook they've had in many a year. And if they want to continue eating good meals, they'd better start giving me a little more leeway. Actually,

I'm at the point where I'm sick and tired of walking the straight and narrow. I'm fed up with the whole damned lot."

"Heavens above Rose, what do you want more leeway for? Being a nun what sort of leeway could you expect? I've never heard you talk like this before."

"Elizabeth, that concert last night changed my mind about a lot of things. Seeing people laughing, talking and greeting each other with such enthusiasm I began to think about our lives here. This morning I studied the nuns around me at prayers, all swathed in funeral black with faces moulded into a perpetual pious bleakness. All of a sudden I thought it would be grand to buy a flaming red dress and dance until dawn. Don't look at me as though I'm the Devil's first cousin. If God made me as I am, and endowed me with the energy to kick over the traces … then he should have warned me before I took the vows. I'm fed up praying for all the sinners of the world. Anyway, every last one of those sinners are out there enjoying their sins to the hilt. I am beginning to have my doubts whether I'm cut out for convent life. Maybe it's not healthy or normal to stifle the natural feelings that we were born with. Oh, for the love of God, Elizabeth, don't look at me like that. By the look on your face one would think I had just indulged in a sexual orgy with the Bishop."

"Rose, it was *your* decision to enter a convent. I'm sure you come out with this outlandish diatribe just to shock me."

Having said this, Elizabeth truly felt like a hypocritical idiot.

Noticing the look of distress on Elizabeth face, Rose was remorseful. Putting her arms around Elizabeth's shoulders, she said, "Elizabeth, let's change the topic. This morning I have an edgy rebellion hammering the hell out of all the pious thoughts that I've been nurturing for the past few years. So far it's been a tight race and at this point I've no idea which side is going to win. By the way, before I become too contrite and title myself the 'Sinner of the World'…I noticed that you were having a high old time with that handsome man from Dublin."

"Rose, don't read anything into those few moments I spent with Terrence O'Dea. We were simply discussing the possibility of young

Patrick performing in Dublin. I agree with you he is a handsome man and he has a pleasing personality which I enjoyed the few moments I spent with him."

"Aye, he has personality plus! He could charm the sparrows out of the trees. I had a good chat with him until Mother Superior spotted us, and then she marched over like an avenging angel and requested that I fetch tea and tarts for her. That put the cap on things–bowing courteously towards her and with a wicked gleam in his eyes, Terence said, 'Dear lady, I hope you enjoy your 'tarts'…I always do.' He winked at me and I winked right back and that took him by *such* surprise…I thought he would drop his drawers." Sister Rose chuckled to herself. "Elizabeth, don't look so disapproving, shure it was the best bit of fun I've had in years."

"Heavens above, Rose, what's got into you?"

"For heavens sake, a wink and a bit of gab with a handsome man is a small reward for the time I've spent here praying for my redemption. Sometimes I imagine the only holiness I have is the holes on my long black stockings; I've darned a trillion holes in those leg coverings. To tell you the truth, whenever we are summoned to the sewing room for an evening of mending I want to run in the opposite direction. Having to listen to Sister Magdalene droning on about all the saintly people that have gone before us. And then to know that she is Mother Superior's ears and eyes around the convent…we also have to darn *her* stockings. There she sits at the head of the table droning away with that smug empty face trying to bring sanctity into our lives. I'm sure there's not a smidgen of sanctity running around her spirit. How could there be? She is just a tattletale for Mother Superior. Honestly, I hate the sight of the nuns sitting bolt upright in straight-backed wooden chairs looking like a colony of penguins. To make matters worse, there's never a titter or a good belly laugh to be heard. I'm sure God had a good reason for providing a laughing apparatus for us and expected us to make good use of it. Now that I think of it there are a few other parts of our anatomy that are rusting away for lack of use. So why do we allow God's good creations to lie dormant?"

"I'm afraid last night's glimpse of the outside world has taken you to a place where you have no right to go."

"Elizabeth, that fresh breeze of freedom targeted you, too!"

"For both our sakes, let's just forget it and go back to where we were. May I join you this afternoon when you go to the garden to pick your vegetables? Perhaps talking this out would untangle the knots in our thoughts."

"I would be delighted to have your company. But I can't promise we'll have *'a toe the line'* conversation. The mood I'm in today I'd rather be in Timbuktu than here."

"Rose, I will pray that peace of mind and soul will be yours."

"Well, while you are praying for me, say one for yourself; you look as though you could do with it."

She left the kitchen with an uneasy feeling. What *had* happened last night to cause such an upheaval to their familiar routine? Had they used the daily routine of the convent as a tool to clout out all natural desires? Elizabeth's uneasiness was fueled by the fact that she and Rose were now traveling a forbidden path.

As she walked along the long dismal hallway pondering their conversation... guilt was weighing heavy upon her. Temptation *had* displayed its attractive wares and whetted desires that had been dormant for a long time. Elizabeth knew she had to straighten out her thoughts before joining Rose in the garden. Deep down she wished that she could allow her thoughts and desires to run wild and enjoy the natural feeling of being a woman!

She made her way into the music room, locked the door having made the decision that today she would not allow anyone to enter. Perhaps meditation might bring peace to the chaotic rhythm of her mind... she closed her eyes and prayed. The thought that Sister Rose might leave the convent filled her with deep sorrow. She and Rose *had* become close friends, a fact they took pains to hide, because it was contrary to convent rules.

The questions she asked herself came fast and furious. Am I a fit person to be a nun? Had she been too complacent by believing that her life had been settled forever? Should she ask permission to go on a retreat, knowing full well that a retreat would only be a temporary escape from reality? How could she leave Patrick to fend for himself? She knew that he loved her and after last night's successful performance, it would be a shame to just walk out of his life. How strange it was that his coming into her life had opened a new vista for both of them. More than ever she was aware that it wouldn't be easy to put all the pieces back into their safe little cell. Ironically prior to the concert the only problem she had was her dealings with Mother Superior, but now a load of undeniable 'ifs' were flogging her conscience with what might have been…and?

Before leaving the music room to join Sister Rose in the garden, she prayed for the wisdom to solve any problems that might arise between them. Life seemed to be a mass of twisted, unrelated mutations…varying from sadness to happiness… love to hatred, followed by spells of calmness. In quiet desperation she endeavoured to toss the rambling thoughts aside as she walked towards the garden to meet Rose.

Rose was digging a row of potatoes and she threw a potato sack towards Elizabeth and told her to start filling it. Elizabeth studied her graceful white hands and holding the old potato bag as though it was a dangerous species she humbly asked Rose for instructions. By no means did she relish the thought of soiling her hands with earth-covered potatoes. However, she didn't think it would be fitting to tell Rose that she had never done work like this before or that when she was growing up a gardener had done such chores. Thinking about the gardener hurled a flashback of the time she had caught sight of Mary the rosy-cheeked scullery maid helping the gardener to fill the freshly dug potatoes into similar bags. She had watched as the gardener and Mary worked in silence, then Mary whispered something to the gardener, which was followed by a burst of laughter. Elizabeth remembered seeing the young maid successfully targeting the gardener's posterior with a potato the size of a turnip. He threw down his spade and chased after her but the young maid lifted her skirts and ran like a gazelle. Elizabeth was amazed at the vividness of the memory. So much so she could almost hear the playful laughter of the young maid.

Rose stared up at her, "Are you in dreamland, Elizabeth? Why are you giving your hands such a careful examination? Don't tell me you had the idea that potatoes came straight from the earth all washed and ready for the pot? Get busy or we won't have time for a bit of a chat. Remember, I have to cook supper after these chores are completed."

Out of the corner of her eye Rose watched in amusement as Sister Elizabeth gingerly held each potato between her thumb and forefinger before releasing it delicately into the sack. After each spud was dropped she scrutinized the dirt still clinging to her two fingers, and her mouth was screwed up in such distaste as though she had just sucked a lemon.

That was all Rose needed to have a bit of fun. "Elizabeth, when you come across some nice long worms remember to toss them back into the plot. Y'know, worms are fine workers in the garden."

She almost died laughing when she saw the look of horror on Sister Elizabeth's face.

"Worms? My Lord, I wouldn't touch a worm for all the tea in China. Really Rose, I don't relish this type of work. Can't you find one of the young novices to help?"

"Yes, we have plenty of young farm girls as novices and every one of them believing that taking their vows would be a gateway to heaven. I don't ask them to help with the garden chores when I have the time to do it, because I enjoy mulling around in God's little acre all by myself. When I plant a few seeds beneath the sod and reap what I've sown, I think I've witnessed one of God's little miracles. Don't you think there is a correlation between the good and evil in humans and the harvesting of crops...after all, we do reap what we sow."

"Rose, would you explain that piece of peasant wisdom? I'm afraid I don't follow you."

"Well, look at it this way, every square inch of this garden is cultivated and nourished to the same degree. I plant the seeds but at harvest time not all of the crops are equally matured, and some aren't even worth keeping. So tell me why shouldn't the whole crop be in the same fine condition? Weren't they all given the same care and nourishment? It's just like families, children born to the same parents, and though most of the family are decent human beings…sometimes the odd one or two may be proper fiends. That is what I mean when I say there is a similarity between the sowing of seeds in a vegetable garden and rearing a family."

"Rose, you have the knack of simplifying the diversified quirks of humanity."

"Shame on you Elizabeth… now you're poking fun at me."

"Of course I'm not making fun of you. Actually I enjoy your unusual way of exploring the quirks of humanity. You seem to unravel the knots without giving one's psyche a lethal blow and in doing so, you leave space for a fresh sowing."

"Elizabeth, I'll put you out of your misery and get one of the young *sinless* novices to finish gathering the potatoes. Then we will have more time to talk. Perhaps we will discover why *you and I* are taking up space on this particular part of the world."

"Rose, today I'm not thinking in a rational manner. I feel that I'm marking time hoping and waiting for the pieces to fall into place."

"Goodness gracious Elizabeth, you are in a strange frame of mind. What has torn aside your customary curtain of complacency?"

"My spirit is not at peace. It is useless to force a solution to a problem one hasn't had time to delve into and understand. Let's walk and enjoy the day and if we don't feel inclined to talk, we'll give our tongues a rest. Our brain might appreciate the silence to clear away the debris that we have burdened it within the past two days."

As the two nuns walked side-by-side, every so often Rose would fiercely kick a stone as far as possible. And every kicked stone…was an unpleasant thought that was too hot for her to handle at the moment.

The late afternoon sun spread its last cloak of shimmering gold across the sky and the oncoming evening dampness chilled the air. Reluctantly the two black figures returned to the bleakness of the convent.

The following day Mother Superior walked into the music room all fired up, because she had just been notified that the Bishop and the

Mother General were on their way to the convent. Walking stiffly to where Elizabeth was sitting at the piano, she inquired if Elizabeth knew the reason for their visit.

Elizabeth assured her that she hadn't the faintest idea why they were coming, and asked, "Why should *I* know?"

"Well, I have a feeling it's something concerning you, because she requested that you cancel all music lessons today. I could well do without a visit from those two! They scrutinize every nook and cranny in the convent as though they expect to find dead fish lurking in corners. Not once have they ever complimented me on how well I run this orphanage."

Elizabeth sat in silence allowing her to rant and rave a few moments longer, and then rising, she said, "If you'll excuse me I'll tidy up around the music room in preparation for their scrutiny."

Mother Superior flounced out of the room, furious because she felt that she had been unjustly dismissed like an errant child.

When the Bishop arrived he suggested that they have a little musical escape from reality and asked Elizabeth if she would permit him to use her brother's flute. Then she sat down at the piano and the Bishop swept his ample body in a mock courtly manner "Let's start the music."

They played for an hour or more and the Mother General applauded enthusiastically when the session was over. Smiling with undisguised appreciation she looked towards Mother Superior, and was taken aback at the baleful expression on that good woman's face. Mother Superior knowing that some response was required then clapped her hands with slothful energy.

Afternoon tea was served in the music room. In respect to the importance of the two visitors it was quite a lavish spread. A young novice nun came in to clear the table, the Bishop said a few words to her, making her so nervous she dropped the cup and saucer right on his lap. The poor girl tearfully tried to retrieve the debris, too young and too naïve to know that the Bishop's lap was supposed to be *unexplored* territory. He was gallant enough to take the blame for this minor disaster saying, "I'm sorry I have a habit of talking with my hands, and like a clumsy oaf I knocked that cup and saucer right out of your hand."

The poor frightened girl looked at him, her eyes overflowing with gratitude. She knew what he had said was untrue, but she loved him for being such a lovely liar.

Sister Elizabeth noticed that the Mother General also appreciated his gallantry. She walked over to the young girl who was still nervously clearing away the dishes and told her to take a few cakes and have a little feast on her own. Then the Reverend Mother graciously thanked the novice nun serving the tea. She added, "At your age, I would have been petrified to serve a Bishop and a Mother General." The young novice bowed her head and thanked the Reverend Mother for her kind words.

Mother Superior, inwardly fuming felt her gorge rising to an unsafe level. She couldn't imagine why they would kow-tow in such a manner to that clumsy young nun. Lord only knows what would happen to the convent if she treated all misdemeanours in such an off-hand manner.

Then, just as Mother Superior thought she had about all she could take for one day, Mother General turned to her and said, "I'm sure you have a lot to attend to, please feel free to leave. Our time is limited and we have to discuss more details with Sister Elizabeth about the upcoming concert in Dublin."

Mother Superior took her leave; as she passed Sister Elizabeth she cast a glance filled with such hatred in her direction that Elizabeth shivered.

With leaden steps and lowered head Mother Superior made her way down the long hall, pondering the injustices that had been thrown at her throughout her entire life. The dislike she harboured for Sister Elizabeth coloured all her thinking. The unhappy childhood she had endured was a miserable contrast to Elizabeth's privileged life in a big house with servants. It seemed Elizabeth was still getting the cream of the crops right here in the convent. Had she known before that the Bishop and Mother General were also musicians, she would not have attempted to have Sister Elizabeth removed. Of course the three of them had tribal bindings… hadn't they all come from landed gentry? With the day's events hanging heavy on her shoulders, she trudged along to her room and lay down on the bed with her face turned to the wall. She felt drained and desperately frustrated and was sorely tempted to let fly with a few of her father's well-used curses.

Bishop Kennedy, the Mother General and Sister Elizabeth sat around the table discussing the offer they had received by mail from Terrence O'Dea. He wrote that an opening for young Patrick was available at the Gaiety Theatre in six weeks' time. As a solo flutist he would be paid a generous sum of money and that it would boost Patrick's confidence to have Sister Elizabeth as his accompanist.

Mother General turned to Elizabeth and inquired what she thought of the proposal. "Of course, the Bishop and I would give permission for you to accompany Patrick, however; it would entail an overnight stay at the Mother House. If you are comfortable with these arrangements, I will notify Mr. O'Dea by return post."

The Bishop said, "It is a well known fact that the roofing here is in dire need of repairs, so any extra funds would be greatly appreciated. Of course, some of the money must be put aside for Patrick. A few extra pounds will come in handy when he leaves the orphanage at the age of fourteen."

Elizabeth replied that she would be happy to accompany Patrick on stage.

"We were surprised at the size of the remuneration, as I am quite sure you are."

"Yes indeed, I am surprised that such a large amount would be paid to a child performer."

"Oh yes, but part of that amount includes your payment," said the Bishop.

"Why would I require money, where would I spend it?"

"With your generous heart we know you will put it to good use, you have my permission to use it as you see fit. Perhaps a new outfit for the boy to wear at the concert would take up most of your newfound wealth."

Elizabeth had a pile of thoughts still in their infancy awaiting her attention; so she was relieved when the Bishop and the Mother General took their leave.

Dear Lord, she thought, everything is happening and changing so fast...playing music with the Bishop and a free flowing conversation with a bit of humour thrown in for good measure. The solemnity of the convent cast such an overall blanket of gloom that the sound of laughter was a rarity. The last time she had laughed heartily was when she watched Sister Rose trying unsuccessfully to chase a bee out of the dining room, culminating with Mother Superior jumping up and making a 'bee-line' for her office...accompanied by the inquisitive bee buzzing the hitherto *'unexplored'* interior of her garments. The austere dining room was rocked with unfamiliar laughter following Mother Superior's hasty exit.

The Mother General tapped on the door of Mother Superior's room and gruffly Mother Superior barked, "Yes, who is it and what do you want?"

"I should like to have a few words with you before the Bishop and I take our leave."

An apologetic voice bid her enter. Mother Superior was lying on the narrow bed with the look of martyrdom spread across her dour countenance. She explained that she was unwell and asked to be excused for not rising.

In a cheerful voice the Mother General said, "I scrutinized your account books today and I must compliment your aptitude for getting the most out of every penny you spend."

Upon hearing these words, Mother Superior's thin lips slowly uncoiled into an unaccustomed smile. And she could feel her heart ticking away at a faster pace within her bony chest.

Then with a slight clearing of the throat, Mother General followed with a verbal clap of thunder. "I want you to come to the Mother House for a two week retreat. A Franciscan priest will be lecturing on finding peace of mind and spirit. I'm sure we will all elicit a better understanding from his knowledgeable observations of human nature."

Mother Superior was taken aback and her eyes filled with despair, she barely whispered, "Why?"

Upon seeing the raw anguish on the poor creature's face, Mother General rather lamely assured her that she and the Bishop would also be attending some of the lectures.

This caused a glimmer of hope to pass across Mother Superior's face. Attending the lectures in the exalted company of the Bishop and Mother General somehow lifted her sagging self-esteem!

CHAPTER NINE
Elizabeth in Dublin

Rose handed a letter to Elizabeth and said, "The postman gave me this letter without a stamp and asked me to make sure that it reached the right person. With a wink, he said to me, 'I'm sure it's for that beauty of a nun who goes by the name of Sister Elizabeth.' He then added, 'Don't worry, I'll be in my last resting place before I ever tell a soul. The man who gave me this letter planted a five-pound note in me' hand and I damn near died from shock! By God, I'll tell you one thing, he was as handsome a man as I've ever clapped me' eyes on.'"

Rose saw the concern in Elizabeth's eyes and immediately tried to calm her fears.

"Elizabeth, I warned him to keep his mouth shut or he'd be leaving this world so fast they won't have time to wrap a shroud around his carcass."

"Good heavens, Rose, this is becoming a dreadful mess. It was foolish of Terrence to put me in this position."

"Elizabeth, don't be alarmed. Henry the postman, is my cousin, you have my word for it that he will never utter a word. It appears that Terrence O'Dea has busied himself getting to know a few of the locals. Anyway, he gave Henry tickets for the concert in Dublin."

Without a word Elizabeth took the letter and went out to the bench in the garden. Rose watched from the kitchen window and wondered why Elizabeth was sitting with the unopened letter on her lap. Rose studied Elizabeth's face and it registered raw sorrow! It had always puzzled Rose why someone with Elizabeth's physical and spiritual beauty had ever entered a convent.

When Elizabeth returned to the kitchen her eyes told their own story. The letter was out of sight quietly and she left without saying a word.

When she reached the music room she went in and locked the door securely. Without further hesitation opened the letter. Terrence wrote that she was in his thoughts all times and that he must talk to her as soon as possible. He went on to say that his feelings for her were so profound that regardless of how hard he tried that it was impossible to sweep them aside. He wanted her to come to Dublin to plan the upcoming concert for young Patrick. The ending to the letter was unusual; he wrote that their relationship… must not interfere with Patrick's future.

In replying to his letter she wrote that she had obtained permission to meet him in Dublin. She also warned him to keep in mind that she was a nun and that it was ludicrous for him to imagine any relationship between them. She ended the letter by stating that the only relationship they had in common was the concert plans.

Terence smiled a knowing smile as he read her letter and thought, little does she know! He was a firm believer that nothing in life was coincidental…there was a reason for everything!

She stepped down from the train and *almost* into the arms of Terrence O'Dea as he stood on the platform with both hands outstretched to assist her down the steps. Elizabeth smiled and as she placed her hands in his she said, "Terrence, I'm no longer accustomed to such assistance."

"I can't imagine you depending on anyone for assistance…still it would give me the greatest pleasure to wait on you hand and foot for the rest of my days."

Little did she realize that he meant every word! No other woman had ever held him in such an emotional bind. His profession had provided him with the opportunity to meet a cross stratum of women… consisting of a bizarre blend of flamboyant *characteristics* and *morals*. Yet here he was pitching his heart into an impossible romantic tangle with a nun. Ridiculous as it was…without any effort she had captured his heart! His many sleepless nights were mute testimony to the depth of his feelings.

On the drive to the office Elizabeth was keenly observing all the sights. The Dublin citizens, oblivious to the steady downpour, strolled along the streets animatedly talking a mile a minute. Terrence wondered if she was remembering the days when she had roamed these streets in her carefree college days.

The yearning expression on Elizabeth's face reminded him of an incident that had occurred a long time ago. So he related the incident to Elizabeth. He had been walking along the street one evening when he noticed an urchin boy with his nose pressed against the window of a confectioner's shop. Above the door of this establishment there was a green and gold sign marked: 'High Class Confectioner'. The window was filled with mouth-watering chocolates and the little boy was so entranced with the display that he jumped guiltily when Terrence spoke to him.

He started to run away…but stopped in his tracks when Terrence said, "Don't those chocolates look good enough to eat?" Putting his hand on the young lad's shoulder he guided him into the shop.

The well-dressed man with the barefoot little urchin in tow caused the girl behind the counter to gape in astonishment. The unwashed urchin with eyes as round as saucers was not the most pleasant sight she had seen all day. Her eyes remained riveted to this tableau. The man told her to fill a box of the best chocolates for the boy. She chose an assortment until the box was almost filled, and, with her hand hovering in mid air over the box, she glanced towards Terrence to see if she should continue. He nodded his approval and when the box was full he handed it to the boy. Without further ado or a word of thanks the boy grabbed it and raced for the door. Terrence hurriedly paid for the chocolates and went out to the street to find the boy. But the ill-lit street was dark and empty and the boy had simply vanished. Terrence returned to the store and asked the clerk if she had ever seen the boy before.

"Yes, he comes quite often and presses his nose on the window until it flattens like a potato scone on a griddle. And do you know, he stares so long you'd swear by the look on his face that he could actually taste the chocolates. Now mind you, I do feel sorry for him, but I have to chase him away. It's not good for business to have a raggedy street urchin hanging around the entrance."

As he related this incident to Elizabeth he was surprised at how intently she was listening. She interrupted him by saying, "Terrence, you made a mistake, giving him chocolates when a good meal would have been better for his little empty belly. The poor child probably hadn't a spare bit of flesh hanging on his bones."

Elizabeth's voice, so filled with compassion, made Terrence realize that he had missed a chance to do something worthwhile for a hungry child. No doubt the boy had devoured the chocolates on an empty stomach with disastrous results. That child's thin face, with eyes too old for the few years he had spent on earth, resurfaced frequently in Terrence's thoughts. However, today was the first time he had ever shared it with someone and the understanding compassion in Elizabeth's eyes spoke volumes for the type of person she was. Terrence sighed, knowing that he had fallen madly in love with a precious woman, albeit at this point in time... unattainable.

Terrence's office had a luxurious ambience; comfortable leather chairs flanked the glowing fireplace and a fine selection of oil paintings were strategically placed around the room. But the piece that held Elizabeth's attention was the magnificent rosewood grand piano. Slowly she walked around the room and the pleasure of what she saw was reflected in her beautiful eyes.

Terrence's eyes followed every graceful movement and his present desire to strip her of the black habit was surprisingly free of carnality. It was enough at the moment just to feast his eyes and dream of the illusive loveliness hidden beneath the dark folds of those garments.

Sensing that as she observed the décor... she herself was being observed, she smiled and said, "Terrence this is a lovely room."

By the expression in his eyes she knew his thoughts were not what she would appreciate hearing at this moment. Their eyes met and Elizabeth could feel her heart beating to an unfamiliar rhythm ... she was the first to look away. Nevertheless she was aware of his rugged handsome face.

"Elizabeth what colour is your hair?"

'Twas a simple question so needless to say he was taken aback at the effect it had.

She blushed and became quite flustered and sharply replied, "The colour of my hair is of no importance to you or anyone else. Now we should start on the music score; you know I must be on the train this afternoon."

Terrence wondered why mentioning the colour of her hair should disturb her so much. There must be a reason, but he had no idea what that might be.

He spread sheets of music over the table and they began the process of choosing music for the concert. Since their tastes were in accord the musical selection was completed quickly. Then they discussed the details of the stage setting and Terrence asked her opinion about his idea of attiring Patrick in a creamy white evening suit. She inquired where such a suit could be found. Terrence said that he had previously discussed it with Kevin, who assured him that his tailor would have it finished on time.

"Elizabeth, can you imagine the scene? The small figure of a boy standing alone on center stage… with the spotlight shining on him like a sparkling star? His tawny head of hair and the cream coloured suit against a background of rich green velvet or perhaps royal blue. Patrick has a magnificent head, truly unique for one so young."

"Yes, you're quite right, for one so young he has a powerful looking head. Isn't it strange how *we* Irish put so much credence in the shape of a head? Indeed it is an unusual way to judge a person's character."

"Well, aren't the Irish a strange breed at the best of times?"

"Yes we are, but we don't mind being a little bit strange, or should I say, different."

The plans for the performance were discussed with boundless enthusiasm as Terrence marked off every detail of the stage plans on a long sheet of paper. As he talked and planned, she understood why he was so successful in his chosen career…*dynamism* poured from him like molten gold.

Finally, with a sigh of satisfaction, he sat back and clasped his hands behind his head. "Elizabeth, you have given me more inspiration than I've had for a long time. You've found a jewel for the world of music; that boy is truly gifted. Well now, that's enough of the concert, we have covered a lot of ground in a short time and you must be hungry. Shall we go out for lunch and finish off the last details when we return?"

"I'm sorry, Terrence, much as I'd love to, it's out of the question."

"Why not? Does that black habit that you wear dictate that you no longer belong to the human race? Elizabeth, keep that scornful look for someone more deserving...such as Mother Superior. I had no right to pass such a snide remark, will you forgive me?"

"Terrence, that humble little boy look that you are presently wearing isn't necessary, yes I'll forgive you."

"Would you consent to having lunch here? If so, my secretary will order lunch from my favourite Cafe. How does that suit you?"

"Perhaps we should finish the loose ends pertaining to the concert right away. Then you can return to your work and I will go to the Mother House."

"Elizabeth, for God's sake, don't be so hard on yourself, why can't you relax for an hour or two? Please don't get upset with what I'm about to say, and forgive me for burdening you with my emotions. But this may be the only chance I'll have to unload the turbulence that has been robbing me of sleep lately. I realize our relationship hasn't a chance in hell of going anywhere; even so, I'm glad our paths crossed. I have never felt this way about any other woman and I just don't know which way to go with the feelings I have."

"That has the incredible sound of a child reaching for the unattainable. However, if it makes you feel any better, I want you to know that I enjoy your company. Meeting you Terrence has wrought changes to my way of thinking and yes... it has been disturbing. Surely you know that after one takes the final vows...such thoughts should take flight forever. I should feel guilty but I don't and knowing that I feel no guilt is the part that is puzzling. And we know that this is far as it goes."

"Elizabeth why did you become a nun? When I am with you, I have the feeling of being in the midst of an unsolved puzzle. It's an awesome feeling; perchance that's my Druid ancestry coming to the fore. You are such a puzzle to me. I would dearly love to unravel the mystery. Have you ever had the desire to leave the convent?"

"Why do you tie yourself in knots pondering improbable reasons for my being what I am? I admire your keen imagination and creativity; however, I dislike answering questions that have absolutely nothing to do with the task on hand. Shall I ever leave the convent? The answer is no! There would be no comfort zone in Catholic Ireland for me. Where could I live in peace and teach music for a living once it was known that I had broken my vows? As soon as that was known a barrage of criticism would fall on my hapless head. So leaving the convent would be akin to exchanging one cage for another."

"Good heavens, Ireland isn't the only place to live. Why not live elsewhere, in a lovely sunny country–such as Spain, Italy or France? Elizabeth, the few moments I spend with you are pierced with unimaginable anguish…it's bloody awful!"

"Why is it so?"

"Well, I realize that I'm in love with you. This conversation clears the air a little. Do you understand what I'm trying to say?"

"Yes, of course I do. Nevertheless I'm afraid the route you are taking will be fraught with disappointment."

Terrence's face was a solid mask of despair, "Elizabeth I will not give up on you! I want you in my life forever and a day. My only hope is that you too will realize that we do have a chance to turn our lives in another direction. Will you consider what I've just told you?"

"Terrence you have allowed yourself to be carried away with romantic thoughts. Although I don't see why I should, I will do my best to explain how difficult it was for me when I first entered the convent. It was a living hell! Just trying to maintain a healthy sanity during that long endless first year was an endurance test. So please don't make my life more difficult by filling our relationship with 'ifs'. At this stage in my life, I can't afford to dream of what might have been."

"Forgive me, Elizabeth, for tormenting you with my needs. From now on I will treasure the moments we have together and respect your vocation."

Her lovely eyes met his and a current of burning desire passed between them… Elizabeth was the first to look away. The fleeting emotion changed and a shadow of sadness swept over her lovely face. Holding her hand he minutely examined each finger as he thoughtfully stroked patterns along each finger. She made no attempt to withdraw her hand…as a powerful emotion pulsated from one to the other!

The secretary entered with the luncheon tray and her inquisitive eyes swept the room. Elizabeth was taken aback with the avid look of curiosity on the woman's face. What on earth had she hoped to find? After she left, Elizabeth inquired how long the woman had worked for him.

"Oh, long enough to keep her psyche tottering in utter confusion. Sometimes she believes she is in love with me and when each day ends and she finds herself with her virginity still *intact,* she switches back to the protective mother role."

"Terrence, if you are trying to shock me, you're not succeeding. Must I remind you that I lived in the outside world for many years before entering the convent."

"Yes, and I'd be delighted to hear about your life before you tucked yourself into the narrow confines of a religious institution."

Little did he know how many times she had pondered that same question and always drew a blank.

The lunch was sumptuous and Elizabeth enjoyed every morsel and she also knew that she was enjoying every minute she spent with this very virile man. He held a glass of wine and mischievously asked her if she would like to have one. She shook her head in disapproval but mischievously she flicked a piece of bread his way.

"Elizabeth, wine is not on the forbidden list. I'm sure you've heard the story told by Jesus to the apostles at the Last Supper? He said that he would not partake of wine again until he reached his

Father's vineyard. I was delighted with that bit of biblical news. I never thought we'd have celestial wine service after we departed from this world."

"I am well aware of what Jesus said. I too will be looking forward to imbibing heavenly wine, at least I'll be in good hands should I over-indulge."

"Thank God your sense of humor is *still* intact."

"Terrance, without humor...I'd be lost."

As he drove her to the train his mood started to hit rock bottom. When would they meet again in private? He had so much he wanted to tell her. Worst of all he had no hope of seeing her alone again.

She offered her hand in parting...and again the fleeting touch sent slivers of desire shooting through him. He found it incredible that a light touch of her hand should arouse such emotion. Although his past had been studded with many romantic interludes, none of them matched the velocity of this extraordinary entanglement.

The train sent puffs of steam into the atmosphere and Terrence stood rooted to the spot until it rounded the first bend. Part of his heart was a passenger on that train!

Oblivious of the rain pelting the pavement, he walked along deep in thought. He headed for his favourite pub, telling himself that a good snort of Irish whiskey and a bit of the old gab might shift his thoughts to a different path.

It was too early for the regulars and the pub was deserted when he entered. Mick, the publican, slid a glass of whiskey along the bar. "Here–put that down before you collapse with misery. In the name of Jaysus, you look as though you've been buried by mistake and had to dig your way out. Terrence, what's the matter with you? Did you lose your loot at the racetrack today?"

"I'm just tired of the bloody rain. I think I need a holiday in Spain. As soon as I have two or three weeks to spare, I'll be off."

"Tell me, which leading lady will you be taking this time? Or have you a couple of beauties stashed away in Spain for your convenience?"

"Mick, I'm turning over a new leaf. I'm going to lead an

exemplary life for a while and that's the God's truth."

"Jaysus, you're either going off the rails or suffering with a strange sickness."

"Christ, if that's all you have to offer in the way of conversation, I'll be off home and have a good night's sleep."

"Sure, you'll be having another drink, won't you? It's not like you to go home on one wing."

"Mick, that's exactly what I'm going to do. Goodnight and may God Bless you because if I stay here listening to any more of your gaff the two us will need more than His blessings."

Mick wondered, 'What the hell had happened to get Terrence in such a foul mood?' Usually it was a pleasure to share the evening with Terrence O'Dea. But tonight his company wasn't worth a pinch of salt.

Mick threw the bar towel on the counter and growled at the other bartender, "What the hell are you staring at?"

"Och, Mick, for a minute there, it appeared to me that you were mucking your way through a mire of uneasy thoughts. Jaysus, you were in such fine fettle until Terrence walked in."

"Is that so? Well, Danny me boy, you'll have the rest of the evening to figure it all out, because I'm getting to hell out of here. You can handle the pub alone tonight."

Mick plunked his cap on his head with such vigor that... had it been full of stones he would have cracked his skull. "Christ Almighty," said Danny to himself, "no one these days can keep a civil tongue."

The young girl who did the daily chores was in the hallway about to leave when Terrence entered his house. She looked surprised to see him home so early, but then his comings and goings were as unpredictable as his eating habits. Ah yes, but wasn't he the grandest man to work for? Granted he was a bit of a conundrum, but then most men were a bit daft at times.

"By the look of you, Mr. O'Shea, you could do with a bit of cheer. There's a roaring fire in the sitting room to warm the cockles of your heart. Your dinner is in the oven and I've baked your favourite fruit dumpling."

"Why did you think of making dinner for me, Peggy? I'm not usually home at this time and you don't usually prepare dinner unless I order it before leaving."

"I just had a feeling that you'd be home early. My poor old mother, may she rest in peace, used to tell me I had the gift of clairvoyance. I think she was right, because today you were twirling through my mind like a merry go round."

"Well Peggy, perhaps you are a bit of a sorceress. For the past few hours I've been suffering from a mental indigestion. Anyway, I appreciate your concern and I will enjoy the dinner. It's such a fierce windy night out there, why don't you take a cab home?"

"A cab? In the name of God, I've never taken a cab in me' life. If I had a few shillings for foolishness like that, I'd have two policemen guarding it."

"Well tonight, pretend you were born to the purple and enjoy a ride home in a cab."

With that, he took a five-pound note from his pocket and handed it to her.

She stared in astonishment when she saw the amount. "Sure that's more than I earn in weeks, I can't accept a five pound note."

"Peggy, take it, that money would have been long gone had I stayed in Mick's pub my usual length of time. So instead of using it to fill my gut with whiskey, I'm sure you can put it to a better use. Off with you now before you drive me to drink trying to explain. Anyway, I need to be alone, I've some tall thinking to take care of."

"Well thank you Mr. O'Dea, and I hope you untangle the snarls in your mind. The old folks say that a mind full of troubling thoughts is akin to a cupboard in need of a clearing out. It's been said... the Irish are akin to the Greeks that they were born old and wise. However, on Saturday nights when I witness some of the Irish rolling home drunk, I know that saying is *far-fetched*. But when I remember the poverty stricken existence that they endure daily, I tend to understand their need for a drink. The Chinese take the edge off of their misery with opium, and the Irish, with unemployment rampant throughout the land, dilute their misery with booze. An Irishman's misery is twofold: when he awakens from his drunken stupor with a rip-roaring hangover he sees his family with the hunger in their eyes wondering if he has a shilling left for food. Riddled with guilt, he filches his brown paper pay docket out of his pocket to find it as empty as his heart! As we all know, England's absentee landlords have wrought a lot of misery on these beautiful green Isles."

Terrence poured himself a stiff whiskey and lowered himself into his favourite chair to do a bit of thinking. He watched the flames flickering and dancing their way to eventual destruction and wondered... was this an analogy parallel for humanity? In youth we seem to crackle and flick through life with flaming colours, then slowly the fire dwindles...until at last the little flame slowly dissipates into colourless ashes.

Holy Mother of God, he thought, here I am trying to avoid thinking about Elizabeth and I find it impossible. She had captivated his imagination more than any woman he had ever known had. He swore that he would leave no stone unturned until he had her out of that convent. He was heedful of the fact that Irish Catholics would never condone an ex-nun marrying, so if they married they would have to live in another country. At the moment he almost wished he had never met her.

CHAPTER TEN
The Beating

Sister Elizabeth went straight to the music room and a few minutes later the door flew open and Sister Rose came hustling in with a grim look on her face.

"Elizabeth, all hell broke loose whilst you were in Dublin. Have you seen young Patrick?"

"No, I haven't seen any one yet. I just arrived a few minutes ago. Why is he ill?"

"Yes, sick at heart is more like it. His poor little hands are swollen beyond recognition. He has been unable to practice since you left. That old fiend Mother Superior caned the living daylights out of him the very day you departed."

"Why?"

"She ordered him to go to the kitchen and scour all the pots and boilers. When he replied that *you* did not want him to do that sort of work, she simply exploded. 'You young cur, I am the Mother Superior here and you will do as I tell you.' And with that she clouted him on the side of the head and told him to go to her office immediately. Then, glaring, she ordered that I leave the scouring jobs for Patrick to tackle when he returned. She left him in such a state he was the most pathetic sight I ever laid my eyes on!"

"Dear sweet Jesus, I think she is going mad. Why does she detest him?"

"Can't you guess? Elizabeth, you are the thorn in her side and she knows that you are fond of him, so she takes her hatred of you out on the poor lad. My heart was as heavy as a sack of wet potatoes when he returned to the kitchen after she caned him. His face was white and his eyes had that hopeless stare. He did not speak…just stood with his arms hanging loosely by his sides. I tried to embrace him and he cringed and whispered, 'Don't touch me'. When he whispered that he hurt all over, I couldn't speak, I just broke down and wept. I told him to go and lie down. Silently he turned and walked out of the kitchen. Sometime later I went to the dormitory to find out how he was faring. The poor wee lad lay with his face under that old gray blanket and wouldn't acknowledge my presence. When I left him my heart was drowning with unshed tears. I was sorely tempted to go down and smother that old harridan."

They heard a tap on the door and it opened slowly and young Patrick came in looking wan and pale. He went over to Sister Elizabeth and stood in front of her without saying a word. She softly stroked his head and gently lifted his hands. She was shocked when she saw the condition of those slender sensitive hands with fingers so badly swollen that they were barely distinguishable.

Sister Rose was in tears and turning to Elizabeth, she said, "This should be reported to the Mother General. It is your duty to do so, Elizabeth, after all–he suffered because he tried to obey your orders."

"Rose, please leave us alone for a few moments."

When the door closed behind Sister Rose, Elizabeth took Patrick in her arms. Their tears flowed in unison and a melancholic cloud engulfed their spirits in deep sadness. Elizabeth wiped his tears with her white hankie and kissed him tenderly on the forehead.

"Patrick, trust me, you will never be caned by anyone in this institution again."

His eyes were devoid of expression as he whispered, "Sister Elizabeth, I don't care anymore about anything…I just want to die. I want to go to a place where I'll never wake up again, a place where I'll never see anyone. My hands and back are sore, and, worst of all, the inside of me is crying. I'm stuck in a place where I don't want to be. Before when I felt sad, I used to dream of running away, but the way I feel today, I don't want to be anywhere."

"Patrick, why is your back sore?"

His face reddened and he told her that Mother Superior had caned his bare buttocks. She gently lifted his jersey and was appalled when she saw welts laced across his white skin. Good Lord, she thought, that woman has surely gone mad.

"Patrick, stay here until I return. I will place a notice on the door that we are practicing so no one will enter; I will return as soon as possible."

She went straight to Mother Superior's office, knocked once and entered without being asked to do so.

Mother Superior stood up from her desk and hissed, "How dare you enter my office without permission to enter?"

"I dared, because you dared to beat an innocent child during my absence. A boy who was simply obeying the orders I had given him before leaving. You knew he had an up-coming concert in Dublin and that his hands had to be protected from injury. Yet you took it upon yourself to destroy those hands and no doubt cause damage to his kidneys by the pounding on his back. Be assured that I will bring this beating to the attention of the Bishop and Mother General. Patrick had permission to discontinue harsh work in the kitchen until after the concert. And you were notified of this…yet; you severely punished the child for doing what he was told to do. I have prayed that God in His mercy would guide you towards a more compassionate way of dealing with these unfortunate orphans. Alas, I have lost faith that *you* will ever change." And without another word spoken, Sister Elizabeth left the office.

Mother Superior's face was ashen and a stream of unspoken venom flooded through her being. As usual she brought that underdog feeling to the fore and blamed everyone and everything for her unfortunate circumstances. She knew there was no way to appease Sister Elizabeth or was she inclined to do so. So there she sat pondering what her next move should be.

Filled with apprehension, memories flooded her mind of the nights she had waited for her father to stagger home loaded with booze. He vented his rage and drunken frustration by beating his children with a thick leather belt. The beatings continued until Gerald, the eldest brother, was old enough to wrestle the belt out of his father's hand. He then beat the living hell out of his father and the two had never spoken again. When Gerald was leaving for America a few years later, he offered his hand to his father in parting. His father refused the handshake and, looking Gerald in the eye said, "Good Riddance." The family never heard from Gerald after that.

Mother Superior's heart was filled with hatred towards Sister Elizabeth, the Bishop and the Mother General. With a heavy heart she walked to the desk and locked the door. Putting her head on her forearms... bitter tears of frustration slowly dampened the black sleeves of her Habit.

Within a week she was notified to report to the Mother House. She was thoroughly reprimanded by the Mother General. Worse was yet to come; the following morning she was sent to a cloister convent in the wilds of Ireland. The length of her stay was undetermined—she was told it would be dependent on her reaction to counseling. However, the duration of her stay would be at least six months... perhaps forever?

On leaving she humbly asked who would replace her at the orphanage. The Mother General tartly replied, "Someone who will add more of God's love to the lives of those poor unfortunate orphans, as opposed to the senseless punishment you engaged in. At the moment we are considering Sister Elizabeth."

The Bishop and the Mother General sensed that Elizabeth didn't want the position of Mother Superior when she suggested Sister Rose for the position. When Sister Rose was advised that she would be the new Mother Superior she was surprised and inquired what would happen when Mother Superior returned.

The Mother General replied that Mother Superior might well stay in the west of Ireland forever.

Later in the music room Elizabeth rocked with laughter as Rose pantomimed her future role as Mother Superior. She walked around the music room with a solemn countenance, hands tucked up her sleeves and laid down the law about how the convent would be run in future under her jurisdiction. She would post an order in the main hallway stating that from now on all Nuns would be forbidden to smoke in the hallways; weekend pub- crawling would be disallowed. All male visitors must vacate the nuns' sleeping quarters before midnight. Flirting with priests would be a thing of the past just in case they might be tempted to forget their vow of celibacy…and if that occurred what would the Pope do about it? Well, he might be tempted to have a fling away from Vatican City to discover for himself the joys of an Irish convent. And wouldn't that be a sight for sore eyes to see the Pope in an Irish pub with his belly full of Guiness's …doing an Irish jig with a spirited colleen dressed in a black habit? Elizabeth enjoyed the pantomime.

"Rose you've chosen the wrong vocation, you would be an excellent actress."

In her role as Mother Superior, Rose made marvellous changes in the running of the convent. Meals were more pleasant and nuns were now allowed to walk in the gardens in their free time. Their solemn tight expressions slackened a bit and when they passed other nuns in the hallways they actually smiled in greeting. Of course the elderly nuns didn't agree with this new mode of conduct… and continued to slither along the hallways like black phantoms with mask-like expressions… their lips never knowing the pleasure of a smile.

One day Mother General arrived unannounced in the nuns' dining room; as was her custom she gave a short talk on their service to God. Before leaving she asked that some special prayers be offered for the well being of Mother Superior. She did not explain the necessity for these prayers, knowing full well that the convent grapevine had already been in action. All the sisters knew that Mother Superior was doing her penance in some forsaken convent in the west of Ireland. They prayed for her as they were ordered to, but pleaded with God to leave her in the wilds of Ireland until He was ready to take her to His mansion.

After the severe beating, it had taken Patrick a few days to regain his usual esprit. However, having youth on his side, he was soon able to smile again. Elizabeth cherished the hours they spent playing the various scores for the concert. As he played, he slipped into a world of his own making, totally focused, composed and confident. It was a complete transformation: it seemed that the shy insecure boy and the boy with the flute were two different personalities.

When the lesson was over, Elizabeth suggested he visit the

Murphys the following Sunday. She knew the love he received from this couple would be of comfort to him at this challenging time. When he arrived at the farm Mrs. Murphy folded him in a warm embrace. The shadow of sadness in his eyes made her wonder what had happened since last they had met. Well, today he would have his favourite dinner, roast chicken, roast potatoes and fresh vegetables and, of course, strawberry pie. Mrs. Murphy believed that a belly-full of tasty food and a bit of love were the cure-all for everything.

For the first time in weeks, Patrick laughed, when Mrs. Murphy said, "You're an important musician now and I'll be the talk of the town when I walk into the concert hall with you. Mr. O'Byrne has given us two tickets, and not only that, he wants us to accompany you and Sister Elizabeth when he drives you to Dublin."

Patrick and Elizabeth had to make another trip to O'Byrne's for the measurements to be taken for Patrick's evening attire. The big black cab stopped and as they alighted from the cab, the same three women wrapped in their wool shawls were enjoying their morning gossip. This second sighting of the nun and the boy took them by surprise.

Aye, but their opinion had changed since the last time they had seen her emerging from the cab. The typical mixture of religious piety and native common sense had now welded their opinion of the nun to a *digestible* size. Hadn't the poor soul paid the price for straying off the moral path? So in deference to the Habit she wore and a feeling of shared feminine sympathy... they bid her 'good day' and respectively lowered their heads.

The door of the shop closed behind the nun and the boy.

One of the women whispered, "Shure, she may have been born to the gentry, but what has the poor soul got out of life? I'd say a helluva lot less than us, except of course, she hasn't the burden of a drunken husband breathing booze down the back of her neck every night in bed. And you can be sure 'tis only the *back of my neck* he breathes on... when he comes home 'one sheet to the wind'. My man was stone drunk on our wedding night, plastered to the gills he was. I suppose the poor sod needed a bellyful of whiskey to tackle what was awaiting his presence in the bridal bed. Did you know that he'd never been out of calling distance of his auld mother? And drunk as he was... he was well aware that she was anxiously holding her breath in the next room... at the thought of *me* ravishing her one and only son. Well there was no rambunctious rattling and rumbling in our bridal bed that night. Sure with the snoot-full he had under his belt he was as limp as a dead fish and didn't smell a helluva lot better."

With that said, off they went to Clancy's pub. As the first slurp of Stout gurgled past their gullet, they resumed the discourse about Sister Elizabeth. Maureen said that she had just learned that the groom had nothing to do with Elizabeth's banishment from her home. He was sacked for mistreating the master's favourite horse. And the person who told her this new piece of gossip had been the housekeeper at the big house at the time. The housekeeper also disclosed that a college friend of Elizabeth's had been given the cold shoulder upon his return from Europe. The servants had been ordered not to give him any information; all they had to say was that she no longer lived at home.

"Well," said one of the other women, "when there is a scandal in this county, it's usually a big one. Aye, do you remember the day Tom O'Connor came home unexpectedly after working in England for a year? Jaysus, he strode through the village as though he wouldn't call the king his uncle. And the village men knowing that Tom's pockets must be well lined with pound notes...tried to entice him into the pub as he passed. But no...big Tom strode happily towards his wee home on the outskirts of the village. Aye, had he stopped for a drink he might have done himself a favour...shure the whole village knew what had been going on during his absence."

"The story goes," she continued, "that his wife wasn't at the door to greet him because she was at that moment cavorting in bed with a handsome young gypsy. Big quiet Tom O'Connor upon seeing this...simply lifted the bare-arsed gypsy out of the bed and carried him out to the pig trough. And merciful God, didn't he hold the gypsy's head down in the trough until there wasn't a breath of life in him!"

Big Tom left the village that same day, and no one has ever clapped an eye on him since. His wife–God only knows what happened to her–she was never seen again. Aye, it's been rumoured that Tom and his wife immigrated to Australia and started a new life.

Now it came to pass that old McGinty's horse died a day or two after Big Tom's speedy departure. The men all brought spades to help old McGinty dig a hole big enough for his horse. 'Twas a nice sunny day and the men passed stories back and forth as they dug deeper into the earth.

Suddenly Brian Connelly, who had gone into the hedge to relieve himself, came running back with his trousers at half-mast… and hardly a breath left in his lungs…as he cried, 'Jaysus, there's a body hanging over the side of the pig's trough!'

The other men leaned on their shovels and laughed knowing full well that Brian loved a bit of fun. Old McGinty said, 'Is that so? Well, give him a shovel and have him do a bit of digging with us.'

'For Christ's sake, go and have a look for yourselves. I'm telling you there's a body draped over the trough as bare-arsed as the day he was born!'

Old McGinty told the men to keep on shovelling and he would go and have a look. It had been many a year since Old McGinty's legs had been used for more than a short stroll to the pub…but by God he came running back barely able to keep his false teeth in his mouth! Leaning against a sturdy old tree with his hands on his chest…he sputtered between gasps… 'Lord God in heaven there's a body in the trough that's about two months late for its burial!'

Sure enough it was the gypsy! The men bandied ideas back and forth as to how they should handle this catastrophe. They decided that big Tom had enough trouble in his life, so the men shook hands and solemnly swore never to tell a soul about their fearful find!

'What should we do with the gypsy?'Brian asked, 'A good stiff drink is what I need. Finding that bare arsed gypsy is enough to drive a man to drink.'

'Well,' says McGinty, 'if we take the time to dig two burial holes the pubs will be closed. So we'll have to bury the gypsy with my poor old horse.'"

"Aye, getting back to that nun," said one of the gossips. "If her fancy man left so early in the pregnancy, maybe he didn't know he'd hit the target."

"Well, if he dipped his wick ahead of the marriage ceremony he should have lingered long enough to find out whether he got more than he had bargained for."

"Aye," said the other woman, "When that eruption gets a hold of a man, sure the devil himself couldn't stop them from having their way with a woman. Me' old mother used to say that women had stronger characters than most men, so it was a woman's duty *not* to let a man have his way with her. The reason being that no man for miles around would ask a fallen woman to be his wife. The man would be off to marry whomever he pleased, with no questions asked. Many a land starved Irishman proposed marriage to some old biddy whose only enticement was a wee plot of land that she had inherited from her parents. Aye, in such a case they could easily overlook the fact that she had a face like a football turned inside out! You know, it's a mystery how we Irish ever survived, what with starvation and famine and all the young Irishmen leaving the country in droves. Indeed it's a wonder we have enough men left to fill a pub."

"By God that's one thing we don't have to worry about–there will always be enough Irishmen to fill a pub. Sure, isn't drink the curse of the Irish? The other curses we have to put up with are the well-fed priests who tell us to offer up our sufferings for the redemption of sins. Aye, they may spiel out sermons 'till they're blue in the face, but it doesn't add comfort to the fact that I have hungry children. Do the priests think of all the empty bellies when they tuck into a roast of lamb on a Sunday afternoon? If it's sins of redemption they are searching for, maybe they should think of some of their own."

"Aye," said the other gossip. "We haven't the energy to commit a good roaring sin with our bellies half empty and a cold fire in the hearth. It breaks my heart to see my wee ones going to school on a cold wet day with not a shoe on their feet. Suffering from chilblains and a runny nose. 'Me poor old mother used to say, that the wealth of this world was ill divided. One day I'll get enough spunk to tell the priest that his sermons flow smoothly from a mouth that's well nourished with blessings of good food. Aye, and I'll tell him that I've never had a chance to taste those blessings."

"Maureen, you'd never have the effrontery to tell a *man of the cloth* all that gibberish. Shure you'd be excommunicated. And with a label like that on your soul, you'd go straight to hell the minute you drew your last breath. God almighty, it makes me shiver just to think about it."

"Don't be daft, the trouble with you is that your imagination takes up more room in your brain than your intelligence! Don't you know that God takes into consideration that most sins are enjoyed by all of us, if they weren't sins, they wouldn't be so much fun. For instance if I had to steal food for my hungry children, I'm sure God in his sensible way of looking at things would never put a black mark on my record. I think He judges us out according to how we cope with the equipment he gave us. If there is such a place as hell there will be a sign on the door marked -'Standing Room Only'. If the sinners from time immortal are all sent to Hell…there will be a lot of vacant seats in Heaven!"

"Aren't you the ripe old sage this morning!"

"Well, sometimes I have to reassemble my thoughts and point them in a fresh direction. Just in case I've been thinking the same rutted pathway too long."

"Mother of God, with all the wee ones you have to look after, where do you find time to ponder all that stuff?"

"I live with day to day misery so I've got to think twice as hard to survive. For instance, this very day I have to think up a new way to cajole the butcher to give me a pound of meat on 'tick'. I haven't a penny to my name until his Nibs comes home with the pay docket."

"You're lucky if you ever see a pay docket, by the time my man gets home, his docket is lighter than a feather. I take one look at his shamefaced drunken face and I know damned well that there will be nothing left for food."

"Aye, you're a soft lump to put up with the likes of that. I'd crack him one over his thick skull whilst he was sleeping the booze off."

"It's alright for you to be the big 'Mick', shure, you have five strapping big brothers to knock the shit out of your man whenever he strays too far off line. The only brothers I have are in America. And we're still waiting to hear that they've finally made a fortune to back up their big talk of how good everything is in America. Aye, streets lined with gold they say…but by God not many of us see greenbacks fluttering from the Christmas letters they send. Aye, it's easy to forget the poverty of the family you left behind when you are living in the land of milk and honey."

"Aye, once in a while one of them will return to the old sod for a holiday and swagger along the roads trying to look like a Yankee. Worse still, they are daft enough to believe we are all staring at them in admiration and envy. When I see a clueless half-assed Irishman swaggering down the road in his brand new clothes, puffed up like a rooster in a hen-run, my sympathy is for the poor old soul who gave birth to such an Ejeet."

"Well, we'd better get back home before it's too late to cook a bite or two for those wee shrunken bellies coming home from school."

Maureen's thoughts were leaden, because she didn't have a bite to put on the table. By God, when Paddy came home tonight, she would let him know that in future he'd better bring his pay docket home unopened. She wanted nothing to do with him in bed until he put some food on the table. Probably he'd head for confession and tell the priest that his wife wasn't fulfilling her Catholic wifely duties. And the priest in his ignorance would appear at the door the following day and read the riot act to her, because it was his duty to do so. Getting back to sinning, I don't think we know of the true story about that nun, so maybe we should be charitable and mind our own business.

CHAPTER ELEVEN
The Dublin Concert

Excitement was in the air the night of the concert. The Murphys came running towards Kevin's car. Kevin, Elizabeth and Patrick had been rather quiet all the way from the convent. When the Murphys entered the car, their cheerful enthusiasm lifted the spirits of the others. On arrival at the concert hall they were delighted to see the *Sold Out* sign on the Marquee.

Terrence had filled the dressing room with an extravagant arrangement of flowers and the fragrance permeated every corner. Kevin, turning towards Elizabeth, whispered, "I've never heard of Terrence sending flowers to anyone unless he was having a torrid affair with her."

"Hush, Kevin, there's a child in the room."

Nevertheless, she felt her face burning as she turned away from Kevin. Good heavens, she thought, this situation is becoming complicated. She decided that she'd better put an end to it before it got out of hand.

All too soon came the knock on the door with the age-old curtain call: "Time!"

Elizabeth made the sign of the cross and then she took Patrick by the hand towards the stage. With a slight nudge from Elizabeth he walked alone to center stage and solemnly bowed. The audience responded with encouraging applause. Elizabeth took her place at the piano…the lights dimmed and the soft sky blue beam of the spotlight glowed on the small slender boy. The silence that followed the clapping of hands filled Patrick with trepidation and he glanced nervously towards Elizabeth; she gave him an encouraging smile for him to start.

Almost against his will Patrick peered towards the darkened hall and then closing his eyes he began to play.

The poignant purity of the music silenced the audience…no

polite coughs or shuffling was heard throughout the entire piece. After the last notes were played a few seconds elapsed, before a thunderous applause reverberated throughout the hall.

Three times he took his bows and still they applauded. Then the velvet curtains closed with a dramatic slowness and Elizabeth joined him on center stage. She felt the trembling of his body and she knew that Patrick's sensitivity was a delicate blend to be cherished and handled with care.

Many came forward to congratulate Patrick on his fine performance. He managed to handle it with poise and self-confidence. Terrence O'Dea came over and put his arms around Patrick's shoulders and said, "Patrick, my boy, I'm proud of you this night. It will take a lot of hard work and dedication but you have a good future ahead of you in the world of music. Aren't you lucky that you're not a boy soprano? They lose their soprano voice as soon as puberty rears its ugly head."

"What is puberty, Mr. O'Dea?"

"Puberty? Ah, Patrick, you won't need anyone to explain puberty, when it hits you. Therefore, it would be useless for me to tell you all about it now. However, I'd be glad to discuss any other problems that might crop up in your life. I will send you notepaper and postage stamps and you can write to me whenever the mood hits you. It's been a long time since I was young, it would be fun to read your ideas of what life is all about at your age."

Patrick was happy talking to Mr. O'Dea; somehow he didn't feel shy with him. And the idea of notepaper and stamps was something to look forward to. He had never written a letter in his life, simply because he had no one to write to.

Life at the convent was brighter and happier since the departure of Mother Superior. Young Patrick was the most affected by her removal. Sister Elizabeth told him about the new rules set down by the Reverend Mother. In future, caning would be abolished; extra chores and curtailment of time spent outdoors would be the new form of punishment. The orphan boys would also be allowed to form teams and play football.

The Mother General had arranged for Terrence and Elizabeth to meet with her in Dublin to discuss details for the next concert. This was good news as far as Elizabeth was concerned, because she wanted the chance to make Terrence understand that there would be no personal talk between them. With her mind firmly set she stepped off the train with the frostiest expression possible.

When Terrence saw her on the platform he could feel his heart leaping with joy. He took her hand but she responded with a formal handshake. By Jesus, he thought, if I know anything about women that tepid handshake is a sure sign that she is running scared. In his heart he hoped that before long she would come to believe that she could find happiness in the outside world. However, he took the cue from her handshake... and assumed a politely formal manner.

He laid out a new score of music for her perusal and went to the piano and began to play. Elizabeth realising that he *was* an accomplished pianist threw caution to the wind and joined him on the bench. They sat side-by-side playing harmoniously together and time flew by on winged feet. This bonding surrounded their spirits and unwittingly set aflame tiny fires of forbidden desires and Elizabeth's defensive straight-laced ideas sank into oblivion.

A sudden knocking on the door brought them back to reality and the secretary walked in. When she saw Terrence and the attractive nun sitting so close on the piano bench an expression of displeasure spread across her face. In a frigid tone she inquired when she should order lunch. Terrence replied, "I will order it later and since I'll be tied up here for a while you may as well take the afternoon off."

That did it! She closed the door with a bang!

Terrence was so anxious to know more about Elizabeth that his thoughts drifted back to conversations he had with Kevin about her previous life. Somehow he didn't believe Kevin when he said that he didn't know her reason for entering the convent. After all he and Elizabeth had been friends since childhood. Terrence wondered if that childhood friendship had perhaps flourished to a romance at some time? No matter how much he probed, Kevin ended the conversation without further disclosures.

His reverie was broken when Elizabeth inquired what was passing through his mind.

"Oh," he lied, "I was thinking about some business I had to attend to in a few days' time."

"Perhaps you should dine alone today, then you will have time to attend to your business matters. I should be on my way."

"No, Elizabeth, I have been looking forward to seeing you and we have a lot more to discuss. After lunch I will drive you to the station. As a matter of fact I'd enjoy driving you back to the convent."

"Heavens no, I don't want to be seen driving with you to the convent. We should have our lunch and then finish off the business on hand. Were you aware of the surprised look on your secretary's face when she opened the door and saw the two of us playing a duet? That silent criticism should make you realize the reaction we would receive if we had lunch together in a restaurant. It is not acceptable in dear old Ireland. Keep that in mind the next time you have ideas about taking a nun out for dinner."

"Elizabeth, you're a darling hypocrite. You know damned well that you've enjoyed snatching a few moments of freedom."

"Yes, there's an ounce of truth in what you are saying. Yes, I've enjoyed these jaunts into the city. Perhaps it will take another decade of moral guidance in the convent to wipe the outside world forever. And that is exactly what I hope to attain."

"Perhaps you should ask yourself this question: are your musical talents being put to the best use in the convent or would they be of more value to the outside world? Granted, you have found Patrick, but think of your other students. The majority have no natural talent and are there because their Mater believes it's the thing to do. I believe that you should be sharing your gift of music with a more appreciative audience, far beyond the convent walls."

"Terrence, I have not found any convincing or comforting answers. My intervals of thinking in the darkness of the night can become a dangerous pastime. Sometimes, when I filter through the dregs of my thoughts I wonder what might have been. Probably that is part of my penance, always wondering 'what if'?"

"Believe me Elizabeth I don't want to destroy the enjoyment of this day, it seems I've hit a discordant note. I'm obliged to walk a tightrope with you in case I tread where angels fear to go."

"Terrence, you are a most discerning person. I enjoy being with you, however; having to deal with that enjoyment has been stressful. I've wondered if it would relieve the stress if I confessed to a priest. Of course the simplest way would be to decide not to see you again. The final question…what is it I feel for you? I'm certainly not in love with you. I only know that when we are together I feel happier than I've been in years."

"All right, you are not in love with me, but you are attracted and don't know why. Supposing that attraction is love in its infancy? We didn't ask for this to happen: we met and bonded in an unusual way. Elizabeth, surely you know that I've fallen in love with you! I've spent many hours weighing the pros and cons and I'm still without direction or an answer. Why can't we give it time and see what develops?"

"Terrence, I assure you there will be no further developments. I will remember you with pleasure for the encouragement that you have given Patrick. For that I will always be grateful. I believe the best solution to this incredulous situation we find ourselves in is to realize that there never will be a happy finale. With the help of God and meditation I will find peace. As the Old Irish saying goes… God never deserts us; we desert Him."

They ate lunch in congenial silence. Frequently their eyes would meet and Elizabeth was always the first to look away. Terrence wished that he could take her in his arms and smother her with the passionate love that was swirling through him.

As they drove to the station, he explained his plan to put Patrick's earnings in a safe place. A portion would be sent to the Mother

House. Terrence felt it would be unnecessary to divulge Patrick's portion to the Mother General. Instinctively, Elizabeth agreed, she was already thinking ahead to the day when Patrick would leave the orphanage.

The train was beginning to puff steam into the moist air. Terrence's heart filled with sadness as their time together finally ebbed away. He reached for her hand and although the touch was warm and tender it was only a minute shadow of his true desires. He watched the train pull out of the station and a wave of empty desolation spilled over him. At times life could be a proper pain in the ass…and this was one of those times, or so he told himself.

CHAPTER TWELVE
Patrick's Departure from the Orphanage

Kevin was examining bolts of new material when the door opened and in walked Terrence with a disheartening appearance hanging over him. His rugged handsome face bore no sign of happiness and his usual bouncing energy was non-existent.

"What ill wind brings you around here in this joyless rainy day? I imagined you had taken off to a warmer clime with one of your current actresses. When I was in Dublin a few nights ago I went looking for you in your favourite watering hole. The bartender said you had been in earlier and that you weren't fit company for man or beast. Then he advised me that I'd be doing myself a favour if I stayed away from you until you'd sorted yourself out. Anyway, now that you're here, where have you been lately?"

"I've been busy with Patrick and his concert and a lot of other things that needed to be done."

"Terrence by the amount of flowers you sent to the dressing room the night of Patrick's debut, I'm sure Elizabeth must be first on your list of chores."

Kevin sensed that his reference to Elizabeth had struck a vital nerve. Kevin placed his hands on Terrence's shoulders and said, "For Christ's sake… Elizabeth is a nun, or have you conveniently tried to forget that?"

"Dry up Kevin, sometimes your tongue rattles faster than a train accelerating down the tracks. If you want to know the God's honest truth, I can't stop thinking about her."

"By God, it has hit you a wallop! You're deluding yourself; don't you know that Elizabeth will never leave the convent? I've known her all my life, so take my advice and think of her as an untouchable friend and leave it at that."

"I won't give up so easily! Or perhaps you are also in love with her? Tell me Kevin, what tragedy happened in her life to trigger such a decision?"

A cloud shadowed Kevin's eyes; "I have no idea. But I missed her friendship more than I can say. When we were young we used to ride over the fields in the early morning. We had a favourite spot where we'd dismount and lie on the grass to discuss our aspirations, and I still remember the peaceful sound of the horses munching the lush green grass. Those youthful days seemed to pass in a flash. Getting back to my friendship with Elizabeth... I went abroad for a year and when I returned she had disappeared. Her mother had died and her father had become reclusive. Whilst I was in Paris I ran into one of Elizabeth's admirers. He had studied law in Dublin and was now touring Europe. He and Elizabeth spent a lot of time together during the last year of college. I'm quite sure he was in love with her. Anyway when I returned to Ireland I tried in vain to discover what had happened to her. Then a short time ago she walked into my shop with the young orphan boy and greeted me as though we had just parted company the day before."

"Kevin, would it surprise you to hear that that I'm in love with her? I'd marry her tomorrow and then we'd get to hell out of Ireland and live happily ever after."

"Well, that makes two of us, I'd marry her tomorrow if I had the chance. Terrence, I know women find you attractive, but you can be sure that Elizabeth will never leave the convent. She has a strong character and the heavens would have to crack open before she broke her vows."

"To hell with it all! Don't be such a killjoy, come on let's take the rest of the day off and drive out to the countryside. We'll find one of those little pubs tucked away in 'god knows where' and forget about the rest of the world. Christ... I never thought I'd see the day when you and I would be in love with the same woman. And to think that she is not available to either on of us... locked up nightly behind convent walls. Now if that isn't a damned good reason for an all-out Bash then I'm the Pope."

"Aye, you're right. The rest of the world can go to hell and back; let's go!"

No one saw hide nor hair of the two men for the next three days. Patrick's earnings from the concerts were adding up to a tidy sum. Terrence kept the account up to date and when he informed Elizabeth of every new addition to the account he was gratified that the news brought her such joy. Terrence surmised the close attachment she had for Patrick was because she had no one else to love. Then one day Patrick and Elizabeth were discussing his earnings and a far away look came into his eyes as he said that soon he would have enough for his fare to America. On hearing this Elizabeth was heartbroken. Even though she understood it would be the best for Patrick's future, it would be a sorrowful parting for her. Ireland was going through difficult times and money was scarce, therefore his musical career would be limited to a few concerts annually.

She told Patrick when the time came for him to leave that she would write to relatives in Boston and New York. They were well off and would take care of him until he found a job. This attachment to Patrick had wrapped around the vulnerable parts of her heart and to disentangle the gossamer tendrils would be difficult!

The Murphys had also written to their cousins in America, asking them to take care of Patrick if he arrived on their doorstep. Again and again, this was the fate of the Irish, those who could afford the fare to America bid farewell to their families and sailed away. They knew they would never clap eyes on each other again—and an indescribable emotion tore at their guts…as they tearfully watched the ocean severing them from their beloved land!

CHAPTER THIRTEEN
The Orphanage Finale

The subsequent business meetings between Elizabeth and Terrence O'Dea led to a close and warm friendship; never again did he mention his love for her. Nevertheless, they *were* drawing closer and Terrence was aware that Elizabeth also felt this emotional shift. He had noticed that whenever her feelings surfaced that she would slide her hands up the wide folds of sleeves of the black habit. Instantaneously like a golden sun suddenly obscured...the camaraderie between them would vanish like a feather in the wind.

When sleep wouldn't yield its healing properties, Terrence lay awake trying to find a solution to the ridiculous situation he found himself in. To spend his life wrestling with the torment of a love affair with a nun was beyond even his scope of imagination.

Exposure to the outside world had done wonders for Patrick's personality and now when he was introduced to people in the concert halls, he didn't fall apart at the seams. Like an unwanted garment... his inmate shyness still clung to him but his self-esteem had risen to a more comfortable level.

As his fourteenth birthday drew near, Patrick began to give more thought to his future. The Murphys had invited him to stay and work with them on the farm. And they had hinted that when the good Lord called them home...that he would inherit the farm.

With a torrent of mixed emotions he awakened on his fourteenth birthday and pushed the old gray blanket aside for the last time! That worn blanket had become a token of despair for Patrick; he had never felt comforting warmth beneath that old blanket. He detested the sight of it... even the greyness of it seemed to symbolise the colourless years he had spent in the orphanage!

Patrick's mood brightened considerably when he saw Sister Rose waiting for him and with a wink and a nod she bid him follow her. Sister Elizabeth was already in the kitchen and she came forward and hugged Patrick…but her smile was melancholic.

The table was set for three and a vase of beautiful flowers adorned the center and Rose had prepared a sumptuous feast of ham, eggs and hot potato scones.

After breakfast Elizabeth accompanied him to the dormitory to help him pack his small valise and she watched as he disdainfully tossed each piece of his orphanage clothing on top of the old grey blanket. He snapped the lock on the valise and proceeded to the hallway with nary a glance backwards at the place where he had slept for all of his fourteen years!

When they were alone in the music room she held his hands and asked him to promise that he would never falter in the pursuance of education. Attending night school, she said, would open his mind and make his life more interesting.

Elizabeth was overcome as she said; "Patrick there will always be a place in my heart for you. I love you dearly and I will pray for you as long as I shall live." Swiftly she turned away and reached into the folds of her habit for her hanky to wipe away the tears that ran unheeded down her cheeks.

Seeing that she was terribly upset, Patrick reminded her that he wouldn't be leaving Ireland for a few years and that she could visit him at the Murphys. He added that he would *never* visit her at the Orphanage, because he never wanted to be inside those walls again as long as he lived!

Kevin was at the front entrance of the orphanage and when he saw Elizabeth he could tell that this parting was a sad one for her.

When they arrived at the Murphys the table was set with Shivaun's best dinnerware. The delicious aroma wafting its way from the kitchen whetted their appetites with an appealing anticipation. Sean poured wine for all and even Patrick was served a thimble-sized glass.

Sean was the first to broach the subject of what Patrick would be doing around the farm. "We have a bedroom ready for Patrick. The two of us will share the chores around the farm and what he earns here will help him towards his fare to America. Of course, Shivaun and I would be happy if he stayed with us forever, but we'll never stand in his way if he decides otherwise. We just want you to know that we love the lad and only have his welfare at heart."

Shivaun sighed deeply, "Lord bless us and save us Sean, why did you have to bring up the idea that someday he will be leaving. Anyway, if he goes off to America and makes a fortune, he'll come back and forth to visit… as often as a bee to the hive."

Before leaving, Elizabeth said that she would visit Patrick whenever she could and asked him to practice his music as often as possible. Sean assured her that they would have many musical sessions because he and Shivaun also loved music. He suggested that Elizabeth would be more than welcome for Sunday dinner. "Of course," he said with a wink "only because we need someone to play the piano."

CHAPTER FOURTEEN
Working on the Farm with Sean

Patrick loved being with the Murphys and his dream of living in America was no longer first and foremost in his thoughts. Sunday, when Elizabeth, Rose, Kevin and Terrence arrived for dinner was truly the highlight of the week. The little house shook with joy, music and laughter. Elizabeth and Rose cut loose from the fetters that bound them all week long. Elizabeth's outings were sometimes tinged with guilt, but in the company of others swept the nagging guilt under the rug ...and just enjoyed the moment!

The sharp edged humour and repartee between Rose and Kevin was hilarious. It was apparent that they enjoyed being together. Shivaun, as she observed the bonding of Elizabeth and Terrence, wondered if they weren't hurtling down a dangerous road.

That night when she conveyed her fears to Sean, he took time mulling over it, then with a thoughtful sigh said, "They are old enough and *hopefully* wise enough to settle the relationship in a sensible manner. But by God, they will have a tough row to sow, before it is all settled!"

Shivaun with her romantic leanings... allowed her thoughts to fly in complete abandon! Supposing Elizabeth turned her back on love and chose to stay in the convent for the rest of her life? Should she try and give Elizabeth a wee push in the right direction? Shivaun couldn't imagine a handsome healthy man like Terrence waiting for years for Elizabeth's decision.

Patrick's mind and body was nourished by the peaceful settings around the farm. He loved going out to the fields when the early morning dew was still glistening on the emerald green grass and the wild rose bushes in full bloom. The fragrance of the roses was a heavenly perfume flowing through the air to proclaim the presence of the Creator!

One day when Sean and Patrick went into the market to sell eggs,

Patrick was introduced to the schoolteacher. The teacher inquired if Patrick was interested in joining the parochial football team. Sean thought that was a grand idea and the following Saturday he took Patrick to the field for his first practice session. Patrick had enjoyed it so much that he could barely wait for the next game. After he'd been playing a few weeks, the coach told Sean that Patrick was one of the best players.

Patrick was still saving money for his fare to America, however; he knew that he would be hard pressed to leave the life he had now.

And then it happened! A young player on the opposite team kicked him so hard in the groin that Patrick lost his balance and fell to the ground. The pain was excruciating and the other players carried him to the sidelines. As he lay there writhing in pain, one of the other players asked Patrick where he lived. Patrick told him that he lived with the Murphys.

"The Murphys? Shure you're not a Murphy?"

"I'm an orphan," said Patrick.

Then the boy asked who his parents were, and Patrick, burning with shame, said he didn't know. Patrick knew that was enough to change his status with the other players.

The coach took Patrick home in his jaunting cart and explained to the Murphys about Patrick's accident. The coach suggested a few days rest and added that the young bully who had kicked Patrick would be expelled from the team.

Patrick was glad when he had recovered enough to commence playing. The other players had all gone and Patrick was sitting on the grass slowly unlacing his boots when the bully who had kicked him came over and sat down.

He said to Patrick, "They say you're from the orphanage and you don't have a Da. Well, I have a Da…and he doesn't like the idea that a bastard like you got me thrown off the team. Shure, the decent folks around here don't want the likes of you… rubbing shoulders with them. You'd be doing yourself a favour if you never set foot outside of the Murphy's farm."

The pounding of Patrick's heart was making it hard for him to breathe and his fists curled into a tight ball. As he was about to smash the ignorant face grinning at him...a voice from behind asked, 'Indeed, what's this all about?'

Silently and fearlessly Patrick glared at his tormentor, "You tell the coach what it's all about and you're bloody lucky he arrived while your face is still in one piece."

The coach tried to stop Patrick from leaving but the lad shrugged off the restraining hand and took off.

The bully appeared to be frightened when the coach shook him roughly and said, "You're a born troublemaker. I warn you... if you or any of the other hooligans in your family ever touch a hair on his head, I'll have you in court."

Patrick was glad to have the time to think as he walked home to the farm. America the land of milk and honey slid easily into his thoughts. Surely there would be more tolerance in such a young country. Furthermore, no one would know his background and he'd just make a new life for himself. Happy as he was on the farm...he now made his mind up to leave for America as soon as he was old enough.

Patrick and Sean worked side-by-side hoeing the potato rows...in peaceful silence. Frequently... Sean would pull a big red and white dotted hankie from his hip pocket to wipe the sweat from his face. Therewith, he would lower himself to a grassy mound and prop his back against the low stone wall.

Time for a pipe...he'd declare, as he mindfully tapped the tobacco into his white clay pipe with the tip of his forefinger. Then he'd strike a wooden match on the sole of his boot...and hold the match to the head of his pipe until tiny puffs of smoke curled into the air. As he puffed contentedly on his pipe...his sea blue eyes would scan the fields and the sky ... and each day he would have a different description of the scene. And he'd say to Patrick, "Feast your eyes on all that's before you, because it's God's way of giving us a wee taste of Heaven's beauty!"

One morning in a serious tone he said to Patrick, "You know you are like a son to Shivaun and me and we would like to see your future settled while we're still on this side of the sod. So, the time has come to have the papers made out for you to inherit the farm."

That shook Patrick to the depth of despair, or was it sadness? To hurt these good kind people was the last thing he wanted to do. He floundered ineptly as he tried to explain that he wasn't sure if he wanted to spend the rest of his life in Ireland. On hearing this, the happiness left Sean's face and they worked in a deep silence for the remainder of the day. Shivaun was at the door to greet them and intuitively she knew that something had upset Sean and Patrick. In her forthright manner she inquired what was wrong.

"Well, it's not cheerful news that I have for you Shivaun. Patrick says he'll be off to America as soon as he's old enough. And to tell the truth I don't think I'll ever know a happy day after he leaves."

"Don't be daft Sean, sure he'll make a fortune in America and have enough money to come back and see us every year. Isn't that so, Patrick?" She wished that her heart were as light as her tone.

Patrick said that the time he had lived with them were the happiest he had ever known and that he would save the money he earned in America to return for a visit.

At the Sunday dinner Patrick disclosed his plans to go to America. A hush went over the visitors and they stared at Patrick as though he had just confessed to a barrel of mortal sins! Elizabeth's face was drained of colour and that was more than he could bear. Rose was the first to speak as she inquired why he was in such a hurry to leave. As he looked around the table at these dear people who had treated him with such kindness he wondered if he had made the right decision. Why leave all this to travel across the ocean where he knew no one?

Worse still, the others at the table knew after Patrick left they would have no excuse to visit the Murphys.

A dozen hankies of the finest Irish linen with his initials embroidered on the corners was his farewell gift from Rose. She had enclosed a note telling him that a few of the stitches had been washed with her tears at the thought of him sailing away to God knows where. Elizabeth gave Patrick her brother's flute and she carefully hid a roll of pound notes beneath the flute. She placed a sealed letter inside the case advising him to save the money for a time of need and added that 'when you feel that you're sitting on top of the world... keep in mind that it turns over every twenty four hours.'

Terrence, Kevin, the Murphys, Rose and Elizabeth were all at the quay to bid him farewell. A solid friendship between this group had evolved all because of their love for this young orphan boy. The ship's shrill warning whistle momentarily silenced the little group and that offbeat sound ripped apart the last shred of the hitherto pretence of joviality. They watched the tall slender figure of Elizabeth accompanying Patrick up the gangplank to share the last wrenching moments together alone.

At shipside, the heartbroken mothers bid farewell to sons and daughters, knowing full well they would never set eyes on them again. Due to the ravages of the English, the only goods the Irish had to export were their poverty stricken citizens.

A short time later Elizabeth walked down the gangplank with a grief stricken face. Any ship leaving the dockside with a loved one aboard arouses abstruse emotions. And so it was for Patrick's six friends as they silently watched the huge steamship make its way out to sea.

As the churning waters severed Patrick from his beloved country... he had the inexplicable feeling that part of him was being torn away!

Terrence took Elizabeth by the hand and led her to the car and she made no effort to disengage her hand from his. The warmth flowing from his hands was a comfort and she would have given the world to feel his arms around her. Although he sensed her vulnerability...he understood that this was not the time to take advantage of it! Nevertheless the current was so strong that he too wanted to take her in his arms and never let her go. A moment later she retrieved her hand from his and her beautiful eyes sent him a silent "thank you." He longed to see her without that horrible black habit and wondered if he ever would?

Kevin and Terrence had made reservations at the hotel for lunch and that suited the others because no one wanted to break the feeling of togetherness.

When everyone was seated at the table, Terrence suggested something to bring a little warmth to the occasion. "I hope you ladies will join us in a toast to young Patrick." Without further ado he ordered sherry, wine and Irish whiskey.

"Aye, and we all need a bit of a lift this sad day…bidding farewell to Patrick almost tore my heart from its moorings. Y'know, in his own quiet way he trod lightly but firmly into the core of our lives. And I'm sure that none of us will ever forget him." Having said this Sean pulled a big hankie from his pocket and blew furiously.

Terrence poured wine for the ladies and was glad to note that neither Rose nor Elizabeth refused.

Somehow Patrick's leaving had intensified the closeness of their relationship and not one of them wanted the status quo to change. Mrs. Murphy was well aware that Sean had looked forward to the Sunday musical gatherings and she had no intention of allowing them to stop. So she invited them for dinner the following Sunday… the invitation was speedily accepted. Elizabeth with tongue in cheek said that she would have to get permission from the new Mother Superior.

Rose replied, "You have my permission… because if *you* don't go, who will escort me? I'll be confined within the convent walls praying that all my past sins will be forgiven …I say past sins because lately I haven't had a chance to start a new list."

"Rose, whenever you feel the need to gallivant, I'll be your chauffeur."

"Thanks Kevin. That's the best offer I've had in years."

CHAPTER FIFTEEN
Aboard the Ship

A cabin boy took Patrick to his cabin and when they opened the door the small cabin looked like a disaster area. Two suitcases were wide open on the floor with the contents spilling all over. Patrick viewed his small valise containing his worldly goods and came to the conclusion that they were minuscule in comparison.

He decided that the bottom bunk would be his, and as he tucked his brand new pyjamas under the pillow, the cabin door flew open. A massive hunk of a man stumbled over the threshold and staggered into the cabin. He appeared to be one sheet to the wind, no doubt having celebrated his departure from the Emerald Isles at every pub along the way.

Giving Patrick a bleary-eyed stare he bellowed. "Who are you, and what the hell are you doing sitting on my bed? Get your arse off, or I'll move it a lot faster than it got there."

Young he might be...but Patrick knew that if he caved in to the demands of this big-mouthed lout that he would be in for a miserable sea voyage. Instead of moving, he looked up at the hulk towering above him and said, "There will be snowballs in hell before I move anywhere to suit you. So if you want a bunk, heave your carcass on the one above."

Instead of retaliating with a stream of invectives, or a punch on the nose, the big man threw his head back and roared with laughter. "Well, I'll be a son of a bitch! By the look of you... you haven't been in the world long enough to become a full grown man, but by Christ and His Holy Mother, you have enough gumption to fill the hold in this ship."

With that said, he spat on the palm of his hand and, pushing it towards Patrick, he bellowed, "Aye, put it there son; if the rest of you sprouts... to match your gumption, you'll be a fine broth of a man.

My name is Barney Donavan and I'm on my to way to America to make a fortune. I have two brothers over there and shure haven't they lined up a grand job for me, aye, I'll be rolling in dollars in the wink an eye."

Having exchanged names he pulled a flask of whiskey from his pocket and took a long swig. Wiping his mouth with the back of his big broad hand, he offered the whiskey to Patrick. Patrick declined... saying he was too hungry to drink.

Patrick closed his valise, locked it and made his way to the door. He barely had time to reach the door when he heard a thump and glancing over his shoulder he saw Barney sprawled out on the lower bunk. He went over to see if Barney was all right and couldn't believe his eyes when he saw that Barney was already puffing his way into a sound sleep. He had passed out! Patrick carefully retrieved his new pyjamas and placed them on the upper bunk.

With a last look around the cabin he stepped out into the long narrow hallway with doors all looking alike. Patrick wondered how would he find his way back? The size of the ship was enormous! Patrick wandered along the narrow hallways...taking many twists and turns, only to arrive back to where he had just come from.

Like so many of the other passengers he was thoroughly confused. With the help of a cabin boy he finally found the purser's office. Realising how young and inexperienced Patrick was, the purser advised him to have his valuables locked in the safe. He also told Patrick he would be wise to stay away from the ship's bars. The Purser then related the story about an Irishman who was so drunk all the way across the Atlantic that he was nowhere to be found when the ship docked in New York. Sure enough, when he sobered up again the ship had returned to Ireland and they found him lying in his cabin groaning like a stuck pig with a gigantic hangover!

"Patrick," said the purser, "A young priest dropped a letter off for you just as the ship was about to leave. Another thing you should know, there is a fine library on this deck, and so if you enjoy reading, you'll find a great assortment of books. I'll be off duty in five minutes, I'll show you where it is."

Although Patrick was curious about the contents of the letter, he put it in his pocket unopened. Before leaving, the Purser, whose name was Douglas, told Patrick to come and talk to him whenever he felt inclined.

The library was furnished with massive leather armchairs. Patrick found the quietness so relaxing that he dozed off and was awakened by the clatter of his book falling on the floor. Douglas spent his free time in the library with Patrick and they became quite friendly. When Patrick confided in Douglas that he had spent his childhood in an orphanage the older man said that he had lived in an orphanage until he was twelve. He showed Patrick pictures of his wife and children and said it was like a dream come true to have a family of his own.

"My children don't realize how fortunate they are, they take everything for granted. I was so badly treated in the orphanage in England that for some time I believed that all people were rotten. Thank goodness I've met so many wonderful people since then that I think differently now."

The night before the ship docked, Douglas gave Patrick his Uncle Peter's address. He described his Uncle Peter as a scholarly man who had lived alone since his wife's death. "I'm confident that he would help you to go forward with your education. Patrick, you should seriously consider enrolling in night school."

Patrick had bonded with this very sincere man and saying farewell to him was not easy. He thanked Douglas for his kindness and promised that he would start school as soon as possible.

Patrick's ticket category was in the lowest bracket so he was among the last to leave the ship. As he walked down the gangplank he was taken aback at the frantic hustle and bustle on the quay below. He had never seen so many people in one spot in his life. How in the name of God would he ever find Sister Elizabeth's relatives in that swirling mass of people? He didn't wander far from the ship, but the surging crowd pushed him forward all anxiously searching for relatives or friends.

Then he began to panic... supposing no one arrived? The Purser had told him there were booths where he could go for help, however he had also told him to stay put, so what *should* he do? Like an unclaimed piece of baggage he stood with his small valise clasped tightly between his feet. The excitement of arrival dwindled into hopeless desperation, as his eyes swivelled from left to right... searching–for what and whom? He moved forward to where the crowds were thinning out. Surely someone would recognize him? Sister Elizabeth had mailed his photograph to her cousin. Just as he was about to give up he saw a man in uniform carrying a sign with 'Patrick O'Grady' printed in bold red letters. A woman and two young men were following with their eyes swivelling in all directions.

Patrick walked towards the man with the sign, "I'm Patrick O' Grady."

The lady and the two young men shook hands with Patrick then guided him towards the exit. The uniformed man who had first met Patrick walked ahead of the group. When they got outside, the chauffeur went towards a huge black motorcar and when they were all seated he tucked blankets over their laps. They must be wealthy to afford all this, thought Patrick.

The motorcar stopped in front of a huge building and it was so large Patrick thought it was a hotel. A young maid came to the car and the chauffeur handed Patrick's valise to her. Giving Patrick a polite smile she said, "Follow me, Sir." They went up a curving staircase to his bedroom. The room was large and well furnished and he couldn't believe that he would have it all to himself. The young maid showed him the bathroom and asked if he would like his bath poured.

As he was about to decline her offer, she hurriedly assured him that it would do him the world of good after his long trip. Patrick hearing the lilt to her words said, "You're Irish?"

"Indeed I am! And so is every one else in this household. The only difference being, some have plenty of money and the likes of us who work for them have damned little! There I go blathering a mile a minute, ignoring what my Da used to tell us, 'don't ever miss the chance to keep your mouth shut."

"What's your name?" Patrick asked.

"I'm Clare O'Toole. It's a bit o' liberty I'm taking, but I think you're a handsome lad." Then with a mischievous wink she added, "If we were on the same footing, sure I'd like nothing better than to tuck my arm in yours and go courting."

And she was out the door like a flash enjoying the young man's blushing discomfort.

A tap on the door brought him out of his reverie. The two lads who had accompanied their mother to meet him were standing in the hallway. There was no welcoming warmth in their voice as they curtly told him that dinner would be served in one hour... adding, "Please be on time, the Mater is accustomed to punctuality."

Patrick sat on the edge of the bed and tried to put the pieces together. Instinctively he knew that he had felt more comfortable with the maid Clare O'Toole than with the two young fellows who had just left. He shrugged these thoughts aside and enjoyed a luxurious steaming hot bath.

As he gazed at his image in the mirror in his brand new suit Patrick wondered how he would be received downstairs. There had been no welcoming warmth emanating from the two young men who had warned him to be on time for his dinner. As Patrick walked down the curving staircase he was aware of an uneasy feeling coursing through him.

At the bottom of the stairway Clare was waiting, and with a 'tongue in cheek' type of curtsy, she proceeded to guide him towards the dining room. But a split second before they reached dining room she whispered, "Don't let the bastards grind you down."

Her remark caused him to enter the dining room with a smile as wide as the ocean. Perhaps that grin saved his bacon, because the two sons were more than a little surprised at Patrick's casual entrance.

The dinner was served and eaten in comparative silence. Occasionally he was questioned politely about his voyage. By the way the inquiries were tossed his way he knew they weren't a damned bit interested. It gave Patrick the feeling of a bone being thrown to a hungry dog.

As soon as dinner was over the two brothers hurriedly excused themselves and left the table. Patrick decided to do likewise, however, the Mater had other ideas.

"Patrick come with me to my sitting room, I have a few items I'd like to discuss with you." He followed her to a private sitting room where an inviting fire was burning brightly. Pointing to an armchair she asked him to be seated. Mary Flanagan studied his face for a second or two, and then she asked what type of work had he done in Ireland. He told her that he had lived and worked on the Murphy farm and had earned extra money working in the concert hall in Dublin.

"Were you–a stagehand?"

"No, I played the flute at various theatres accompanied by Sister Elizabeth."

"Good Heavens, do you mean to tell me that the Mother General allowed Sister Elizabeth to leave the convent and play in a Dublin theatre?"

"Yes, and the Bishop and the Mother General never missed any of our concerts."

"Have you any idea what sort of work you are capable of doing here?"

"I will work at anything. Later I intend to continue my education."

"How much education *do* you have?"

"To tell the truth, I haven't had too much. I was held back two years."

"Why were you held back, were you ill?"

"I wasn't physically ill, but I was heartsick."

"Why would a child be heartsick? For that matter I can't imagine a child understanding the meaning of heart-sickness."

"You're right, at that age I couldn't give it a name…but now that I'm older I know I was heartsick."

"I see. What caused this condition?"

"It's something I've been trying to forget. But since you ask, I will tell you. Mother Superior detested me, and in turn, my heart wasn't overburdened with love for her. She assigned me to kitchen duties. Every day after class I had to report to Sister Fatima who was in charge of the kitchen. Sister Fatima was one of God's misfits and she was a real Tarter! She clouted me with ladles, heavy bladed knives and the odd time she smacked me on top of the head with her fat ugly hand. Sister Fatima and Mother Superior made my life a living hell. Everything changed when Sister Elizabeth started giving me music lessons. It opened up a world I'd never known."

"Am I to understand that you have no more than a seventh standard education?"

"Yes."

There was no understanding or kindness lingering in her face as she listened and he didn't have long to wait before she lowered the boom.

"Good heavens what sort of employment do you expect to find with such a limited education?"

"As I said before, I'll take any type of work. In the meantime I have enough savings to pay for my keep. I'll not be a burden to you or anyone else."

"That, I'm afraid, is easier said than done. Sister Elizabeth should have warned us what to expect. You are a nice young man…but I'm afraid you would be out of place living here." Then clearing her throat followed by a polite little cough, she continued, "My son's college friends are frequent guests here and perhaps you would be out of your depth in their company. If you know what I mean."

Patrick with pounding heart replied, "I know exactly what you mean. You say that Sister Elizabeth should have warned you? With her way of thinking, she would never have imagined that a warning was necessary. Prior to my departure she endeavoured to make me understand what human nature is all about. She was concerned that perhaps my views of people might be warped because of the hardships I endured at the orphanage. I'm grateful that through our many discussions she managed to extricate me from a quagmire of negativity. I thank you for meeting me; however my presence seems to be an unwelcome burden. I'd appreciate it if you would tell me where I might find a modest priced lodging house and I will leave immediately."

"Good Lord, do you think I would ask you to leave on your first day in a new country? What would Cousin Elizabeth think?"

"Trust me, I will write and tell her that you met me and that I had dinner at your home and that is all she needs to know."

"Patrick, you may be lacking in formal education, but you seem to have learned more at your young age than some people learn in a lifetime. I truly wish I could handle your presence in my home in a different manner, but it is impossible. Please stay here tonight and rest after your long voyage. Tomorrow I will take you to a boarding house in the center of the city. The owner is an Irish lady, whom I've known for years. She runs a clean lodging house and serves wholesome meals, it will be within your means. I'm sure she will ask one of her lodgers to find a job for you."

"Thank you, I will stay the night. It wouldn't be wise to leave in the dark of night to look for lodgings. What time should we leave tomorrow?"

"We'll start out right after breakfast. Patrick, did the Bishop give you information about your parents? I remember Elizabeth saying that it was the custom to give the orphans such information when they reached the age of fourteen."

"I was told that the forms pertaining to my birth had been destroyed by fire."

"Ah, that is sad indeed. Yet on the other hand…perhaps no news is good news. How old were you when you entered the orphanage?"

"From the day I was born."

"You are eighteen years old now?"

"Yes."

"When my cousin Elizabeth entered the convent it was quite a shock to all of us over here. She had a good future ahead of her in the music world. Furthermore, she was a beautiful young lady."

"She is a beautiful woman, and even the black Habit she wears does not detract from her natural beauty. She is beautiful in many ways and I will never forget her as long as I live. Sister Elizabeth unfettered the despair from my soul and filled it with hope." As he said this Patrick felt a deep loneliness and wished he was back in

Ireland having Sunday dinner in the Murphy's cozy home.

"Patrick, under the present circumstances of our meeting, you may find it hard to believe what I'm about to say. Truly I wish to God that my children were endowed with some of your natural wisdom. Unfortunately they take after their father, who unfortunately has become a self-centered snob. Furthermore, he used my inheritance to further his political and social climb up the ladder. I'm afraid my youthful dreams of what life was all about has eroded into jaded cynicism. Patrick, you'll be better off living elsewhere, because this is not a happy home."

Somehow Patrick felt more kindly towards her and he reassured her that what she had discussed would be held in confidence.

CHAPTER SIXTEEN
The Boston Lodging House

The green and white sign above the door was marked, 'Cassidy's Lodgings.' Through the car window Mrs. Flanagan anxiously watched her chauffeur banging the brass knocker on the door. Finally the door was flung open and a short plump woman with rosy cheeks glared at him and asked, "God in heaven, I'm not deaf, is it the door you're trying to break down, you big ejeet?"

"Are you Mrs. Cassidy?"

"Of course I'm Mrs. Cassidy, who in the name of God do you imagine would be answering the door to my own house? A butler?"

Before the chauffeur had time to recover from this onslaught, Mrs. Flanagan and Patrick were at his side.

"Hello Biddy, do you remember me?"

"Holy Mother of God, if it isn't Mary Flanagan herself. Aye, the years have treated your face kindly. What in God's name brought you to this neck in the woods? Hopefully, it's because you've decided to leave that frozen-faced upstart you were daft enough to marry. Anyway, come on in and have a cup o' tea. And who is this young man you've brought with you? Shure, and hasn't he the map of Ireland written all over his handsome kisser?"

"Biddy, I'd like you to meet Patrick O'Grady. He is a friend of my cousin in Ireland. I'm hoping you have a room for him. He will be in need of a job as soon as possible, but don't concern yourself about his rent, I will take care of that until he can fend for himself."

"Well, I haven't a room right now. However, one of my lodgers is leaving the day after tomorrow and Patrick can bunk in the hallway until the room is vacant. Mary Flanagan, surely you had a spare room for the lad in that mansion of yours?"

Quickly Patrick accepted the offer to sleep in the hallway and with a slight edge to his voice, he added, "There will be no need for Mrs. Flanagan to pay for my keep. I have savings that will hold out until I find a job."

"Aye, that's the spirit me' lad, the less you depend on other people to carry your load the stronger you become. God almighty, just hearing that Irish brogue of yours …makes me long for the sight of my old hearth and home back in Donegal. Isn't it a bloody shame that the Irish have to leave the Land they love best, just to earn a living? Aye, when the English shake the last bit of earthly dust from their feet, they'll have a helluva lot of explaining to do. I don't think 'His Nibs' at the pearly gates will take too kindly to them once he's had a squint at their record. It's a black burning shame they should feel…turfing the rightful owners off the land that their families had tilled for centuries. Lord God in heaven if I get started on the injustices of this world, I'll wear me' tongue out before I finish the telling."

She bid them take a seat, and went into the kitchen to infuse the tea. Biddy returned with a tray holding an appetizing array of soda bread, hot scones and homemade preserves. Her best china, which was only used on Sundays and special occasions, was laid out on a white lace tablecloth. Biddy bustled around with such energy that the stillness of the room scattered into insignificance when she entered.

Biddy asked, "Where has your driver gone?"

"Why? He is waiting in the car of course," said Mrs. Fianagan.

"In the name of God, why is he sitting outside, do you want him to freeze his backside?" With that she flung the door open and called out to the man to come in for his tea.

In a low tone he said, "Thanks for the invitation, but, I'm one of the staff and we don't sit down to tea with our employers."

"Well now, I'll tell you something me' boy, in my home, *no one* and I mean *no one*…tells me who I should invite to my table. Shure God made us equal and that's the way I intend to keep it! If anyone say's a word, I'll brain them with a teapot."

Anticipating with glee the effect this might have on his mistress he followed her into the little parlour. Standing with his cap slapped dutifully against his chest he glanced apprehensively towards Mrs. Flanagan.

His mistress, with a tight smile struggling across her face, bid Paddy take a seat. But he knew by her ramrod straight back that she was far from pleased. He could barely wait to return to the big house and relate the day's events to the other servants. So anxious was he to get the hell out of this farce that the hot tea burned as it passed over his windpipe. Soon after that he excused himself, saying that he should go out and start up the engine. Since smoking on duty was not allowed, he stood behind the car and furtively lit his pipe. Well aware that his mistress would be in a flaming temper on the drive home he needed the solace of a few good draws on his pipe. Aye, she would be in no mood to put up with any shenanigans this day. All because he had borne witness to her being taken down a peg or two. Biddy taking control of the situation and her refusal to kow-tow had been an unexpected pleasure for him as he contentedly puffed away at this pipe.

After they left, Biddy plied Patrick with questions, some of which he decided not to answer. He would follow Sean Murphy's advice to keep his mouth closed until he knew more about the person he was talking to.

With that in mind he answered fairly and squarely the questions that he thought deserved an answer. So when Biddy inquired about his family in Ireland, Patrick told her straight off that he had lived in an orphanage until he was fourteen and had no family. For some unknown reason that put a halt to further questioning.

She thoughtfully scanned his face and saw a shadow pass over that ought to be dealt with. "Patrick, whatever happened to you in the past, good bad or indifferent should be taken care of in a sensible manner. If any of those memories cloud your thinking, get rid of them. You can only handle one day at a time. Come with me and I'll show you where you'll sleep for the next few days."

She made up a nice clean bed in the alcove at the end of a hallway and pulled a clean flowered curtain across the threshold. "There now, you'll be warm and cosy here until the other lodger leaves. By the way, do you drink?"

"No, I never drink. I had a glass of Port wine once after a concert in Dublin. I enjoyed the flavour, it was nice and sweet."

"Well, that's a relief to know you don't drink. Because the rules in my house are as follows, no lodger comes home roaring drunk twice in a row. The second time it happens he will get turfed out so fast he won't know what hit him. I give them fair warning when they rent a room, and if they don't take it seriously...out they go. I overlook the first time because I take into consideration the fact that the poor souls are homesick for their folk's back home. Do you know that I've heard full grown men cry like a child in the solitude of their rooms during their first weeks in America? Aye, and many a time I wanted to go in and comfort them, but I knew that would hurt their pride. I'm sure they would be hard put to face me the following morning knowing I'd borne witness to their tears. So as a wee bit of comfort I put an extra egg or sausage on their plate."

"Mrs.Cassidy, I'll always be grateful to Mrs. Flanagan for bringing me to your house. Of course, I must find a job as soon as possible."

"What sort of a job are you looking for?"

"I'll be glad to take any kind of work. I worked and lived with the Murphys on their farm after I left the orphanage and I earned money playing the flute. I'd be much obliged if you would direct me to where I should go to look for work?"

"Well, I'll speak with Tom about finding a job for you, he is the quietest of all my lodgers and very dependable."

"I thank you."

"So what you need right now me' boy is a good walk by yourself in the fresh air to get your thoughts sorted out after all the excitement of landing in a new country. I'll have a fine dinner ready when you get back. Maybe before the other lodgers return you could have a little snooze. How does that suit you?"

"Great! I won't stray too far in case I get lost."

"Och, you won't get lost! And if you do wander in the wrong direction, ask any policeman to bring you back to Biddy's lodgings. The majority of the police in this district are Irish and they all know me. Now take yourself down to the end of the street, then bear left and you'll find a nice park. On the odd Sunday after mass I wended my way there to watch a pair of white swans. My God, they are beautiful and as graceful as a toe dancer. An elderly man informed me that when swans mate they remain faithful to each other for life. Now that's more than you can say for a lot of married couples, isn't it? But you know when I heard that I wondered how anyone tells if they remained faithful to the same mate because they all look alike. Off you go Patrick, for if I keep on blathering there will be a few empty bellies waiting around my table tonight."

Patrick took a deep breath of fresh air and could hardly believe that he was actually walking in the United States of America. The weather was nippy, yet the sun was bright in the heavens above. As he walked, his mind was filled with what lay ahead of him in this land of opportunity. Where would he work, and what would he do if they asked him for references? His thoughts veered off in many directions. He could almost hear Terrence O'Dea's deep voice saying, 'Patrick, why are you wearing your heart out worrying about something that hasn't happened yet? Keep in mind that God hasn't asked you to handle tomorrow's program... and he may decide *not* to give you a tomorrow. Now wouldn't that be a helluva waste of time worrying about a 'tomorrow' that you'll never have the chance to use?'

Patrick found the park and he sat down on a wooden bench facing the pond. An elderly man who was sitting on the other end of the bench greeted Patrick with a smile and hello. The white swans gliding effortlessly without even ruffling the water seemed to hold the man's attention. A few minutes elapsed before the man opened a conversation about the gift and beauty of nature. Then shaking his head in puzzlement he said, "There it is for all to see and yet so few take the time to stop long enough to refresh their spirit with the beauty of it all."

Patrick replied that he had always admired the natural beauty surrounding him and that when he was a child he used to lay on the grass looking at the clouds and drawing imaginary skyscapes.

The elderly man upon hearing Patrick's Irish brogue inquired how long he had been in America.

And was taken aback when Patrick replied. "This is my second day."

"Well, young man, just make sure that you don't follow in the footsteps of so many of your race and become a Barfly," in a clipped English accent the man replied.

"What is a Barfly?" asked Patrick.

"A Barfly is a man whose posterior is in constant contact with a bar stool and the smell of booze never evaporates from his pores."

"Well Sir, I don't drink and have no intention of going that route."

"Well for your own sake I hope that you remain steadfast to that intention. You'd be better off reading good literature or perhaps enhancing your education by attending night classes."

He knocked on the door of his lodgings several times before the door was flung open and a flustered Biddy appeared. "In the name of God you don't think I'll be running to the door every time you want to get in. Shure the door is never locked. Come on in and keep me company in the kitchen while I'm getting dinner ready."

She placed a steaming cup of tea and a scone in front of him. "Knock that into you, it will stave off your hunger until dinner is ready."

He watched as she shunted back and forth preparing all sorts of vegetables and he asked if she would like some help.

"Now, what would any man know about preparing food?"

"I know, because I worked in the kitchen every day at the orphanage."

"Hmm' and how did that suit you?"

"I didn't mind the work, but I detested the old nun who was in charge of the kitchen. She hated me and walloped me every chance she got."

"Aye, a proper old bitch. I say it's the unnatural life they endure that sours them. They have no one to love but themselves and they are convinced that God in the heavens is jotting down every pious minute of their lives. Come to think of it, I've never been too sure how much love they dish out to God or themselves. Patrick, come over and show me how handy you are in the kitchen."

The two of them worked in harmony and when the chores were completed, Biddy with a satisfied sigh sat by the fireside and put her feet up. "Patrick, off you go to the parlour and find yourself a good book to read until suppertime."

As far as Patrick was concerned he had no doubt that Biddy already had a heart as large as a full moon! He also knew that she couldn't afford to be too soft with a house full of men and as she had told Patrick earlier, she took no nonsense from any of them. She made sure they had nourishing food and she kept their clothes clean and mended.

CHAPTER SEVENTEEN
Patrick's First Dinner at the Lodging House

Like homing pigeons, Biddy's lodgers headed towards their specified place at the dinner table. They didn't all troop in at the same time which left Patrick in a quandary as to where he should sit. Biddy came in with a steaming tureen of soup, and upon seeing Patrick standing like a lost duck, she bid him to sit in the chair at the far end of the table.

Then with a clearing of her throat denoting an important announcement, she said, "Will you hold your tongues until I introduce Patrick O' Grady. A fine broth of a lad if ever I saw one, and he just arrived from Ireland the day before yesterday. And, while I'm at it, let me tell you this... if I catch any one of you taking Patrick to the Bookies or Pubs, you'll be searching for new digs."

One of the lodgers replied, "Away with you, Biddy shure none of us would take a lad so young into pubs or betting shops. Shure, he still has the look of the Alter boy about him."

"Paddy, that's blarney! You'd take your guardian angel on a booze tour if you were hard up for company. Anyway, I've given you all fair warning: just mind your P's and Q's as far as this young lad is concerned. Now let's ask our heavenly Father to bless this meal and to also bless some of you Ejeets that are badly in need of it."

The other men ribbed Patrick in a good-natured manner about his Irish brogue and in turn Patrick wondered how long they had been in America because their brogue was *still* as thick as a fog.

Each man thanked Biddy for the fine dinner as they were about to leave the table. Of course Paddy always had to have the last word, "Biddy, sure and I'd marry you for your cooking alone, and the rest of you I'd learn to endure. So should you ever feel like tying the knot, just say the word."

"Paddy, if you had one intelligent thought in that fat head of yours, it would be as lonesome as a spinster in bed on a cold winter night."

As the lodgers were leaving, a dark-haired man who had not participated in the light-hearted banter at the table approached Biddy. "I found your note on my dresser."

She nodded to him and quietly said, "Tom, this young lad needs a job and I'm sure you are the very man to find one for him. He got off the boat two days ago and hasn't a friend on this side of the ocean. What do you think his chances are?"

Tom turned to Patrick and asked the question that Patrick was beginning to dread, "How much schooling have you had?"

"Not very much. I didn't have the opportunity to further my education because I was in an orphanage from the day I was born. I left the orphanage when I was fourteen and then I worked on a farm. I hope to start night school after I'm settled in a job."

"Well, that will be a step in the right direction. Just make sure you don't misfire by following another route. I'll have a word with my boss today and find out if he can find a job for you."

Patrick thanked him, and Tom, eyeballing him for a second, replied, "The only thanks I need are for you to toe the line and do a good job. Don't start pub crawling every time you have a pay docket in your hand."

Without another word Tom turned on his heel and walked out.

Biddy smiled happily, "I'll bet he'll find a job for you faster than you can wink an eye. He is well thought of by his boss. Tom isn't the type to show up late for work with a hangover and he's as different from my other lodgers as night and day. Aye, he's a bit of a loner, Saturdays he's off to the library and when he returns with his books he goes into my little parlour and reads for hours on end. Lord Bless us, when he is through reading, shure his eyes look like two pee holes in the snow. He is not given to loose gabbing, but when he has something to say it's usually worth listening to. He uses words as though they were priceless jewels, not to be scattered like the seeds of a dandelion fluttering in the wind. By God, I'd miss Tom if he moved away from this house."

True to his word the following day Tom took Patrick to meet his boss. John Doyle had a solid build, broad shoulders and a chest thick as a beer barrel. He had the most penetrating eyes that Patrick had ever seen. When he was through questioning Patrick about his work experience, he walked towards the window and stood there looking out at God knows what. In the meantime Patrick remained standing in the center of the office… feeling akin to a fly flapping away the last of its life on flypaper.

John Doyle whirled around and sat down at his battered old desk. He wrote swiftly on a slip of paper, put it in an envelope, and with a swipe of his tongue across the glued edge he handed the envelope to Patrick. "Give this to Donavan the foreman and be sure you are on time tomorrow morning or you'll be sacked before you even start. Good luck to you and don't take crap from any of the other workers. Start out the way you're gonna end up… be your own man."

Patrick taken by surprise at the abrupt ending had almost forgotten that he didn't know how to get back to his lodgings, worse still he didn't know the address. He stood there like a dolt, "Mr. Doyle, I don't know the way home nor do I know the name of the street that I live on."

"Jaysus, how long have you been in the country…a minute?"

"No sir, I arrived three days ago."

"Three days? Christ, I'll have to find work for you to do for the rest of the day. Tom will take you back to your digs when his shift is over. Well now, since you're dressed in your Sunday best you can't work with the men. Do you know anything about sorting out business papers? Look at this bloody mess, I haven't seen the top of my desk for months."

"Well sir, the only papers I ever sorted were sheets of music in the music room at the orphanage."

"What in the hell were you sorting out music for?"

"I played the flute in Dublin concerts and I worked with Sister Elizabeth the music teacher. She was my accompanist when I played in concerts."

"A flute player? Christ almighty, have you ever done a day's hard work?"

"I worked on Murphy's farm after leaving the orphanage. They fed me well and I built up my strength there with good meals and peace of heart."

"Patrick, for the rest of the day see what you can make of all this mess. I'll let Tom know that you will be going home with him at the end of the day."

Patrick started on the pile of papers, not really knowing what he was supposed to do, but his methodical mind helped him reach some semblance of order. When the boss returned a couple of hours later, everything was neatly stacked in rows across the desk and all dates in rotation.

John Doyle thumbed through the lot and slowly a grin spread across his Irish kisser, and he said, "Patrick, if you wore a skirt I'd hire you on the spot as my girl Friday."

By the look on Patrick's face he knew the remark wasn't sitting too well. "Listen lad, a sense of humor is a useful weapon, so make sure you have it *'on the ready'* at all times. Now tell me, have you had anything to eat since breakfast?"

"No sir, but I had a big breakfast at Biddy's lodgings."

"Aye, Biddy is proud of the fact that no one ever leaves her table hungry. I was a lodger there when I first arrived from Ireland. Mind you though, her tongue is razor sharp, her heart is as big as a barn door! Come on and I'll get you out for a bite to eat. After all I don't want old Biddy on my back berating me because I let you starve."

They went to a little Italian Café, not too far from the 'Doyle's Brickyard'. Maria the owner came over and greeted Mr. Doyle with a big smile, "Johnny boy, where have you been? We've missed you."

Guiding them to a table covered with a brightly coloured cloth she said, "Ah today you're lucky, we are featuring your favourite dinner."

Without further ado she went to the huge dark wooden sideboard, poured two glasses of red wine and brought them to the table.

Patrick left his wine untouched and John after drinking to Patrick's good health, said, "I'll tackle your glass when I'm through this one."

Maria returned with an enormous platter of food and the mouth-watering aroma was such that Patrick could barely wait to taste the colourful array of food. He hadn't the slightest idea what he was eating... having never seen or tasted anything like it...but every bite was delicious. John Doyle watched with amusement as the young lad worked his way through each course. Maria, standing a few feet away, was beaming as the young lad devoured his meal with gusto!

Finally John Doyle pulled the big square napkin from inside his collar and made a sound that was halfway between a burp and a sigh and he told Maria that an angel must have taught her how to cook.

With a smile as wide as a crescent moon, "Johnny, as the old saying goes...'the Irish are born with honey on their tongue, don't worry I'll never grow tired of your sweet words. Who is this young fellow you have with you?"

"Aye, this is Patrick, another Irishman, and he has only been in the country three days."

"Three days? Mama Mio, does he speak English?"

"Well, he speaks *Irish English* and as everyone knows, Irish English is softer and easier to listen to than English-English."

"Irish English...English –English, me I only speak a leetle English. Maybe I speak Irish English, I don't know."

"You speak English with an Italian twist. Maria, when the English speak their own language they sound like they have a *whole* plum in their mouth. The reason we Irish speak English with a brogue is because it is a foreign language that was forced upon us. The English cast their avaricious eyes across the Sea to Ireland and stole our land and went as far as to forbid us to speak our own language. Next, the Catholic religion was taboo and our priests were hunted down like animals. Any person caught giving food to a starving priest was harshly punished. Our own language had a beautiful poetic cadence, but the strangers' language was harsh on our ears. So the Irish softened up the strangers' language and gave it a lilting tone, 'twas easier on the eardrums. Napoleon said that 'English' was the language of shopkeepers...y'know, I think he hit the nail on the head."

As the two of them were about to leave, Maria handed a small parcel to Patrick and said, "This is a little gift. Take good care of her and she will always take care of you."

They walked back to the office together with few words spoken because Johnny Doyle was deep in thought.

When the whistle blew at the end the day, the Boss took Patrick down to the brickyard. The workmen were a tired looking group. Having hauled bricks all day they stood in line waiting to be checked out by a thin-faced officious looking man. No friendly greetings were passed between *this* man and the workers.

As Patrick stood against the wall waiting for Mr. Doyle to find Tom amidst the milling group of workmen, his eyes wandered over to the thin-faced man. Instantly he disliked the dour looking man because he reminded Patrick of the tall thin man who used to take the coffins away from the orphanage in the big black hearse. At this point the man looked straight at Patrick and bore him such a baleful glare that Patrick felt a shiver rippling down his spine.

Tom walked over to Patrick and in a very low voice said, "Mr. Doyle wants you to work in the office for a while. Now I'll take you over to the timekeeper, he's the miserable old bastard at the wicket. He hates everyone, including himself. Are you hungry? I waited for you to come down to the yard at noontime and I would have shared my lunch with you."

"Mr. Doyle took me to an Italian Café for lunch."

"Doyle must have taken a liking to you, I've never heard of him taking an employee out for a meal. Anyway he wants to keep you in his office. Perhaps he intends to find a white collar job for you, if that is the case then you should consider starting night school right away."

Biddy was anxious to hear all that had happened to Patrick and was more than pleased when he said that he had been hired. She went over to Tom, shook hands with him and said, "Tom, you are a good man and may God's blessings be with you always."

Tom's habitual guarded expression was replaced by a warm smile and his step was lighter as he took his leave.

"Patrick, you can move into your room this evening, the other lodger has gone. Come with me and I'll show you where it is."

When Patrick moved his meager belongings to his room he remembered the gift from Maria. He sat on the edge of his bed and opened the parcel. It was a small-framed picture of the Virgin Mary with the child Jesus in her arms. Patrick studied the picture and wondered what it would feel like to have had a mother to hold him tenderly in her arms. Lord almighty, he thought, every day in a lifetime is an odd mix of moods… forever shadow-boxing between light and dark.

"Well auld son, how did you fare today?" asked one of the lodgers.

Before Patrick answered he looked towards Tom and the guarded look upon his face was all he required to know that he should keep his business to himself.

Patrick said, "Yes, Danny, I got the job."

The following morning he and Tom travelled together and as usual, the latter had little to say. He cautioned Patrick not to get too friendly with the other workers until he had tested the waters.

Every Saturday Patrick and Tom went to the library. One Saturday Tom suggested a walk through a park on the other side of town where Patrick had never been. Patrick was so impressed with the beauty of the park that on the way home he memorized the streets to make sure he would know how to find his way again. Later he told Tom that during the good summer months he would take his book to the park and spend the afternoons there.

Tom agreed that would be healthier than sitting inside the library. "Just let Biddy know and she will make a lunch for you to take to the park."

Patrick spent wonderful afternoons in the park and met many friendly picnickers. One Sunday an Italian family arrived with parents and grandparents and loads of children. They spread a colourful tablecloth on the grass and proceeded to sort out the food and wine. The children ran barefoot in complete abandon around an *invisible boundary* encircling their family. The women hustled and bustled as they prepared the food, while animated laughter and conversation filled the air. Patrick was fascinated; he had never seen anything like this before. An aged man with eyes as dark as a beetle and snow-white hair added to the merriment playing cheerful music on his accordian.

When they caught Patrick looking their way they smiled and waved for him to come over and join in their meal. He was too shy to accept the invitation, so a young fellow about his own age came over and pulled Patrick into the circle. Patrick was amazed at the array of food. One of the younger girls gave Patrick a plate overflowing with food and a glass of ruby red wine. Totally bewildered with the energy and welcome he swallowed the contents in one gulp. He almost choked as the wine passed down his windpipe as though it was running a marathon from the top of his head to his feet. To tell the truth it made him giddy enough to join the men in their games. The women laughed merrily and cleared away the remains of the picnic. It was one of the most carefree, delightful days that Patrick had ever experienced.

One Sunday he and a fellow by the name of Douglas started talking as they watched the graceful swans. Douglas, an American whose mother was of Irish stock, told Patrick that he enjoyed listening to his Irish brogue. As they were about to part, Patrick asked Douglas if he knew of any schools he could attend in the evening.

"Yes, there is a school not too far from here, let's go and I'll lead you right to it."

When they arrived at the school there was a sign on the door stating that it would be open every night from six o'clock until ten o'clock and closed from June until September. Patrick was relieved that he didn't have to register immediately, because he knew that it would take a bit of courage to do so.

Alas, September rolled around faster than Patrick wanted it to! And here he was standing at the entrance of the school in the pouring rain too damned nervous to open the door and walk in! But finally he proceeded up the wooden stairway. His steps were light and barely audible and he wished that he were anywhere else but here.

And what followed when he opened the door to the classroom was an experience he wanted to erase from his mind!

CHAPTER EIGHTEEN
The Donnybrook

Patrick peered through the steamy window of the Bar and Pool Hall to see if any of his fellow lodgers were inside. Since he had never walked into a Pub before, he was apprehensive about entering alone. As he stood rooted to the spot watching the pelting rain running down the window... the door swung open and a whiff of boozy smoke assailed Patrick's nostrils. A man with a few too many under his belt heaved his cumbersome body unsteadily over the threshold.

Patrick hadn't the slightest inkling as to the results of drowning his sorrow with whiskey, but he was going to give it a damn good try tonight! His self-esteem had gushed down the drain after that shenanigan at the school tonight. Christ, hadn't he made a real clown of himself? Walking up that flight of stairs, fingernails clamped into the palm of his hands and a heart jumping like a spit on a hot griddle! *Even* the door to the schoolroom had felt like a ton weight.

His courage decreased with every creaky step up the wooden stairway. Then, just as he was reading the sign on the door – 'Quiet-Class in Session' – he inadvertently turned the door handle. In a split-second the door flew open and he was inside the large classroom. Having just left the darkness of the ill-lit street, it took him a few seconds to adjust his sight to the brightness of the classroom...and there... a sea of inquisitive eyes met his. His first instinct was to cut and run, but before he had time to do so, Jan, the smiling young teacher approached and asked if she could help him. This friendly greeting did not lessen the panic he was feeling at the moment.

With a bone dry mouth and his tongue glued to the roof of his mouth... Patrick answered in a voice that sounded like a constipated duck. "Yes, I would like to start evening classes."

"Please take a seat, I will be back in a moment with an application form for you to fill out. We need a little information. Your name please?"

"Patrick O'Grady. What kind of information might you be looking for?"

"Oh, just a few questions about your previous education and background." He cringed... his education? Christ, he had never been inside a schoolroom since his fourteenth birthday. Background? That was something he wanted to forget.

As soon as Jan left the room, he bolted for the door as though a couple of hornets were doing somersaults in his crotch! He didn't breathe until he reached the bottom of the stairs.

Then walking along the deserted street, with the rain pelting his hapless body, he dejectedly thought of Jan going back to find that he had disappeared faster than a hole-popping gopher. Poor Patrick berated himself unmercifully as the gutless wonder of the world! Why did I run like a streak out of hell?

A deep and lonely dejection oozed into every corner of his heart and soul...and once again he found himself fluttering back to a past that he wanted to forget. Gut deep sadness deluged his spirit and warm tears coursed unheeded down his cold wet face. 'So men shouldn't cry... if not, why not?'

In the past few months he had gained the courage to enroll in night school. However, when Jan inquired about his background his confidence vanished like a feather in the wind. Aye, he said to himself, I've come a long way since my departure from the orphanage, but I still have a long way to go. Now he knew that his protective shield had been as fragile as a house of cards.

And with that Patrick swung through the pub doors and with a 'don't give a damn attitude' stood inside hoping to find a welcoming face.

And he didn't have long to wait. Barney a fellow lodger came over and giving Patrick a friendly punch in the midriff, asked, "And what in the hell brings you out on such a windy rainy night? Shure you've been standing so long at the entrance I thought you'd fallen asleep. Come on over to the table and join us."

God Almighty the men looked in surprise as Patrick sloshed

down the fiery shot of whiskey in one gulp! It took Patrick's breath away and he thought that he'd never regain his voice … when his eyeballs finally rocketed back into their sockets he realized that the lodgers were staring at him in amazement!

Barney was the first to talk, "Jaysus, you shure had old Biddy fooled, she said that you never indulged in booze. Shure that shot of whiskey hadn't time to get familiar with the bottom of the glass before it slid down your gullet."

Patrick had another and as he downed each fiery draft… all desires for an academic career scattered in the wind!

The men talked about their families in Ireland and the beauty of the country that they might never see again. And before too long the drunken nostalgic tales had a few of the lodgers ferociously wiping their eyes on the cotton mufflers that was always part of their daily apparel.

In the midst of the tales being told, a swarthy, dark haired man approached the table and suddenly conversation ceased. He was flanked on each side by two rough looking characters with faces that looked as though a steamroller had flattened them out. He greeted the Irishmen with a tight smile showing teeth as white as piano keys. There was a discerning shift in the lodger's behaviour as they returned his greeting.

Without being invited the man sat down beside Patrick and said, "So you're O'Grady? My cousin who owns the pool hall …tells me that you're a great pool player. I'm thinking of setting up a few games for you a couple of nights a week with some guys who like to gamble. The stakes will be high, I'll give you a good cut in the winnings, okay?"

"No, it's not okay. I play billiards for enjoyment, I don't play for money."

In a voice that could cut through steel the Italian hissed, "Is that so? I've got news for you Paddy, I'm not accustomed to taking no for an answer. Maybe you'll need a little more time to work that through your thick skull. I'm Tony Zarboni, you can be sure… I'll keep in touch with you."

"I don't need time to think, and my name is Patrick…not Paddy… and maybe if I give *you* enough time, your thick skull will sort that out."

The lodgers continued to sit in wary silence and watched as Patrick stood up and made an unsteady passage to the door. It was still raining when he reached the street and Patrick was aware that his head, eyes and feet were not performing, as they should.

Just as he rounded the darkest corner of the road, the two henchmen who had accompanied Tony Zarboni grabbed him from behind. They pounded his face and body with hammer-like fists. Patrick did his best to land a few blows but the battering soon put an end to this valiant but feeble effort.

When Patrick came to…he found himself in a prison cell with both his body and mind in a tortured state. Completely confused he wished he could return to the bliss of the unconscious state. Bloody stains painted a grotesque mosaic on his tattered clothing and as he absorbed this mess his spirit dropped to a new low! He reconstructed the events of the previous evening and he realized that the caper at the school was minuscule in comparison to the aftermath.

At this point the jingling of keys attracted his attention and a guard opened the cell and hollered, "Get your arse off the bench and follow me. So you're Irish, eh? Well, I'm from the auld sod meself. Be well warned that this very day, your case is going before the toughest Irish judge in the whole country. He shows no mercy to an Irish Barfly charged with drunken brawls. He declares it makes him ashamed of his own kind."

Patrick, with the last remnants of his self-esteem taking a slippery path to an island of 'never to be', gingerly made his way to the prisoners' dock.

CHAPTER NINETEEN
Meeting Terrence in Dublin

Elizabeth's heart was beating to the same frenetic rhythm of the train as she tossed ideas around in an effort to find the right words to explain her reason for leaving the convent. She never considered herself a weakling, nevertheless; she cringed when she thought of the forthcoming meeting with the Bishop and the Reverend Mother.

In due time the metallic chant of the wheels lulled Elizabeth into a deep sleep. When the train came to a shuddering halt in Dublin station she awakened with a jolt. In a dazed confusion she straightened her voluminous garments and looked around to see if the other passengers had observed her abrupt awakening. Needless to say, they were all too busy gathering up their luggage. She remained seated until most of the passengers had disembarked and watched as they stepped down to the platform and were greeted with welcoming hugs and handshakes. The exchange and warmth of the greetings had a strange effect on Elizabeth and she found herself longing to return to this world where one's emotion could run *naturally* free. Surely it was natural to laugh, cry, and be loved. Otherwise why were we given the means to do so? Sadly, she realized how much of her natural self had been obliterated in the effort to become a good nun.

As she alighted from the train the conductor solemnly tipped his cap in due respect for the Habit she wore. Ironically she thought…little did he know that today would be the last time she'd wear the Habit. Or would it? Fragments of indecision were still swirling and intermingling with the newness of her first day in a world that she had left behind so long ago.

Terrence was nowhere in sight and she was the only one left on the platform. The ghostly silence that followed the departure of the passengers added to her feeling of abandonment and her thoughts overflowed with misgiving. Had Terrence second thoughts about their relationship? If so, surely he would have the courage to tell her. With a heavy heart she decided to go straight to the Mother House. As she approached the street hopefully she looked right and left but there was no sight of Terrence. She signalled to the driver standing beside the only cab at the curb. Just as she was about to enter the cab, she was pulled out again.

The driver stared in amazement at the sight of a man tossing a nun around in such a manner. Before he had time to intervene the two were engaged in a whispered conversation.

With an apologetic clearing of his throat the driver inquired if she still needed the cab. Immediately Terrence gave the driver money to reimburse him for the loss of his fare. The driver seeing it was a five-pound note shook his head in disbelief and muttered… "Jaysus, that's the quickest five pounds I've earned in my whole bloody life." And off he went with a smile a yard wide.

"Where were you going Elizabeth?"

"I was on my way to the Mother House to face the tribunal. I assumed you had a change of heart. Hence, I planned to return to the convent and vowed never again to become entangled in a ridiculous situation such as this."

"Good God, you can't be serious? For heavens sake, I had a business meeting that ran overtime. I apologize for being late, I thought you would understand."

"Terrence, I think my judgement is not at it's best right now, forgive me for doubting your intentions. Before leaving the convent I felt it necessary to tell Rose what I had in mind. I simply couldn't leave without telling her that we might never see each other again. The sorrow in her eyes was heartbreaking. She put her arms around me and tearfully said that her life in the convent would become unbearable without our friendship. Through her tears she managed to smile and told me to follow my heart's desire."

"You surprise me, I had no idea that you were going to tell her so soon."

"Well, when I did tell her, she said that she had known that we were in love. Then she said that she would leave the convent if she had some money or relatives who would support her decision to leave."

"Don't worry about Rose, she is a good-looking woman. If and when she leaves the convent, I'm sure she will find a good man to take care of her. That bit of mischief that is always lurking in her eyes would be enticing for most men. I'm sure you must have noticed that Rose and Kevin hit it off pretty well? They share and enjoy the same sardonic sense of humor. Perhaps we should try and drum up a romance between them?"

"Terrence, I think we should mind our own business. Kevin has a family business to look after so they would have to live in Ireland. Their married life would be marred, because of the lack of tolerance shown to those who broke the vows they had made to God."

"Kevin has nephews who are waiting in the wing to take over the family business. Elizabeth, why were you disturbed when I mentioned that those two were attracted to each other? Was there ever a romance going on between you two when you were young?"

"We were very close friends. Don't you think we have important business of our own to discuss? For instance, the outcome of today's meeting with the Bishop and Mother General might destroy *our* plans."

"How could it? Surely you'd never be persuaded to change your mind? Spirituality is not confined exclusively to those in a religious order. I think every marriage requires a good dose of healthy spirituality to keep it intact."

"Terrence, you are overlooking the fact that I'm *still* bound by my vows."

"I was under the impression that we had made a final decision, however; now you sound unsure of the direction *you* should take. Isn't our love strong enough to offset your doubts?"

He had noticed that in times of stress or indecision she had a habit of lowering her eyes and slowly examining her long slender hands. So he waited patiently until she lifted her eyes and then without speaking she searched his face in an attempt to shore up her dwindling confidence.

"Please understand that the isolation in a convent subdues one's spirit. It will take time to rid myself of the rigid rules that have been part of my life for so long. Terrence, I need your understanding and patience."

"My dear, I love you so much it hurts. Yes, that may be a hackneyed saying, however I can assure you it describes exactly how I feel. My happiness is interspersed with longing and of course the dread that something might happen to keep us apart forever."

She studied his face for a moment. "I love you with all my heart. It's a great pity that our moments together are fraught with doubt regarding our future."

"Let's go to my office and I'll have our lunch sent over."

The luncheon was consumed in comparative silence, each with their thoughts, doubts and hopes vying for survival.

Terrence asked if she had given any thought to their honeymoon in France.

"Indeed I have not! I cannot allow myself to think of such things until this meeting is over."

For the time being he knew it would be better to close the subject!

Before she left he asked if she would permit him to buy clothing for her, adding that it would be less of a hassle if she wore street clothes when she shopped for her own personal wardrobe. With a wry smile, he added ... "Just think of the raised eyebrows if the sales clerks see a nun entering the fitting room and emerging a minutes later wearing a fashionable ensemble?"

"Terrence, I think it's a bit premature to purchase clothes for me."

"Elizabeth, why are you wavering? If the Bishop and the Reverend Mother detects any weakness on your part they will double the effort to coerce you to capitulate. For both our sakes, please don't take a step backwards."

"I will keep all of this in mind. We must leave now."

"May I drive you to the Mother House?"

"No, I will take a cab. I need time alone to collect my thoughts before the meeting."

"Will you take a cab to my home as soon as the meeting is over?"

"Yes, if that's possible, I can't tell when that will be, because I've no idea what's going to happen. I will get in touch with you one way or the other."

"Elizabeth, I love you."

"I love you Terrence and I will love you forever."

When it was time to leave, he held out his arms and she walked right in to his warm embrace. He kissed her tenderly and neither of them wanted the moment to end. Although the flow of love was strong, the moment was impregnated with foreboding.

CHAPTER TWENTY
The Ritualistic Disrobing

In a chilling voice, the Reverend Mother asked Elizabeth to explain why she was late.

"Do you realize that the Bishop had to leave otherwise he would have missed an important appointment? I can assure you he was far from pleased. You stated in your letter that you are contemplating breaking your vows. Do you realize the gravity of this action? Needless to say, I have no intention of accepting your request. I will make arrangements for you to go on a meditative retreat…and there you will have time to reflect on the seriousness of your actions."

"Reverend Mother, I know this is distressful for you and I'm truly sorry. However, I have examined every angle and my decision is final. A spiritual retreat would be of no help. So with your permission may I return to the convent and clear out the few things I have there?"

"Indeed you will do nothing of the kind. You will do as you are ordered. You will retreat to the cloister convent for meditation and months of complete silence."

"I'm sorry, I must disobey your orders and that is final."

"The vows you took were *also* final, or have you forgotten that? Is your spiritual commitment to God of lesser importance than the one you've made with this man?"

"Reverend Mother, I haven't taken this step lightly and I've spent many sleepless nights before arriving at this decision."

"I should like to point out a few facts that perhaps you have conveniently forgotten. First and foremost, keep in mind that you sought refuge in the convent to avoid the accursed classification of bearing a child out of wedlock. It had a traumatic effect on your parents. They never recovered from the shame of their first grandchild being illegitimate. Your dear mother, *may she rest in peace,* died a short time after your child was born. Yet here you are once again… ready to embark on a path leading to further destruction of your soul."

Elizabeth was visibly moved and tears were glistening like jewels on the tips of her long lashes. A moment of sadness and then with determination, she said, "Reverend Mother, now I am convinced that I should not have taken the vows. Yes, shame and desperation forced me to seek refuge behind the walls of a convent. My family had disowned me, where else could I go? The tight moralistic custom of Catholic Ireland to which they adhered to was evidently stronger than their love for me. I have come to the conclusion that those who point the finger of guilt in the *name* of religion haven't the slightest knowledge of God's all forgiving love. Some people's religion consists of a judgmental blend of God's truth spiced with a version of the Church's method of keeping control. My only role as a nun was to teach music to those who could *afford* to pay... and sadly that didn't include orphans. Then young Patrick came along with his rare musical gift and I was allowed to bring his talent to the fore. Of course that privilege was granted...because his concert earnings... fattened the convent coffers."

"You should be thankful for the gift of music bestowed upon you and Patrick."

"I give thanks every waking moment for the joy of music. In all due respect, may I remind you that my God-given gift also contributed financially for the necessary repairs around the convent."

"Your cynicism disturbs me, I would never have expected this attitude from you."

"Reverend Mother, now that I'm leaving I would appreciate knowing more about my child's birth. Where did my child go? I believe I've the right to know. All these years my heart ached to know something about the child I carried in my womb. All those long lonely nights as I lay in bed unable to sleep, I was constantly worried about the whereabouts of my child."

"Have you told this man that you are now entangled with that you gave birth to a child out of wedlock?"

"Yes, he knows. However, he believes that one's past should be a *learning* experience and that all experiences, good, bad or indifferent should be utilized to expand the future growth of one's character."

Mother General acknowledged this statement with a slight clearing of her throat. The silence that followed was more powerful than any spoken word.

Finally, and with sadness the Reverend Mother said, "Elizabeth, I know very little concerning the birth of your child. As you know I arrived here several years after you entered the convent. I learned a few facts about your fall from grace when I was appointed as Mother General. I was informed that you had given birth to a son and that the files were destroyed when the record's office went on fire. I was also told that your father requested that the child be removed from your presence immediately after the birthing and on no account should you be allowed to see your baby. Upon hearing this I felt a pang of sadness. I simply could not imagine carrying a child for nine months and having it taken away without ever feeling its warmth. However, your father donated an annual amount of money to the convent orphanage, needless to say, his bidding was carried out as ordered. I have the no idea where your son was taken."

"My child was a boy? Even that's enlightening. Somehow I had a vague memory of a young nurse referring to my child as a 'he'. It's a tragic twist of fate that because of my father's wealth he had the power to dictate who should raise *my* son."

"Elizabeth I'm sure your father thought it would be to your benefit not to know the whereabouts of your child."

"His actions were not for my benefit, he was driven by what the scandal would do to his social standing. I never realized that my father had such cruelty lurking behind his customary benign expression. He and I were never close, because he had a way of warding off intimacy without actually requesting one to stay at arm's length. How could he inflict such sorrow on his first and only grandchild and me? Not knowing the whereabouts of my child is a sadness I will carry in my heart forever."

"Elizabeth, the times we spent in each other's company has

always been a pleasure for me, therefore I feel that I must spare you the tribunal Council. That is a customary procedure for all nuns' contemplating leaving the convent. As far as I'm concerned these rituals are a 'hair-shirt' of oral condemnation. I find it repulsive to bear witness to another human being standing alone, whilst a group of nuns lash her with verbal contempt. Sad to say, I've had to witness this many times since becoming Mother General." With a desperate attempt to hide the emotion that was savagely twisting within her breast, she said, "Go now Elizabeth, may God grant you a renewal of peace." With that said, Mother General gave her a sealed envelope.

Elizabeth was the first to move…the two women briefly embraced and then without a backward glance Elizabeth opened the door and made her exit.

An elderly nun waiting on the threshold of the outer door glared at Elizabeth and with a voice cold enough to freeze a blacksmith's anvil, ordered Elizabeth to follow her.

A tight garter of fear tenaciously grasped Elizabeth as she followed the nun along the gloomy hallway. Finally the grim-faced nun stopped before a heavy wooden door, and taking a ring of keys from the folds of her Habit she unlocked the door and thrust Elizabeth into a darkened interior. The door clicked shut and Elizabeth found herself alone in a sombre, unlit room. The cold dampness pervaded the whole space. She cast her eyes on the sparse furnishings. Along one wall a row of straight-backed chairs were placed behind a long wooden table. On the opposite wall a crucifix almost twelve feet tall with the tortured face of Jesus sadly gazed down on Elizabeth's hapless head.

Riveting apprehension shot through her like a bolt of lightening…what was she supposed to do in this room, pray, sit down, meditate…or? So she remained standing in the centre of the room awaiting the unknown. It seemed ages before the door opened and a group of dour faced nuns filed in. They avoided eye contact with Elizabeth as though the very sight of her would corrode their shield of piety. Like judges in a court of law, they sat ramrod straight on the wooden chairs, praying in a low primitive sounding chant.

Silence followed for an eternity; at least that's how it felt to Elizabeth who remained standing in the center of the room. Then a tall sallow-complexioned nun approached Elizabeth and told her to disrobe completely.

Elizabeth, amazed at such a request said, "I have no other clothes."

"Do as you are told... you will find articles of clothing in a paper bag on the table."

Turning her back to the nuns she disrobed in abject humiliation. The pounding of her heart was loud and frantic as she peeled each piece of the Habit from her body. The fear she had felt earlier was suddenly replaced with defiance! She stripped and tossed each layer of the Habit in a heap on the floor! Standing cold, naked and completely humiliated she knew that this was her darkest hour. An indelible scar ...never to be erased...and tears of shame poured forth drowning her anguished spirit in despair.

She attempted to reach for the clothes on the table behind her trying not to expose her frontal nakedness to the nuns. However, in desperation she had to turn to face them and discovered that she was alone. Having witnessed her naked humiliation they had departed in *stealthy* silence.

An envelope was pinned to the brown paper bag. She opened the envelope and found a one-pound note and instructions not to leave by the front entrance. "Leave by the back door." And written in black ink... *"May God forgive you for breaking your vows."*

The bag contained cotton knickers, a petticoat made from reused flour bags and a dark gray ill-fitting dress, a black felt hat that almost covered her eyebrows. She was grateful for the absence of mirrors! She donned the black shapeless coat made of thick heavy material.

Remembering the envelope Mother General had given her; she reached into the deep pocket of her habit still lying on the floor and pulled out a five-pound note. This last bit of kindness from the Mother General had a shattering effect; her throat thickened and once more the tears flowed forth in complete abandon.

Elizabeth walked along the hall and in defiance to convent rules that nuns must walk softly she allowed every step to hit the floor loudly with a sharp click!

When she reached the tree-lined avenue leading to the road she pondered how she would make her way to Terrence. Since cabs and motorcars were a rare sight on the roads of Ireland, she reproached herself for not allowing Terrence to come and fetch her.

Turning onto the country road she spotted a motorcar similar to Terrence's. Her heart skipped a beat as she ran towards the car. A short distance from the car she heard the engine start and the car sped away. She called his name… the wind tauntingly tossed it into the air.

Had he seen her and decided that what he saw wasn't what he had expected? After all, he had never seen her dressed in street clothes. What difference did it make what he thought? She was alone with no place to go. A feeling of desertion took hold, leaving her vulnerable to negative thoughts. Was this all part of a punishment? Would the Jesus she had known forgive her for the sin she had committed in youthful ignorance? Right or wrong, she felt comforted by the belief that God's love *was* non-judgemental.

The country road was deserted and the only sign of life had been a small jaunting cart loaded with a family of six and they waved a cheerful 'Good day' as they passed her by. Once more Elizabeth was alone with the whispering trees, the happy song of the birds… intermingling with her own sombre thoughts.

Exhausted from lack of sleep and the recent trauma, she sat down on the grass close to a hedge. No sooner had she sat down than she heard the clip-clop of a horse and cart coming down the roadway. The man, with a gentle "Whoa Nellie, old girl" stopped the cart close to Elizabeth. He offered to take her as far as *he* was going and she accepted gratefully. When they were well on their way, he remarked that her apparel was heavier than the bright day called for. She replied that she had expected bad weather and was now paying for her faulty judgement.

"Aye, you won't be the first one to suffer for misjudging Mother Nature in her many shapes and guises. Now since we'll be travelling the same road for a spell we may as well introduce ourselves. I'm Tom Cormac Jordan."

"My name is Elizabeth, and I thank you for your kindness."

"Well, if you don't mind me saying so, you appear to me as though a bit of human kindness would do you the world of good. Aye, and you don't have to talk if you don't feel like it. Just feast your eyes and nourish your spirit with the lovely green countryside that we're passing by. One sensible idea that we Irish had was to place the seats on these jaunting carts sideways to allow us to see more of the natural beauty as we pass. Y'know I believe that God provided us with mountains, sea, sunshine and rain, to remind us daily that He has His hand on the tiller."

"What a wonderful way to express the gift of nature."

The rest of the journey was a silent affair. Meeting this woman dressed as she was…had rolled Tom's thoughts back to that day many years ago, when *his* daughter had arrived home wearing a similar outfit.

The cart stopped at a low wall built with stones that had been gathered when the fields were cleared. Pointing to a white washed cottage, he said, "This is my little home, will you come in and meet my wife and have a cup of tea with us?"

He knew full well that his wife would size up the situation and act accordingly when she caught sight of Elizabeth's drab outfit. He wondered if Elizabeth would divulge that she had just left the convent. Aye, he knew it would lighten her burden if she talked it out, instead of keeping it all locked inside.

Annie was sitting in a chair in the garden with a basket of mending by her side and looked up when she saw Tom with the tall woman coming towards her. Annie's heart almost thumped out of her ample bosom as the searing memory of her daughter seeped through the corners of her mind.

But she managed a welcoming smile, "Aye, I see you've brought a visitor. And shure I hope the fine weather has whetted your appetites, because I have a good dinner ready. Tom, before the day gets any older, will you tell me who your friend is?"

"Aye, this is Elizabeth, we were both going in the same direction so I offered the lady a ride in my cart. Glad am I to hear that supper is ready. I'm ready for a good belt tightener."

"Go and wash up and rid yourself of the road's dust."

Then turning to Elizabeth she said, "By the look of you, my girl, I think a little rest would do you the world of good before supper. It's said that food never sits well on a tired stomach."

She led Elizabeth into a small bright bedroom. It was a cosy room with white lace curtains billowing inwards with the summery breeze. The bed was covered with a colourful handmade quilt. Above the bed hung a picture of the Sacred Heart of Jesus and on another wall The Blessed Virgin holding her child. On the dresser were two photographs–a photo of a very young nun and the other frame held a picture of an attractive woman with a boy by her side. Annie fussed around the room straightening up things that required *no straightening*, and Elizabeth detected that something had upset Annie.

"Mrs. Jordan, I thank you for your kindness but I fear that I'm intruding."

"Not at all, I'm glad to have the diversion, we haven't had many visitors of late. Here's a towel and a basin of water to freshen you up a bit." And without thinking Annie added, "Rest awhile and put the last few hours out of your mind. It's over and done with, try and give yourself a little while away from thinking. I know that's easier said than done. Anyway when you're ready I'll have a hearty supper waiting for you."

"Yes, I'm weary and a rest would be wonderful. Later I have to make my way to Dublin." Then stumbling for words, Elizabeth burst into tears.

Annie held her in her arms; "I'm not going to tell you to stop weeping... weep until the well runs dry. Tears can be a natural source of healing. You don't have to talk unless you feel the need."

When the weeping had run its course, Annie, with the corner of her spotless white apron, wiped Elizabeth's tears. Annie's gesture brought a glimmer of a smile to Elizabeth's face. As a child, whenever she had fallen, she remembered running to the kitchen, assured of the greatest sympathy from Nellie the cook. Nellie would make a great ado over the small cuts and bruises and always ended by wiping Elizabeth's tears with the corner of her big apron.

"I'll bring you a cup of tea and fetch a clean cotton dress fresh off the line. Mind you, it won't be the latest fashion, but it will make you feel a lot better than that heavy stuff you're wearing. Tomorrow I'll go to the shop in the village and buy a few things for you to wear. Elizabeth, I'm mindful of what you are going through right now, because years ago my darling daughter came home dressed in similar clothes. Aye, like you she had decided to break her vows and home she came…looking like a wee bird with a broken wing. The earlier vision of a glorious calling…made no sense to her now. Also, the final grilling she had to put up with leaving … left her wounded in body and soul. Aye, she was a very sick girl for many months."

"Is she still living in Ireland?"

"No she isn't, when she was strong enough to face the world again it appeared the locals had no intention of letting her enter their *decent* world. She was a marked woman unfit to mingle with decent folks, so they thought. Whenever my daughter ventured forth to the market in the village, they stood in tight little groups with their shawls pulled up to their faces, whispering insults that could have been heard in Dublin. Aye, may God forgive them for their ignorance and unforgiving hearts. Mind you, the same ones should be praying to God to forgive them for their own barrel of sins. Anyway, she couldn't bear it and it made her ill all over again. When we saw the toll it was taking, we took our savings to pay her passage to Canada."

"What did she do when she arrived in Canada?"

"She landed in a place called Quebec in the cold month of January. The streets were covered in snow and she told us that she couldn't see over the snow banks that lined the streets. Horse drawn sleighs delivered butter and milk. She wrote and told us that the milk froze and pushed up the caps and the milk was a solid lump two inches above the bottle. Aye, she had never seen the likes of it before. That first winter she almost froze to death, because she didn't have warm clothes for that climate and no money to buy any. Of course, we knew nothing about the hardships she endured. Later she wrote that for months she cried herself to sleep every night, because of the homesickness that had taken hold of her. But thank God, within a year she married a good man and now has three children. We have never seen her since she left Ireland."

"You must miss her." Elizabeth said.

"Aye, indeed we do! We've never been able to save enough money to go to Canada. Every Christmas she sends a hundred dollars, and for us that's a fortune indeed. Here I am rattling away like an engine with steam to spare and you're still waiting for your tea. Anyway, Elizabeth, I thought it might ease your burden to know that we understand what you're going through. Put your trust in God… He never deserts us…although many a time we desert Him. Who knows, maybe God had a hand in leading you here to us. Aye, there's a reason for everything."

Annie went out to fetch the tea and when she returned with the tea and warm scones lathered in butter, she found Elizabeth still sitting on the side of the bed, staring straight ahead. Annie reached out and gently patted Elizabeth's hand and placed the tray on the side table and left without speaking.

Elizabeth drank the tea, ate a scone and all the time…pondering how she could indulge in such normal functions when her life was in chaos. That was the last thought she remembered before drifting into a deep sleep.

When she awakened the room was in total darkness and she had no idea where she was.

Hastily she threw the blankets back and stepped out of bed…her legs buckled and she fell into a bottomless pit of blackness.

The room was gyrating like a carousel and Elizabeth found it difficult to focus on the person who was bathing her face. Gradually the messed up world she had momentarily left came swirling back and with it came all the unanswered questions and doubts. Where was Terrence? Somehow she remembered seeing him, if so, why was she here in a stranger's house? She remembered; he had sped off in his car as she approached it. Was it possible he hadn't recognized her…or? The answer to that she painfully avoided. Nevertheless, as of now she knew she was alone in the world, penniless, without a relative or friend…suddenly she was wracked by uncontrollable sobs.

Annie drew her into her arms and rocked her until the sobbing subsided.

"You slept such a long time we became alarmed. I knocked on the door and when you didn't respond, I peeked in and sure enough you were still sound asleep. About an hour later we heard a loud thump and found you lying on the floor unconscious. Holy Mary, Mother of God, it scared the living daylights out of us."

"I'm so sorry to have caused such worry. I was exhausted in mind, body and soul. Words can't express how thankful I am for your kindness and understanding."

"My dear, helping another human being is an opportunity to fulfil in a small way, what God expects of us."

"Elizabeth, today I'm going to the village, wouldn't it do you the world of good if I bought some clothing for you? Shure, a new frock would set you on the right track again. Mind you, in our little town there won't be any stylish fashions, but I think it's time you had a change."

"That's very kind of you, you're right, it's time I had something else to wear."

Elizabeth handed over three-pound notes and asked Annie to buy whatever she could for that amount of money. She watched from her window as Tom patiently waited by the horse and cart until Annie came bustling out. Childlike Elizabeth eagerly awaited their return. She tried to imagine what it would feel like to don ordinary apparel again.

The articles of clothing Annie purchased fitted very well. The dress was a nice shade of green and highlighted the tawny hue of Elizabeth's short-cropped hair. She dreamily passed the new comb through her thick short tresses and wondered how long it would take to grow to a fashionable length. She was aware that the shortness would be a dead give-away to anyone knowledgeable about the rules and regulations of the convent. What would Terrence think if he ever saw the almost boyish cut? With a shrug she put that thought back into limbo!

When Annie caught sight of Elizabeth's black snub-nosed shoes she heaved a sigh of despair, "Lord bless us and save us, if those shoes were fitted with a pair of oars you could row yourself all the way across the Irish Sea. You've still got a pound- note and a bit of silver left, tomorrow Tom will go to old Dennis the shoemaker and see if he has a pair of shoes for you."

The following day Tom hitched up old Nellie and with Elizabeth's black lacing shoes in a brown paper bag and set off for the shoemaker's house.

Old Dennis with one eyebrow cocked half way up his forehead asked, "Where in the name of God are the feet that usually fit inside these shoes? Tom you've known me for a long time and you know damned well to make a pair of shoes I need feet to make a proper fit. Off with you now and bring back someone with their feet attached."

"Well, you see, it's like this–the person with the feet attached isn't feeling too sprightly these days, so that's why I'm here to get you started on a pair of new shoes for her."

"In that case she won't be in need of a pair of shoes until she is up and at it again, will she? So you and old Nellie just wend your way back home and bring the feet in as soon as the owner feels sprightly enough to walk again."

"Dennis, I've a tale to tell, and since we've known each other all our born days…I know that what I'm about to say… will be between us. Now to make a short story longer…I have a lady staying with us who finds herself in the same predicament as our daughter Shannon did all those years ago. In other words she left the convent and has broken her vows. I'd say that her spirit is at low ebb. Even though she is not fit to leave the house her feet would be a lot warmer inside a pair of shoes."

"Aye, Tom, she has to be shod, I'll be out your way tomorrow."

"Thank God for your understanding nature, I'll be off now and there will be a grand dinner waiting for you the 'morrow and a healthy shot of Irish whiskey."

"Jaysus, Tom with an invitation like that…I might be over to your place before the rooster has finished the first crowing."

"Good man you are, I'll tell Annie she'll be a couple of hens *short* tomorrow, one for the dinner and the other for you to take home. I'll bid you 'good day' and be on my way."

Halfway home Tom pulled over to the side of the dirt road to allow a motorcar to pass. He looked at the motorcar with great interest because cars were a rare sight in Ireland. It stopped and a handsome man poked his head out of the window and inquired if Tom had a minute to spare.

"I have indeed," said Tom, "as long as what you have to say is worth the time."

The man shut the engine off and walked over to the cart. Tom, eyeing him up, thought, 'God didn't spare any parts when he created this man. Handsome of face and strong of build and a gift that many a woman would likely take a tumble to.'

"Good Day to you. I'm wondering if you could help me find a missing friend. A farmer who lives at the crossroad said that he noticed a lone woman walking this way a few days ago. Have you seen her?"

"Well, I'll answer that when I know who you are and what your connection is."

"Ah, so you have seen her?"

"I haven't said one way or the other. Are you related to this person you're looking for?"

"I'll join you in your cart and tell you my tale of woe. Should I move the motorcar or will it be all right where it is?"

"Ah, don't bother yourself with the car, the travellers on this road are few and far between. And shure if anyone passes by… their curiosity will slow them down…as soon as they catch sight of me talking to a man with a motorcar. Aye, they'll take the story back home to the family and you can be shure the telling of it will be a yard longer than it should be."

"I'm Terrence O'Dea and for the past few days I've been searching these roads for this lady. So you could lighten my burden by telling me what you know and take me to her."

"Terrence, I'm Tom Jordan and I just might take you to her when I know your reason. You see she has been ill and I've no intention of piling more grief on the load she has right now."

"For the love of God, take me to her! I may as well tell you, if everything went according to plan we had hoped to marry. Has Elizabeth told you that she *was* a nun?"

"Aye, we know the whole story except your part in it. 'Tis strange indeed, but in the short time we've known her she has crept right into our hearts. There's no doubt that the reason we understand Elizabeth's situation so well is because a few years ago our daughter left the convent. Lord God in heaven, sure the villagers never gave her a minute of peace after she left the convent. Aye, so tormented was she that she left for Canada as soon as she could. I'm telling you this so that you know what a burden these women have to carry once they break the vows."

"Tom, take me to Elizabeth please. I must talk to her as soon as possible."

"Aye, I'll tell you what I'll do, follow me on foot to the farm, keep out of sight until I have a talk with my wife and Elizabeth. When that's over with, I'll return to the roadway and let you know how the land lies. I'll be on my way and don't take too much for granted, she may not be ready to see you."

Terrence followed behind the cart and when they came to the bend in the road, Tom signaled him to stop. Then the horse and cart continued clip clopping to the little white cottage.

Oblivious to the sunny sky and the joyful singing of the birds, Terrence, with furrowed brow paced back and forth. He was burning inside for the sight of her once more, but also very concerned about the toll this had upon her. He looked towards the path leading to the cottage and saw Tom approaching. Terrence could tell by Tom's expression that he wasn't bearing good news.

"Well, here I'm no further ahead than when I left you. Elizabeth's first reaction to my news was a mixture of surprise, happiness then fear. God only knows why she should fear meeting you. Furthermore, she refuses to wear the black shoes that she wore in the convent and with a lost look on her face she declared that she couldn't receive anyone in her bare feet. So until old Dennis the shoemaker finishes making her shoes, she'll be barefoot, so put that all together and maybe you'll twig on to why she hesitates to set eyes on you right now. Y'know the mind of a woman is a conundrum for most men to unravel and then we end up marrying them in spite of it all."

"Tom, if we are lucky enough to marry the right one, the unravelling can be a wonderful occupation."

Whilst the two men were talking Annie came hurrying towards them with a yard wide smile and breathlessly she said, "Tom, after you left, Elizabeth walked to the end of the pathway and watched the two of you out on the roadway. She came into the house in tears and said she was sorry that she had refused to meet Terrence. Now, for the love of God, come along before she changes her mind again."

As the three approached the stone fence leading to the cottage, Elizabeth came to meet them…wearing a green dress and her bare feet making their appearance below the hem of the dress. Terrence thought she looked magnificent. But he was shocked to see the pallor on her face. When he caught sight of her tawny coloured short hair glistening in the sunlight he was delighted.

His only desire was to take her in his arms and care for her, but all she offered was her hand. He took her hand in his and never wanted to let it go. No words were spoken; none were needed! The love that emanated from one to the other was powerful indeed!

Tom and Annie left them alone in the garden in a world of their own.

The two lovers strolled hand in hand through the garden amidst the symphony of birdsong and the sweet fragrance of the flowers filling the air. Elizabeth broke the silence by saying that she had been convinced he had changed his mind about their relationship.

"What are you talking about? I had no idea what happened to you.

I've been searching for days, needless to say, my quest for information at the Mother House went unanswered."

"Terrence, when I left the Mother House I was in despair. I walked out to the roadway and saw your car. I hurried to reach you but when I was within a few feet of your car you drove off, why?"

"Good God, Elizabeth, I didn't see you. I've been driving along that road every day hoping to find you and not once did anyone in nun's attire pass me by."

"I was not wearing a Habit. I was dressed in an outfit that I shall remember until the day I draw my last breath and the humiliating circumstances attached to it."

Her face clouded over with the memory and her smoky green eyes filled with tears. Terrence knew then she would be in need of tender care for a long time to come. He took her in his arms and held her close.

"Elizabeth, I bought clothes for you, I hope the size is correct. You can do your own shopping when we return to Dublin. I've booked a suite for you in the Hotel."

"Thank you, I would like to stay here at least another day. Tom and Annie have been so very kind to me."

"I will come for you whenever you're ready and as far as I'm concerned it can't come fast enough. Have you any idea the torment I've been through the past few days, not knowing where you were?"

"Terrence, that applies to both of us, I never want to relive the past few horrible days."

"My dear, I will do my best to erase it from your memory."

They embraced and then went into the house to tell Annie and Tom about their plans. The table was set with a white linen tablecloth and Annie's best china. A mouth-watering aroma flowed through from the kitchen.

"Well there you are, now I hope the two of you are as hungry as I am. Sit yourselves down and I'll fetch some Guinness stout to whet your appetite."

Tom came in with the stout and two glasses of Port wine for the ladies. Terrence watched Elizabeth's reaction to the glass of wine being set down in front of her…she twisted the stem of the glass a few times before taking a tiny sip.

"Lord in heaven I'll miss you Elizabeth, it's been a long time since we've had company in this house. After Shannon left it seemed like we were the sole survivors in the whole county. However, Tom and I are good company for each other and the only dark cloud that hovers over us is the fact that we will never see Shannon again."

"If Shannon refuses to ever set foot in Ireland again, why don't you two go over to Canada and visit her?" Terrence asked.

"Tom and I are not getting any younger so the few shillings we have put away are for the time when we are too old to do the work around this wee bit o' land. Anyway the fare to Canada is more than we have saved, so a trip over there is out of the question. At least we know she is happy and we get a letter every week without fail."

When dinner was over Elizabeth asked to be excused for a few moments. She went to the little bedroom and opened the parcel of clothing that Terrence had bought. With childlike curiosity she unwrapped the parcel. She hadn't experienced a surge of anticipation like this for a long time. The first garment was a Donegal tweed skirt in blended tones of green, blue and fawn, and a soft shaded green jacket. Hastily she removed the garments she was wearing and slid her body into the soft silks of the lingerie, which Terrence had also purchased. Like a river hastening to reach its source, a sensuality, which had been restrained too long seeped through every part of her. Catching as much of her image as possible in the small oval mirror hanging above the chest of drawers, she was pleased with the results.

She made her way back to the others and suddenly felt shy about making her appearance in her brand new outfit.

Terrence held out his arms and she walked right in to his embrace. Her heart was pulsating at a rate she had never before experienced…as he whispered in her ear, 'You are beautiful. Put me out of my agony and tell me when I can take you back to Dublin."

"I will be ready to leave tomorrow. Annie and I need time for a good farewell talk."

"Tom has a natural down to earth honesty that's a treasure to behold. Later I will tell you of a plan I have in mind for the two of them."

Terrence returned the following day and found Annie and Elizabeth sitting in the garden in deep conversation.

Annie with a broad smile on her face said, "Aye, you didn't let the grass grow under your feet too long before returning for your lovely lady. I'll be off now, I'm sure you have a lot of talking to do."

When it was time to leave, Annie invited them to come for dinner the following Sunday and Elizabeth happily accepted. The fact that they would soon meet again soon made for an easier parting. Silently, Terrence placed an envelope containing two tickets for passage to Canada on the table, to fulfill the dream of being reunited with their daughter once more.

They drove all the way to Dublin happy to be together and felt no need for conversation. When they neared the city Terrence suggested going to his home before registering at the hotel to collect a few items that he had bought for her. Elizabeth remained in the car when he arrived at his home. Terrence, observing her reserved expression, understood this wasn't the time to ask her to be alone with him.

Elizabeth felt an unusual sensation when she gave her family name to the man at the front desk. In her wildest dreams she had never imagined she would be registering in a hotel again. Terrence could tell that this abrupt transition from nun to civilian was affecting her greatly. He became alert to the fact he would have to be tactfully patient until her convent days were a dim memory.

She bid Terrence goodbye and followed the bellboy to her room. He placed her valise and as he was about to leave she gave the lad a pound note. He studied the note and timidly told her that he had no money for change.

"I don't want any change."

Upon hearing this, the poor lad looked at her in confused disbelief, "Mother of God, if this isn't an answer to a prayer. Lady, it's like this, our rent is due and my Ma has to hide behind a cupboard when the Agent bangs on the door to collect the rent. She has been up to this caper every day for the past week. Aye, it breaks my heart to see her so fraught with worry when she hears him banging on the door. Jaysus, my Ma would kill me if she found out I'd told this to anyone. She warns all the family that what happens between us should be our business and not spread around for the gossips to feed on. Lady, I thank you for this kindness."

Later Elizabeth went down to the lobby to meet Terrence and she told him the story of the rent collector. Terrence turned to the lad and thanked him for the good service and handed him a few pound notes. The lad was almost speechless and all he could mutter was, "Thank you Sir... and may your last breath be a long way off."

Terrence smilingly repeated the young lad's blessing to Elizabeth, "By the way I know his father; he works the odd night at my favourite pub. The poor man hasn't had a steady job for ages and that young lad's wages is supposed to feed a family of seven. 'Tis no wonder our countrymen are departing from these shores in droves... Ireland is a land of desperate sorrow with rampant hunger and a dearth of employment."

Terrence took Elizabeth all through his home and she loved every part of it. She wished with all her heart that they could continue living in this lovely home, but that would not be possible. Alas, she knew they would have no peace here. The Irish would never condone the marriage of a woman who had broken her vows to God.

They discussed their plans to shop for suitable clothing for Elizabeth. "At the moment I'm not exactly broke, so spend as much as you want. I never worry about money until my banker taps me on the shoulder and tells me that the well is running dry. By the way, I'm anxious to have you meet my brother Jim. He and I have a lot to discuss. I have asked him to look after my business here in Dublin until my plans are more settled. Shall I invite him to have dinner with us tomorrow night?"

"Yes, I would love to meet another member of the O'Dea family. I hope I can find something to wear that will suit the occasion. This transition in my lifestyle is happening so quickly that it's difficult to keep abreast."

"Elizabeth let's get married as soon as possible. What do you say to that?

"We can't marry here in Ireland, so tell me, where should we marry? Furthermore, Terrence O'Dea I haven't agreed to marry you!"

"It's too late for you to act coy. What do you think of this idea? I have a friend who is a priest in Paris; he and I went through college together. He would perform the marriage ceremony and then we could spend our honeymoon roaming around France. Later we could set sail for America."

"Where should we go to in America? I have cousins in New York and Boston and it would be lovely to meet up with them again." She paused before adding, "Of course, if their Irish 'mindset' is still in place, they may not want to renew our kinship."

"You will never know unless you make the effort to meet them. So choose the destination and that's where we'll go."

Jim joined them the following evening and Elizabeth found him to be pleasant with a finely tuned sense of humour. He agreed to be their best man at the wedding.

Elizabeth began in earnest to take the long road back to a world she had left all those years ago.

Their wedding was a quiet affair. The priest, Jim, Elizabeth and Terrence celebrated with a champagne dinner that lasted until the wee hours of the morning. Elizabeth was as happy as a child listening to the conversation studded with wit interspersed with serious talk. It brought home to her the need she had to communicate with others of a like mind.

Terrence was a sensitive and gentle lover and the suite became their romantic haven for the next few days. Meals were delivered daily until one day they decided that it was time to see the sights of Paris. It seemed everything they shared had a magical touch; their love had a deep dimension.

CHAPTER TWENTY-ONE
The Lovers in America

Crossing the Atlantic in the month of January was usually a stormy affair. The two lovers however were enjoying the solitude of the deserted deck. The waves smashed against the ship with savagery, disgorging sea spray onto the decks with untamed fury. Elizabeth and Terrence walked briskly with the top half of their bodies forward, bracing themselves against the fierce winds. Periodically they sought shelter in little doorways scattered along the deck, and, clinging breathlessly to each other, kissed with lips seasoned with salty sea spray.

That night Elizabeth told Terrence that she wanted to find Patrick as soon as possible, because she had received only one letter since his departure. However, the regulation forbidding nuns to receive correspondence had put an end to further news.

As the days passed, Elizabeth was more at ease with her entry into the outside world and the good sea air had done wonders for her complexion. He prayed that when they arrived the news about Patrick would be what she wanted to hear. Elizabeth's love for the young lad was strong indeed!

Mary Flanagan was at the dockside to meet them and she seemed to be at a loss for words. The lovers had no idea that Mary had been shocked when she received the letter from Elizabeth that she had broken her vows. And the second letter from Paris that she was on her honeymoon... had Mary running off to seek the priest's advice. She wanted to know if she would be sinning if she allowed them to her home? As a good Catholic, wasn't it her duty to let them know that they had committed a grievous sin?

The priest, old in years and wisdom, advised her to treat them with understanding and kindness. "Now is the time to give a little of *'that'* which we all hope to receive at our final judgement... *unconditional love.* Mary, surely you've lived long enough to know that 'to search for a friend without fault, is to remain friendless.'"

As Mary waited for the passengers to disembark from the ship, she was concerned about how she should greet them, with pleasure or with a hint of reproof in her demeanour? Sure, it was all right for the priest to tell her to cast out all judgmental thoughts; he didn't have to deal with the issue. How would her family handle it? Not that one of them gave a damn about being fair to those in trouble; they were only concerned about keeping up with their so-called '*betters*.' Mary's father had often said that those who strove to keep up with their so-called '*betters*'... were sadly lacking in self-esteem.

Mary, upon seeing the handsome couple cast all reproofs aside. Just the way they looked into each other's eyes left no doubt that they were madly in love. Mary had always remembered Elizabeth being a real beauty, so tall and slender, with a graceful manner of walking. Today she looked outstandingly attractive; her short-cropped auburn hair was alight with colour.

Mary was startled when Elizabeth asked why Patrick wasn't there to meet them. Guiltily she admitted that they had lost touch since he had gone to live in Biddy's lodgings.

Elizabeth, with a look of alarm, asked why he was in a lodging house. Mary replied that Patrick had to live there to be closer to his work.

"How long did he live at your home?"

"Only one night."

"Why one night? And you have never been in touch with him since he left your house?"

"I'm sorry to say we haven't been in touch."

"Dear God, and to think that I gave him your address because I thought you were the one person who would open her heart to this poor unfortunate lad. Do you have Patrick's address? I will get in touch with him immediately."

"Yes, I have his address. An Irish seamstress who does work for me also does sewing for Patrick's landlady and she said that Patrick and his landlady were planning a trip to Ireland soon."

"Going to Ireland? Why didn't you write and tell me? How on

earth did he save his fare in such a short time?"

"I have no idea, I just heard this rumour a few weeks ago. Elizabeth, we must go home now. I'm sure you two must be tired after your long voyage."

At this point, Terrence, who had been silent throughout this conversation, decided it was time to make a suggestion. Turning to Elizabeth he said, "Would you prefer going straight to our hotel?"

Mary cried, "For heaven's sake, I have told my friends and family that you were arriving. How can I explain that you are going to a hotel...rather than stay with me, your cousin?"

"You didn't bother to write and tell me about Patrick's speedy departure from your home. I'm sure he must have sensed that he was unwelcome, hence his speedy departure. I am deeply disturbed about all of this, that young man's welfare is most important to me. And as far as you are concerned, Mary, I don't want you in my life at this time."

Terrence was seeing a part of Elizabeth that he had never seen before.

Ignoring Mary's pleas to go home with her, they hailed a cab and were on their way to the hotel well known to Terrence where he had stayed on previous visits. Elizabeth was delighted with the beautiful suite, and the great view from the large windows.

"Terrence, this is like having a piece of the world all to ourselves, cut away from the rest of humanity."

"Yes, I have you all to myself and that is something I could enjoy for the rest of my days. I love you more every minute I'm with you."

"My happiness is complete, just knowing that we love with such natural honesty. I hope it never ends!"

Terrence took her in his arms and the last thing he was considering at the moment was food, and he was surprised when she suggested having lunch. So he suggested having lunch served in their suite, accompanied by a bottle of wine. When the waiter left the room, Elizabeth asked if the consumption of wine in the middle of the day would become a habit. Terrence replied that from now on they could indulge in their likes and dislikes as they pleased.

Before the day turned to darkness they ventured forth to find Biddy's Lodging house. The cab driver was Irish and told them yarns of the many immigrants that he had taken to Biddy's throughout the years.

"Aye," said the driver, "it would break your heart to see the poor devils coming off the ships not knowing which foot to put ahead of the other. No relatives to greet them and the sadness of leaving their families in Ireland still resting heavy in their hearts. I find them standing at the dockside, wondering which way to turn and their expressions would brighten when I'd ask if they needed lodgings. In their joy of having one of their 'own' talking they believed that any man speaking with an Irish brogue had to be honest. Aye, I know of many a poor 'greenhorn' being taken to a bug-ridden hovel, managed by an old hag ...who would toss a bit of change to the con man who had led the poor innocents to her hovel. Often the con man would wheedle a dollar from the new arrivals, assuring them he would have a job for them within a couple of days. Needless to say they never saw him again."

This disheartening news of the tragic outcome of the arrival of Irish immigrants made Elizabeth realize that Patrick had been fortunate not to land in the clutches of such dishonest men. Perhaps she should write and thank Mary Flanagan for at least finding a decent boarding house for Patrick.

They had barely knocked on the door and it was flung open and Biddy stood on the threshold eyeing them up from head to toe. "And who would you be looking for?" she asked.

"Are you Biddy Cassidy? We are friends of Patrick O'Grady."

"In that case you're welcome, so in you come. Patrick has gone to the library. Heavens above, he spends half his life there reading for hours until his eyes look like two pee-holes in the snow. Patrick can't put a book down until the last page. Ah well, he's better off reading than spending his time keeping the barstools warm. Are you friends or relations of Patrick?"

Elizabeth almost made the mistake of saying, "I'm Sister Elizabeth," and Terrence saw the hesitation and answered, "I'm

Terrence and this is my wife Elizabeth."

"Well, since you're friends of Patrick's, I'm happy to make your acquaintance. Take a seat, and I'll infuse the tea."

But before Biddy had time to go the kitchen, they heard the front door close and Patrick walked into the small parlour. The colour drained from his face as he recognised the two. It took time for him to adjust to the fact that Elizabeth was not wearing the nun's habit.

Biddy excused herself and made herself scarce by saying that she had to make a short trip to the grocery shop. Aye, there was something in the air, she thought, and it was none of her business–so she decided to give them time alone to work it out.

Elizabeth walked towards Patrick and took his hand, "Patrick, I'm so happy to see you again. We have so much to catch up on, are you free to come to our hotel and have dinner?"

"I can't believe you're here. Why didn't you write and tell me that you were coming to America?"

"I wrote to you and mailed it to the Flanagan address, I had no idea that you had moved. My cousin Mary met us at the dock and told me that you had moved here. Evidently she didn't bother to forward my letter to you. I'm truly shocked at her behaviour! Had you received my letter you would have known that Terrence and I were married in Paris a month ago."

Patrick seemed to be having difficulty absorbing all this news. "Long ago in the orphanage I loved to play make believe games. I would imagine you and I fleeing from the orphanage and that we would live together like family in a real home. So now that you're married how should I address you? I've never had an aunt, should I could call you Aunt Elizabeth?"

"You may call me Elizabeth or Aunt, whatever comes easy to you. I'm surprised that my departure from the convent doesn't faze you in the least?"

"Your happiness means more to me than rules and regulations."

"Patrick, my dear, that's exactly what I needed to hear from you." And without further ado she swept him into her arms in a loving embrace.

Observing this strong bond was certainly a moving experience for Terrence. He knew that Patrick would always be a part of this newfound family. And three musicians should make an interesting relationship.

Biddy had returned from her short shopping spree and came in to the little parlour carrying a tray filled with her freshly baked savouries. The conversation was light and cheerful until Biddy remarked that she and Patrick were considering a trip to Ireland.

"Patrick, why do you want to return so soon and why have the two of you decided to go at the same time?"

"Aye, it's a long story with a few twists to it," said Biddy. "I have a friend who is a highly respected judge. He helped untangle a business deal for the owner of a shipping company who was a good friend of his. The judge refused to take money for his work so the ship owner presented him with four first class tickets for a trip to Ireland. The judge invited Patrick and me to accompany him to Ireland. Just imagine we'll travel first class and all our expenses will be paid during our stay in Ireland. Now tell me, who could pass up a chance like that? The judge is a Dublin man himself–he studied law there. By God, since the judge got to know Patrick he has taken a liking to him and that I'm glad of."

This last piece of news had a strange effect on Elizabeth; her cup clattered into the saucer and she looked absolutely distraught. Terrence was alarmed and wondered if all she had been through lately was beginning to play havoc with her equilibrium. He touched her hand and anxiously asked if she was feeling ill. She shook her head, saying that perhaps she was feeling the effects of the journey across the Atlantic. Nevertheless, Terrence was aware that something had seriously upset her. Patrick also detected that things had gone wrong somewhere along the line…but what?

Before leaving they made arrangements to call for Patrick the following day, which was a Sunday.

"Patrick attends mass every Sunday, so you can either go with him or take him to a church close to your hotel. I don't want him to start missing mass. Another thing, why are you staying in a hotel?

Didn't your cousin Mary Flanagan have room for you in that big house of hers?"

"We wanted the privacy of a hotel; that way we can come and go as we please."

"Aye, she shuffled Patrick out of her home faster than blowing out a candle. By God, she's a poor excuse for an Irish woman, allowing herself to be dictated to by her snotty sons and that weakling of a husband that she was daft enough to marry. Do you know that when Flanagan married her he hadn't a pair of socks that weren't holier than the Pope. Aye, but as soon as he had his hands on her inheritance he strutted around like a rooster in a hen-run. As the old saying goes...put a beggar on horseback and he'll ride to Hell."

"Yes, she treated Patrick badly... but that's all over and done with and I am thankful that she found good lodgings for him. Have you set a date yet for your trip to Ireland?"

"No, we haven't and I have a lot to do before I'll be free to leave."

CHAPTER TWENTY-TWO
Meeting the Judge

Elizabeth and Terrence attended mass at the big church in the downtown area. When they came out of the church they watched and listened to the parishioners, passing greetings back and forth as they made their way down the stone steps. New marriages, new birth—and ultimately those who had passed on were discussed in full. Voices would be lowered as whispered tidbits of the latest scandal was divulged, followed by "tut-tutting" and the sign of the cross being made in the hopes that God in his mercy would forgive the poor immoral sinner.

When they arrived at Biddy's they found Patrick anxiously walking back and forth outside the lodgings. When he caught sight of them his whole face lit up, and he hurriedly made his way to the cab. It was a beautiful morning and Elizabeth suggested a walk through the city streets and parks. The area was familiar to Terrence, so he took great pleasure watching the other two as they took in the unfamiliar sights.

After an exhausting long walk they went back to the hotel and Terrence suggested having lunch served in their suite. Since this would be a great opportunity to talk in private they all agreed. On the way they informed Patrick that they had reserved a room for him in the hotel. Biddy had been in touch with Mr. Doyle to find out if it would be possible for Patrick to have the week off. She told him that he had visitors from Ireland; he agreed on one condition… that she would invite him for a roast lamb dinner.

On hearing this bit of news, Patrick said, "Now that's great news! I'd love to spend more time with Elizabeth…and get to know her better, now that she is no longer a nun."

The words had barely left his mouth and by her expression he knew he had said the wrong thing. Evidently her departure from the convent was still prickling her conscience unpleasantly!

Left alone in his suite Patrick was amazed at the luxurious

furnishings as he walked around the room giving everything the once over. He sat on the velvet chair, then the sofa and eventually threw himself on the bed and enjoyed the unexpected bounce. Upon the well-polished desk there was an exquisite ink well, a gold pen and embossed writing paper. He could barely wait to write letters to the Murphys and Sister Rose on the gold crested writing paper. He could just see their faces when the postman handed those letters to them.

He entered the bathroom; he was amazed at the size of the large bathtub. Quickly peeling his clothes off he turned the taps on full blast! It took ages to fill such a huge bath and when the water was a few inches from the rim, he gingerly stepped in…savouring the soft warm water as he lowered his body slowly until it was *totally* immersed! He marveled at this turn of events in his life: such luxury and comfort…he had never imagined in his wildest dreams. If being rich, brought such comfort… he'd work like a Trojan to reach that goal.

During luncheon, Elizabeth encouraged him to talk about his life since his arrival in America. He told them about his office job and how glad he was that he didn't have to work in the brickyard. He said that Mr. Doyle has persuaded him to enroll in night school. As he said this Patrick's face reddened at the memory of that first feeble attempt to enroll because he had been ashamed to admit that he had no knowledge of his parents. Therefore, rather than relate the history of his orphanage years, he raced out of the school and ended up in a pub frequented by Biddy's lodgers. He had had whiskey for the first time and he never wanted a repeat performance!

He finished off the tale by relating his ill-starred meeting with Zarboni the Italian hustler. It came out later that a fellow lodger had bragged to Zarboni that Patrick could beat anyone at billiards. Patrick began to recount the tale.

"So Zarboni propositioned me and suggested arranging games and that I'd get a cut in the winnings. I told him I wasn't interested and when I refused his offer the conversation at the table died a sudden death! Zarboni fixed his dark eyes on mine and tried to eyeball me into a fear filled submission. Seconds ticked away and then he nodded to his two burly henchmen who were flanking him on each side and they turned on their heels and left the barroom.

"None of the fellow lodgers made a move, they sat as though glued to their chairs. I pushed my chair back and made my way to the door. The street was deserted but just as I turned the corner of the darkened street, two men grabbed me and started to rough me up. I tried to protect myself from the hammer-like blows and yelled for help. Anyway I must have lost consciousness...because the next thing I knew was in a police wagon and spent the night in jail."

"The following morning I was led into the courtroom and the judge gave me a tongue lashing about Irish immigrants who couldn't pass a bar without falling in and later staggering out with a belly full of booze and empty wallets. I tried in vain to convince him that I wasn't a boozer.

"'Your name is Patrick O'Grady?'

"'Yes Sir, it is and it isn't...but O'Grady is the name I've had all my life.'

"'What kind of answer is that? I want to know your legal name.'

"'Sir, when I applied for papers to migrate to America I discovered that O'Grady was not my real name.'

"'So, what is your real name and why don't you use it now?'

"'Because I don't want to.'

"'You are in a court of law, and your legal name is what we require.'

"'My legal name is Michael Fitzpatrick O'Reardon. I lived in an orphanage until I was fourteen and there I was informed that my name was O'Grady. When it was time to leave the orphanage I was presented with a letter with information regarding my legal name. After leaving the orphanage I considered using my legal name. I decided not to, because no kin by that name had ever come forward to claim me and they had fourteen years to do so. There was no honour attached to that name, so why should I use it?'

"Well now, the judge stared at me a good few minutes in silence, then he brought the gavel down hard on the bench and in a deep toned voice announced that court was adjourned.

"He walked towards me and ordered. 'O'Grady, follow me to my chambers.'

"By this time my stomach was churning…wondering what was going to happen next. When we entered his chambers, he pointed to a chair in front of his desk and told me to be seated. He sat at his desk and for a few seconds his eyes never left my face, and I began to feel most uncomfortable. After this thorough scrutiny, he inquired if my parents were in America and what county I came from in Ireland.

"Before I'd time to answer he added, 'O'Grady, I want the truth and nothing but the truth.'

"I related snippets of my life at the orphanage and how you had introduced me to the wonderful world of music. He wanted to know all the details of the people I knew after leaving the orphanage and where I had lived since arriving in America. He seemed amused when I said I lived at Biddy Cassidy's lodgings.'

"'Well, in that case, I'll forget about last night's brawl and let Biddy take a strip off your hide. I have known Biddy for many years. When one of her lodgers gets in trouble with the law, she has their valise at the front door faster than a dime rolling down a manhole. I think I'd better drive you home and explain the circumstances to her…otherwise you may be looking for new digs. By the way, the two hooligans that were arrested with you are bad news, so stay clear of them. Should they contact you again let me know and I'll make sure they give you a wide berth.'

"We drove over to Biddy's and sure enough she gave me a real tongue lashing and told me to go and wash and make sure there was no prison vermin clinging to my clothes. As I left the room she was in the process of pouring a couple of healthy shots of Irish whiskey for the two of them

"Later, she made a fine dinner for us and beamed when the judge told her she was the best cook in America. Before leaving, the judge invited us for dinner at his home for the following Sunday. Since that day onward, Biddy and I have dinner at his home frequently. The judge has a beautiful piano and a harp: he plays both instruments with great sensitivity. I look forward to our duets with keen anticipation and so does he."

Terrence noticed a look of concern pass over Elizabeth's face as Patrick's story unfolded. And her lips trembled as she asked, "Patrick, when are you leaving for Ireland?"

"No date has been set, because Biddy has to find someone she can trust to take care of the lodging house."

"Well, now that we are together again, I hope you will not leave too soon."

"I'm sure the judge would love to meet you."

"Yes, I'd like to meet him before we leave."

Patrick looked up in surprise, "Leaving? I thought you were going to stay here."

"Oh, we haven't decided, but there is a lot of the world we'd like to explore. Who knows we may end up living in New York; it depends on Terrence finding musical contracts here."

"Now that you're here I'm not so keen on going to Ireland, because you were the only reason I wanted to return. I missed you so very much."

Elizabeth and Patrick were waiting in the lobby for Terrence to finish making dinner reservations at the front desk. And then Patrick heard his name being called. As he turned around he saw the judge hurrying over towards him.

Oblivious to the fact that Elizabeth and Patrick were together, he said, "Patrick, what on earth brings you here? Why aren't you at work?"

"I am here with friends from Ireland. I would like you to meet Elizabeth. She was the music teacher at the convent."

The moment was frozen in time as the judge and Elizabeth stared at one another in shocked silence.

The judge was the first to speak; taking her hand in his, he said, "Elizabeth, I can't believe this is happening, after all these years I've been hoping and praying we'd meet again. When I returned from Europe and you had disappeared, I tried to track you down. Surely you are not the nun …Patrick has been talking about?"

Elizabeth gently disengaged her hand and replied, "Yes, I *was* a nun until a very short time ago. I believe the term is…I've broken my vows."

"My dear your vows aren't the only thing you have broken; when I couldn't find you… my heart was broken. You must have known that I loved you and hoped to marry you on my return from Europe?"

Elizabeth had turned very pale and asked Patrick to excuse them for a minute. Hurriedly turning to the judge, "My husband will be here in a moment, would you care to join us for dinner?"

"Your husband? Good God, I didn't know you were married?"

"Terrence O'Dea and I were married in France a few weeks ago."

Mike's expression changed to anguish, "Elizabeth, to find you after all these years and to discover that you're married…is quite a blow."

Patrick was aware of the charged emotion of this encounter and wished that he could make a hasty retreat. He was relieved when Terrence approached and taking Elizabeth by the arm he apologized for keeping her waiting.

Then with a curious look at the other man, he said, "Elizabeth, a couple of days in America and you've met a friend already?"

"Yes, Mike O'Reardon and I attended college in Dublin and we have not seen each other since graduation."

The two men shook hands and eyed each other with *cautious* curiosity.

Mike inquired if they were here on holiday.

And Terrence replied, "Yes and no…I am a musical entrepreneur and I'm in the process of rounding up contracts in my field of work."

Terrence noticed that Elizabeth had lost her usual calm and he wondered why meeting this man had upset her. Curious to find out the reason, he invited Mike to join them for dinner. Indeed Mike was *also* curious to know more about Elizabeth and Terrence.

The dinner was a pleasant affair…a combination of Irish anecdotes studded with humour and nostalgia.

Mike wound up the evening by saying that the Irish folk talk more about Ireland after leaving … than when they actually lived there. Memories of their family and homeland encircled their hearts forever and the retelling the tales of long ago kept the past fresh and alive!

After dinner whilst Terrence was making arrangements at the front desk, Mike took Elizabeth aside and whispered, "Elizabeth I must see you alone as soon as possible. It concerns young Patrick and what I have to say is for your ears only. At least for the time being."

Elizabeth was alarmed at his serious demeanour and experienced a feeling of foreboding. Immediately she went over to Terrence and said a few words and returned to Mike and in a sombre tone agreed to meet him the following day. Mike took his leave with a taut smile that belied his anguished spirit.

The mood of the three as they walked to their rooms was subdued and Patrick wondered what had happened to change the tempo of the evening. Terrence seemed to be grappling with something unpleasant and Elizabeth's thoughts appeared to be in a far off place.

When she told Terrence that Mike wanted her to come alone the following day, he swung around and asked, "Why, what's going on?"

She shrugged her shoulders and said that she had no idea. "Mike and I were friends during our college years, I simply could not refuse his request."

Nevertheless her offhand answer belied the apprehension that had taken hold of her!

The next day, the proprietor of the Café greeted Mike like a long-lost friend. Bowing to Elizabeth he led them to a private alcove quite a distance from the other diners. The judge ordered wine and was slightly surprised when Elizabeth lifted her glass and wished him good health.

But she wasted no time getting to the guts of the matter! "Mike, I think I know why you had to talk to me alone. And I'm amazed that this could happen just as I begin a new chapter in my life. Yesterday when Patrick disclosed how the two of you met in the courtroom and the discussion that ensued about his name...somehow I knew that my life was in for big change. When Patrick began his music lessons I felt sorry for him because he was such a lonely little boy. It didn't take long before I realized that I anticipated his arrival in the music room with great pleasure. Yes, I loved him, and it tore me apart when he had to leave. Now that his legal name has been established…I know why I loved him so dearly. He is *my* son, am I correct in that assumption? How much does he know? How did you discover this information about Patrick? And another thing, how does he handle the fact that the two of you have the same name?"

"I haven't told Patrick my full name. He knows me as…Mike O'Reardon. And he finds that amusing…once in jest he said that if someone had fancied up *my* name a little more that we could pretend that we were family."

"Ah, so he doesn't suspect anything yet?"

"Good heavens, of course he doesn't. I will now disclose the details of the information I received from my good friend Liam Pearce. Liam is a Dublin lawyer and his father was the doctor that delivered your child… excuse me *our* child. Dr. Pearce revealed that you had given birth to a child a few months after you entered the convent and everything had been shrouded in secrecy to protect your family's name. He said that your parents refused to see you or the child and would not allow you to return home with or without your baby. Against your father's wishes, your mother pleaded with Dr. Pearce to make sure that your name and mine were on the birth certificate. And that the child would receive the certificate only when the time came for him to be released from the orphanage. But fearful of your father's rage she begged Dr. Pearce to have a bogus certificate made out with the name, Patrick O'Grady. She gave no explanation why this was the chosen name. Liam's father and a chap by the name of Patrick O'Grady graduated from medical college at the same time. It appears that Dr. Patrick O' Grady accompanied your mother to many of the balls and was a regular visitor at her family home when she was a beautiful young girl. What happened to that romance is a mystery because she married your father before she was twenty-one years old. Why did she choose the name O'Grady as the fictitious name for our son?"

"Mike, when I was a young child I loved playing with my mother's jewelry. One day, when I was rummaging through her jewel box, I touched a tiny clasp and a secret drawer flew open. Inside was a picture of my mother with a handsome man and on the back was a message... 'To Anne, with all my love. Patrick.' Knowing I would be reprimanded for playing with my mother's jewels, I replaced everything and left the bedroom. I've never thought about that picture until this moment. In some obscure manner perhaps it clears up the mystery of *our* son acquiring that name."

"Elizabeth, why was I kept in the dark about your pregnancy? You knew I loved you. It's hard to believe that the few romantic days we spent together after graduation could wreck so many lives! All my letters were returned unopened. When I arrived back in Ireland I went directly to your home, the servant girl told me there was illness in the house and visitors were not being received."

Elizabeth's happiness of the past few months was slowly ebbing downstream as once again the torn pages of her life were being turned...spelling out those long kept secrets! Her fall from grace due to a premarital pregnancy had destroyed her parents' life... and had caused her son to endure years of untold misery. With tear filled eyes she looked towards Mike for comfort.

"My dear, I don't have to tell you how distressed I am. Elizabeth, had you known all this a few months ago, would you have married Terrence? Just think how different it might have been for us had we known sooner. We as his real parents could have married."

"Mike, that is fantasy, I love Terrence and nothing will change my love for him, so let's put that aside. We must find a way to disclose this to Patrick and Terrence, I'm sure they will be shocked. Do you have the birth certificate with you?"

Reaching into an inside pocket he pulled forth an envelope and handed it to Elizabeth. She held it to her bosom and then, with a deep sigh, she opened it. Mike couldn't tell by her expression what she was thinking; nevertheless he remembered the emotional thump *he had* experienced when he read it for the first time.

Elizabeth tried to speak but the words were muffled by the sobs she could no longer withhold. He held her tenderly in his arms and put his hankie in her hand. With a childlike gesture she swiftly scrubbed away the tears.

"Mike, at this moment a bittersweet mixture of sadness and happiness is running rampant through every fibre of my being! It's difficult to believe that people in the service of God…lied to me in such a manner. Had I known that Patrick was my son, I would have taken him and departed from the convent. Poor little fellow he suffered so much at the hands of Mother Superior and Sister Fatima. How will he react when he learns that we are his parents? I'd also like to know, why are you and Patrick going to Ireland?"

"Primarily the reason for my trip was to find out more about his birth. When I got to know him better I knew that his self-esteem was marred by the fact that he was illegitimate. We've had a few philosophical conversations about taking charge of one's life, regardless of the past. I had hoped that this trip would cement our relationship. When we return I hope to engage a private tutor to bring Patrick up to college entry level. He has an amazing native intelligence and I'm positive that he will do well. I do know that he has an extremely sensitive character, so only God knows how he will react when we reveal the facts."

"We should both be present when this unfolds. Don't you think so, Mike?"

"Yes, I agree. By the way, have you told Terrence that you had a child?"

"Of course! Strangely enough he has never asked who the father was. Sometimes I think that Terrence shadow boxes with the notion that Kevin O'Byrne is the father."

When they returned to the hotel Elizabeth left Mike in the lobby, while she went to her suite to see if Terrence and Patrick had returned. They had not, and hadn't left a message to say where they had gone.

She went back down to the lobby and decided to take a chair where she could watch for the arrival of Patrick and Terrence.

She saw Mike pacing back and forth; evidently, by the grim look on his face he was rehashing something unpleasant.

The unusual occurrences of the day had brought back memories that had occurred after Elizabeth's disappearance. As he paced he was thinking about his ill-fated marriage to Sheila whom he had known briefly in college. Alas, it wasn't too long before Sheila discovered that spending seven days a week as husband and wife was not her idea of a wonderful way to spend her days. Spoiled and self-centered, she indulged in her own wild pursuits...parties in London and weekends in Paris were the stuff her dreams were made of. Her romantic interludes were not unknown to Mike and frankly he didn't give a damn! Divorce in Ireland was impossible so they lived together off and on with reasonable tolerance.

Then one dark autumn morning Mike received a telegram from England that Sheila was dead. He was told that she had been galloping wildly across the moors and had been thrown from her horse. For a long time after Sheila's death, Mike's 'persona' seemed to be encased in a melancholic cloud. Although he was aware that the marriage had been a mistake he tussled with the idea that perhaps tragedy was stalking his life. And before the year was out...he closed his law practice and was on his way to America.

Elizabeth was having agonizing thoughts bearing down on her! Such as...how would Patrick react to the fact that she was his mother? In the eyes of the world she was a *fallen* woman! After all he had trusted her in every way and now she had to bring him down to earth with the revelation that she too had blots on her record.

Suddenly she was jolted out of her reveries when Mike leaned down and asked, "Were you trying to avoid me?"

"No, I'm watching the entrance for Terrence and Patrick to arrive. I also appreciated the time alone to sort out my thoughts that were scuttling back and forth like scampering mice. Mike, are you concerned about how our son will handle this information? Such a strange sensation to hear myself say those words...my son!"

"Elizabeth, I'm sure he will sift through it in a sensible manner. I've noticed that he is a good listener and also takes time to digest what he hears. Patrick can be quite emotional at times, however; he is not easily swayed."

"You two have formed a close relationship since that extraordinary first meeting. It is strange that his first misdemeanour should land him in prison and you being the judge that day. You said that you berated him for being a 'Barfly', not knowing that you were addressing your own son. There is a reason for everything, but this is truly one of the *most* unusual."

"Indeed it is, and I sincerely hope that it is a good omen for all of us."

Just then the pageboy passed calling for 'Mrs. O'Dea.' Elizabeth accepted the note from the silver tray and anxiously read the note.

"Good heavens, we must have missed them whilst we were talking. They are in the dining room, let's go and join them."

During lunch they listened to Patrick and Terrence's description of the places they had visited.

When Terrence started to discuss plans for the rest of the day, Elizabeth interrupted him by saying, "Terrence, I'm sorry but *we* have something important to discuss with Patrick. I would like to return to our suite where we may talk in private."

"You said *we,* am I included?"

Terrence, noticing his wife's harried expression, immediately stood up. "All right let's go."

Patrick and Terrence were the first to be seated, but the other two remained standing side by side in front of the tall windows. Terrence, in a halfhearted attempt to lighten the unease that seemed to permeate the atmosphere, said, "Well now, we don't want to spend such a beautiful day inside …so perhaps we should commence this discussion."

Mike crossed the room and put one hand on Patrick's shoulder, "What I'm about to tell you will be startling news; however, I hope it will bring happiness to all concerned. Patrick, I have your birth certificate and I know who your parents are."

A mixture of joyous apprehension passed over Patrick's face. "Are they alive?" he asked.

"Yes, very much alive and not too far away from you."

"What do you mean, have you met my parents?"

"Elizabeth and I are your parents."

An inexplicable intensity spread throughout the room! Patrick and Terrence stared in amazement at the two standing side by side in indecipherable amazement!

But no one was prepared for Patrick's reaction; the colour drained from his face and in a strangled tone, he asked, ... "May I have my birth certificate?"

They handed it over and he perused the contents of the document. Any hopeful anticipation of the situation evaporated as Patrick's contemptuously asked, "Why did you two keep this secret all these years? Surely you don't imagine that I should be happy about this belated revelation? It appears to me that you had to leave Ireland and your friends before claiming me as your bastard son. You abandoned me to ensure that your shame would never be known until you were safely away from Catholic Ireland's moral condemnation. The hell that I would endure was of little consequence to you."

He started to leave and Elizabeth wracked with heart- broken sobs, pleaded, "Patrick, please don't make such a hasty judgement. I beg you to listen to what we have to say."

He shrugged free of her hold and was about to open the door; Terrence swiftly blocked his way. Putting his arms around the sorrowful young man he pleaded with him to stay. Patrick refused...so Terrence forcibly brought him back to the center of the room and held him in front of Elizabeth.

"Look at this woman whom you admired and loved all these years, can't you understand how this new information has affected her? Give her a chance to tell her side of the story."

"Patrick, I only discovered this very day that you were my son. I was shocked! To think that you and I had been so close all those years in the orphanage and never knew that we were mother and son. Please allow me to explain how this information has come to light at this time."

As she pleaded, he kept his eyes downward cast as though the very sight of her was repugnant! Seeing no response was coming from him, she continued...

"When you appeared in court before Mike, he discovered that you and he bore the same family name. Needless to say, that kindled his curiosity. You aroused his sympathy when you told him that you were an orphan. He also knew that you were deeply hurt and ashamed not knowing who your parents were. Mike wrote to a lawyer friend in Dublin to try to demystify your parentage. His friend gave him the startling news that you were his son. Prior to that he had no idea that he had a son! His lawyer friend Liam discovered that his father Dr. Patrick Pearce attended me during my confinement. Dr. Pearce and my father were close friends; therefore my father was assured my fall from grace would be kept confidential. In this case it appears my father used his money and influence to have your birth and my shame shrouded in secrecy. When I told my parents that I was pregnant my father told me he never wanted see me again. Well, after your birth I took the vows and you know the rest of the story. I want you to know Patrick...that your father and I were in love when you were conceived. Our brief romantic interlude... caused tragedy for all three of us. Neither of us knew that I was pregnant when he left for Europe. However, when he returned I had disappeared and my parents refused to reveal any information about my whereabouts. After many fruitless inquiries he gave up the search. Sometime later he left for America to practice law."

Terrence intercepted at this point and pleaded with Elizabeth to say no more.

"Yes, I must finish, I want Patrick to know all the details so that he will understand the circumstances leading up to this day."

Patrick walking towards the door said, "I've heard all that I want to hear, I'm leaving."

Elizabeth lashed out in fury and said, "Patrick you will stay here and listen until I'm finished! I refuse to allow this occasion to become another blight in our lives."

Terrence patiently led the young man towards his mother although he refused to look at her; valiantly she began to tell her story. "I was seriously ill after your birth and when my health was restored I implored the Bishop to give me information regarding the child I had borne. He said my child had been adopted and that he did not know the adoptive parents. I asked if my child was a boy or a girl. The Bishop sadly shook his head and declared that he had no idea because a fire in the office had destroyed all the records. Patrick, when you started taking music lessons, you tread softly into my heart and before long I loved you dearly. You suffered so much in the orphanage and I tried to alleviate some of those hardships. Believe me, I had no idea you were the child I had yearned for all my life."

She reached out to him but he recoiled as though her touch was loathsome.

Elizabeth, with an anguished cry said, "Patrick, don't make the mistake of walking away! Don't you understand that enough mistakes have been made?"

The two men stood in grief-stricken silence, both in love with the same woman...and having to witness such a sad scene. Terrence suggested that perhaps it would be an idea to give Patrick some time alone to think things over.

"Patrick would you consider discussing all of this in private with your parents?"

"I have nothing further to discuss. All I can say at the moment is this, at least I know who I am."

Without a backward glance Patrick left the room...closing the door softly behind him.

At the closing of the door, Elizabeth's body crumbled and forlornly she reached out to the empty space that her son had just vacated. Terrence and Mike both rushed to comfort her, this action brought home to Mike that she belonged to Terrence and had no need for *his* attention.

Mike looked out the window and he watched the solitary figure of his son crossing the street; and he wished he could go down and join him. A feeling of severe loss pervaded his spirit and he made up his mind that he would not allow Patrick to walk out of his life forever. He comforted himself knowing that he knew he could depend on

Biddy to take care of Patrick and keep him posted on Patrick's activities.

Patrick walked for miles, oblivious to the evening darkness slowly wiping away the last patches of daylight. His thoughts twirled in chaotic confusion as he waded through the pros and cons of all he had heard. How much of today's happenings should he reveal to Biddy? Was it possible the judge had told her? Perhaps he should break all ties and move to another lodging house? Yet it saddened him to think of parting from Biddy because he had grown so fond of her.

At last, tired and hungry he stood in front of his lodgings and was thankful to see that it was in complete darkness. He hoped to reach his room without having to talk to Biddy. His first footstep on the stairs produced the usual squeaky creak, and in the stillness of the night it sounded like a clap of thunder! He bent down and carefully removed his shoes and treaded softly one step at a time.

A shaft of light appeared at the bottom of the stairs and Biddy whispered, "Patrick, come down here, I want to speak to you."

"I'm very tired, Biddy, can't it wait until tomorrow?"

"No, I have something of importance to tell you."

Still carrying his shoes in his hand he entered the little parlour and was surprised to see the fire burning brightly, because it was Biddy's custom to let it die down to glowing embers before she retired for the night. But now the dancing flames were casting flickering lights around the room, and when his eyes adjusted to the darkness... he was startled to see the shadow of a man sitting in the big leather armchair.

The shadow shifted in the chair and the man said quietly, "Patrick, I've been waiting here for hours, so don't run off again until you hear what I have to say."

Biddy left the judge and Patrick alone and went to the kitchen where she prepared a tray of savouries. She knew a bite to eat would be a welcome treat when they were through talking. Reaching for a bottle of Irish whiskey, she poured a good measure into three glasses, adding a dollop of honey and thick warm cream. Aye, a good hot toddy would do them the world of good! And after the tale that Mike had told her… relating what had taken place today…she knew that a good hot toddy would cheer young Patrick up too! So there stood Biddy in the kitchen preparing three strong whiskey toddies and simultaneously imploring the Virgin Mother to assist Mike and Patrick to do the sensible thing.

Having walked so many hours, Patrick was so tired that he simply slumped into the first available chair.

"Patrick, I want you to pay attention to what I'm about to say and please listen with an open mind. I know your mother is a strong-spirited woman, but after you walked out today all her strength departed. She is beside herself with grief and is taking all the blame for all the tragedy in your young life. Your mother requires understanding and love…not condemnation! All three of us are aware of the many hardships you endured, but surely you must know that Elizabeth suffered too. She said that many nights she wept for the child she had never been allowed to hold in her arms. It's difficult to believe that her father's need of social standing was more precious than the love he presumably had for his only daughter. Elizabeth also had the guilt of her mother's death to contend with…she has convinced herself that she was responsible for her mother's early death. I want you to know that I loved Elizabeth then and she will always be dear to me. Alas, it seems that our paths didn't cross in time and she is now married to Terrence. Patrick, you must allow your mother to be part of your life. She is a wonderful human being! I hope and pray that you can mend her heartbreak soon and tell her that you are proud to be her son."

"Mike, I need time to think, I just want to be alone for a while. I plan to leave and find a job in another city. However, before I leave I will say goodbye to Elizabeth and thank her for the goodness she added to my earlier life. And of course, surely you know that in the short time we have known each other I do feel close to you. This mess is not your fault; you never knew that you had fathered a bastard son. Parting from all of you will cast a dark shadow on my life."

"I see no need to change our relationship, however; you're free to make your own choice. Why must you go away from here? You have your music to think of, which by the way is surely an inherited trait from Elizabeth and me. Patrick, come and live in my home for a while. It will give you time and space to get your thoughts and feelings in order. In the meantime, I want you to get in touch with Elizabeth as soon as possible. It's time to close the book on the suffering you two have suffered for so many years."

"I will visit her in a couple of days. Perhaps by then the jagged edges of my spirit will have smoothed out a bit. Thanks for the invitation to stay with you, but right now I want to stay at my lodgings for a few days. You have my word that I'll not leave town without telling you. I am also sorry for the harsh words I used today. Mike, could we all meet at your home next Sunday?"

"Of course we can! I'm sure Elizabeth will look forward to seeing you again in a less contentious setting. In the meantime don't do anything hasty. Keep in mind our trip to Ireland, the Murphys must have received your letter by now and would be greatly disappointed if you cancelled the trip. Furthermore, we can't let Biddy down now that she has made up her mind to go. Patrick I'm glad that we've had this chance to talk, and from the bottom of my heart I thank God for allowing us to meet. The only sorrow I have is this, I wish it had happened the day you came into the world!"

Biddy slid her bottom along the wooden pew and with rosary beads in hand she commenced the well-worn ritual of thumbing from bead to bead. But her thoughts were not focused on saving her soul… instead they were devoted to the happenings of the past week. She had prayed that Patrick would stay here and not take off with a heart full of bitterness and now she thanked God for answering her prayers. Biddy cared deeply for the judge and the lad and knew that they needed each other like the fields need rain.

Biddy sat ramrod straight, neat and trim in her Sunday best, waiting for the vacant seats around her to fill. Truth to tell, she would have preferred to be home alone in her little parlour, instead of in church. She wasn't in the mood to listen to the familiar hackneyed sermon from the priest. So taking her mind to a more pleasurable level she smacked her lips in anticipation of a whiskey toddy slowly warming her insides as it slid down the hatch.

After ditching that irreverent thought she took to observing the parishioners as they sidled into their pews. It seemed to Biddy that the minute the parishioner's backsides hit the seat… their faces took on an expression of piety. 'Piety and Sunday best clothes appeared to be a weekly duet for most of them. Biddy was sure that the majority would take their faults and foibles back home as soon as they left the sanctity of the church. Aye, for example, across the aisle sat Lizzie Kearney looking as though she had just been canonised by the Pope…and for the time being ignoring the fact that she was the worst gossip in the street.

'God forgive me,' said Biddy to herself, 'Shure and I'm daft pouring over stuff like that…it's me' own soul I should be trying to get in order.' Sighing she knew that it would take more than what she was endowed with to straighten out her soul.

CHAPTER TWENTY-THREE
The Finale

Mike and Patrick were standing at the bottom of the church steps in what appeared to Biddy as a very serious conversation. This didn't bode well as far as she was concerned because the meeting at the judge's home today could change all of their lives forever.

She greeted the two men with a smile that spread across her face like the sun appearing from behind a dark cloud. It seemed to be infectious, immediately their faces brightened and as Mike assisted her into the car, he said, "Biddy, your happy face is a sight for sore eyes!"

When Terrence and Elizabeth arrived, Mike was perturbed when he observed how ill she looked. "Elizabeth you look very tired, are you alright?"

She replied that she had not been sleeping well the past few nights. A look of alarm passed over Patrick's face when he heard this and he went towards her and asked if his senseless behaviour had been the cause.

"Patrick, when you walked away that day my life was at its lowest ebb! Yet it made me realize more than ever how much you mean to me. I believe it's time to start a healing process, don't you?"

"Yes! I was confused and angry that day. Now it's time for a new beginning. With this change in our relationship, I have no idea what to call you. My father said I should continue to call him Mike, however; he decided that I should now be known by my real name. I'm sure it will take time before I become accustomed to being called Michael. No doubt these changes will be difficult to explain to Mr. Doyle and some of the lodgers. May I address you as Elizabeth?"

"Yes, of course!" Elizabeth held out her arms to her son and with an anchor-sized lump in his throat, at last the young orphan lad was in his mother's arms. 'Twas a moving emotional moment for all concerned.

Biddy went to the kitchen to put the finishing touches to the dinner. At the moment she yearned for the privacy of her own little parlour. After seeing this loving reunion between Patrick and his mother, Biddy's tears ran unchecked down her cheeks. As she sliced the big Spanish onion she thought, 'By God it's not often a mixture of happy tears and onion tears race down my cheeks at the same time.'

EPILOGUE

As I bring this story to a close I look again, as I have done many times in my lifetime, at the photographs on my desk. The stories connected with these photos were told to me piecemeal by my grandmother Lynn. Her husband, my grandfather, was Michael O'Reardon the orphan boy who eventually became a world renowned Flutist.

The first is the wedding portrait of Judge Michael Fitzgerald O'Reardon and Rose O'Hanlon (formerly Sister Rose). The judge and Rose became acquainted after she arrived in America to run Biddy's Boarding House.

The second portrait was taken in London, England when Michael (formerly Patrick the Orphan) graduated from the Royal Academy of Music. Elizabeth, Terrence, Rose, The Judge and the Murphys are in the photo and if you look closely you will notice Biddy in the background, weeping into a hankie the size of a tablecloth.

Last, but not least, the wedding portrait of Elizabeth and Terrence in Paris.

The End